THE STONE OF DESTINY

THE STONE OF DESTINY

Paul Doherty

CRÈME de la CRIME

This first world edition published 2020
in Great Britain and 2021 in the USA by
Crème de la Crime an imprint of
SEVERN HOUSE PUBLISHERS LTD of
Eardley House, 4 Uxbridge Street, London W8 7SY.
Trade paperback edition first published
in Great Britain and the USA 2021 by
SEVERN HOUSE PUBLISHERS LTD.

British Library Cataloguing in Publication Data
A CIP catalogue record for this title is available from the British Library.

ISBN-13: 978-1-78029-114-7 (cased)
ISBN-13: 978-1-78029-750-7 (trade paper)
ISBN-13: 978-1-4483-0488-2 (e-book)

All Severn House titles are printed on acid-free paper.

Typeset by Palimpsest Book Production Ltd.,
Falkirk, Stirlingshire, Scotland.
Printed and bound in Great Britain by
TJ Books Limited, Padstow, Cornwall.

To my beloved Grandson Caspar Doherty of Sheffield.

HISTORICAL NOTE

I n 1296, Edward I of England, the so-called 'Hammer of the Scots' swept into Scotland to crush all opposition. He was tired of playing the role of the 'honest broker' between the different claimants to the Scottish Crown. Edward terrorized his opponents with fire and sword, by land and sea. A grim, harsh King, Edward struck at the very heart of the Scottish nation. He seized their most sacred relic, the Stone of Scone – the Stone of Destiny – from its royal abbey. Edward took the stone for himself: a crude, cruel and, in the long run, very unsuccessful campaign to crush all sense of independence amongst the Scots. Nevertheless, Edward I had sown dragon's teeth. Scotland would never forget its rightful treasure and so more blood would have to be spilt . . .

(The quotations before each chapter are from *The Death of Pilate*, a Medieval Miracle play from the Cornish Trilogy.)

PART ONE

'I am without equal about the rest of the world.'

April 1360. The Parish of St Erconwald's, Southwark

The world had ceased to be a dark, murky prison full of stench, fresh with flame, all weeping and shrieking. The Great Pestilence was dying out. Its victims, with swollen buboes in groin and armpit, no longer crawled the streets. No longer was Southwark the teeming, filthy encampment of venomous demons, no longer a place of horrors. Order was being reimposed. Adele Puddlicot, crouching in the desolate, dark cellar of her rotting tenement in Weasel Lane, not far from the approaches to London Bridge, realized this. Adele was truly frightened, deeply concerned by what was happening. The season of the plague was over. Everything was about to change. The parish of St Erconwald's had once been a desolate, neglected haunt: its priest had long gone, seizing what paltry treasure he could before fleeing for refuge in the southern shires. The priest, like others, was searching for a hiding place, a refuge well away from the horrors of the plague. The Great Pestilence had prowled the narrow runnels of the parish, moving like some great jawed monster, sweeping to the left and right with its poisonous sword. The dead had become more numerous than the living. Corpses were dragged out and stacked like so many slabs of putrid, maggot-infested meat. The stench of corruption drifted everywhere. Houses lay empty. Doors and windows pulled open. Of course the dark-dwellers emerged from the blackness to plunder, steal, rape and ravish. Little good it did them. Within the week they had died, gagging on the contents of their own bellies.

The darkest night had descended over St Erconwald's. However, in early summer the resurrection began. The Great Pestilence sloped away as if sated, and the Good and the God-fearing thanked the Lord and began their work. Burial pits were dug long and deep. Funeral pyres roared at night. Sewers were emptied and cleaned. Rotting, empty buildings were pulled down. True, no parson or priest occupied the parish church and house. Nevertheless, leading parishioners recalled ancient privileges granted to St Erconwald's. The parish had been given the right to convoke a grand jury to investigate, summon, question, reach a verdict, and so impose judgement. A grand jury had in fact been empanelled to hear all complaints, pleas, allegations, accusations and grievances. Adele Puddlicot had heard of this and then, more alarming, how warrants had been issued for her arrest. She had warned her son, or so she called the Boy who lived with her. She had sent him away, telling him to hide in some mumpers' castle deep in the slums of Southwark; that was the least she could do. Adele was now hiding herself. She took a deep drink from the wineskin, closing her eyes as she wondered what she might do.

Months previously, Adele had moved through Southwark like a Queen of the Night. She was a corpse-dresser. She prepared cadavers for burial. People generously paid her for that. They'd leave the corpse of some loved one out on the streets. They'd hand over a fee and she would cart the corpse away on her barrow, ostensibly to have them buried deep in some lime pit. In truth Adele would, as soon as she could, take the coin and dispose of the corpse in some rotting lay stall. Adele herself seemed impervious to the pestilence. She'd worked at the very heart of the raging pestilence yet she suffered no infection herself. Adele in fact became fascinated by the dead and the dying. Some of the latter would come crawling in to this tenement in the hope of solace and comfort. They would creep in here offering coins, presents, even themselves. Adele would grasp them by the arm and, in doing so, she became aware of how beautiful the human skin felt. She had once bought a piece of silk, smooth and soft; human skin was similar, particularly that of young women. One of her victims, a pretty streetwalker, a whore whom Adele had found slumped on the corner of Weasel Lane, had nudged Adele into the realization of her fantasies. Adele had helped the whore back to this dark cellar, garnished and refurbished by the items she had plundered from different houses. Once back, the young woman began to sob. She would not stop. Adele, leaning beside her, tried to stroke her face and smooth silky neck; this disturbed her humours. Adele had swiftly recalled how the fleshers and flayers of Newgate carry out their tasks. This was no different. Adele, frustrated by what she saw and felt, grasped a mallet; one swift blow to the front of the head and the whore had ceased her moaning. Adele however continued to caress her victim's soft fleshy shoulders and so it had begun. Adele loved nothing better than to peel the skin of the freshly dead as well as those on the verge of slipping through the veil. Adele would help them on their way. She saw this as a mercy, an end to their suffering as well as a means to continue her own pleasure. She peeled her victims and tenderly treated the skins as a housewife would valuable cloth or precious linen: she kept them in the drawers of a beautifully crafted cabinet looted from a merchant's mansion close to London Bridge.

Adele did not know why she was so fascinated except, when she retreated into herself, she would recall that terrible day so many years ago outside Westminster. Oh yes, she could remember it so clearly. A cold, harsh day with a gibbet soaring up above the execution platform outside the abbey gates. Despite being well past her sixtieth summer, Adele could still experience that fear-drenched day. The executioners in elaborately horned masks, their long leather aprons smeared with blood, then her beloved father garbed in nothing more than a filthy shift. A place of terror! The braziers on the execution platform glowed like the fires of hell, tongues of flame leaping up to be drenched by a hard frost. Royal men at arms, archers and hobelars, a mass of steel, guarded the scaffold. And so the end: her father Richard Puddlicot, who had first been dragged in a barrow from the Tower, was readied for death. Bruised and bloodied, he was stripped of his filthy shift and made to climb the long narrow ladder to the hangman now waiting on the one alongside. Once there, her father was cast off to dangle and dance, a grotesque, gruesome shadow against the light evening sky. Adele, her mother and other kin had been forced to stay and watch her father's corpse being cut down then carefully peeled by a flesher from the Newgate meat market.

Adele recalled her father in his prime, the adventurer, the robber, the great friend of the monks of Westminster, who had been his firm allies in that audacious robbery of the Crown Jewels stored in the cavernous crypt of Westminster Abbey. Her father had been most successful and plundered the royal treasure hoard to his heart's content. He had even brought some of the plunder to the family home in Farringdon Ward. Deep in his cups, he had decorated himself with the royal regalia of Scotland: the crown, the orb and, above all, the Black Rood of St Margaret's, which contained a fragment of the True Cross. Oh, how her father had glorified himself! Of course it all ended in disaster. Royal clerks, mailed and dangerous, prowled through the city like lurchers. They were the King's mastiffs and they tracked, hunted and cornered her father. The dragged him out of sanctuary and committed him for trial before a military tribunal in the Tower. Richard Puddlicot had been found guilty and paraded through London in a wheelbarrow. He had then been condemned to death. They hanged her handsome father but worse, they skinned him, flaying his corpse, peeling it as you would an apple. Adele's mother, racked with illness, had pleaded for the skin to be given to her for burial along with her husband's mangled remains: this had been refused. Instead, the King had ordered that Pudlicott's skin be nailed to an abbey door close to the crypt, a hideous warning to any other would-be robber.

Adele closed her eyes then opened them, she was sure she had heard a sound. The Boy? She called him her son and he played the role: in truth he was an orphan, an urchin, a street-swallow who had befriended her some years ago. The Boy had helped her in her work. Adele would entertain him by allowing him to watch her flay the corpses and, when it was finished, she would pipe on her flute and do a silly jig to make him laugh. However, all that was in the past. Times had changed, as they did so abruptly during her childhood. Life's candle had burnt away. Adele had found herself as an orphan, forsaken by all because of her father. She had passed from one harsh convent to another. She had drunk deep of the waters of bitterness and eaten the harsh bread of rejection.

Oh, Adele comforted herself, she had lived by her wits and, if she had to die, she would go bravely into the dark. She was no coward, nevertheless she had become wary. A week ago the

Boy had informed her of how a proclamation, pinned to the door of St Erconwald's, had promised a reward for the arrest of 'Adele Puddlicot, thief, reprobate, murderer, witch and warlock and self-styled corpse-dresser.' Adele Puddlicot was formally summoned to answer sundry charges levelled against her. Once the Boy had informed her of this, Adele had immediately fled here, what she called her little palace, adorned and furnished with the plunder snatched from corpses and their houses. Precious goods, cloths and artefacts had been loaded on to her barrow and brought here to enhance her comfort. Adele tried to relax but she heard that sound again. She rose and fumbled for the arbalest, the crossbow primed and ready on top of a coffer. As she seized this, the door to the cellar crashed open. Figures garbed in cloak, cowl and mask thronged into the cellar. Adele raised the arbalest but this was knocked from her hand. She was pushed and shoved up and out of the cellar, more hooded figures waited for her in the street. Adele twisted and turned. As she did so she glimpsed the Boy, white faced, round eyed, standing in a pool of light thrown by one of the lanterns.

'Judas,' Adele screamed at him. 'You little, miserable . . .'

A blow to the mouth silenced her and she was dragged away. The escort pulling her cruelly with coarse ropes lashed around her chest and middle. She stumbled down the narrow, reeking lanes, slipping and slithering on the greasy, dirty cobbles. Cats raced across her path in hot pursuit of the legion of rats which still roamed free. Somewhere a dog howled at the moon. In corners, doorways and alcoves, Adele glimpsed the destitute with their pallid white, skeletal faces, clacking dishes held out before them: these were swiftly withdrawn as this group of sinister-looking figures emerged out of the dark. One of these outcasts however, glimpsed Adele. A rock was thrown followed by pieces of ordure. The escort drew their swords and the hail of filth abruptly ceased.

They turned a corner going down the alleyway past The Piebald tavern and up towards the soaring mass of St Erconwald's. The ancient church stood an ominously dark building against a sky now brightening under the first signs of dawn. They reached the church steps, Adele was pushed and shoved up into

the porch. She moaned at the sight which greeted her. The
sombre atrium of St Erconwald's was now lit by flaring cresset
torches and large lanternhorns. A court had been set up on a
makeshift dais. To the right of this ranged two benches with
a high stool placed in the centre before the judgement bench:
the top of this table was covered by a velvet cloth and orna-
mented with a crucifix, a rusty sword, a tattered Book of the
Gospels and a freshly fashioned noose.

Adele realized what was going to happen. This court was as
dreadful and dire as King's Bench in Westminster or any
commission presided over by a justice. The parish of St
Erconwald's had decided to exert itself. Adele realized she could
not plead for mercy, seek a pardon or even bribe her way out
of the closing trap. She had acted like a Queen of the Night,
now this was judgement day. Adele was forced to sit on the
stool, a guard either side of her. One of the hooded figures took
the judgement chair, the rest sat on benches. The court was
ready. The judge banged hard on the table, blessed himself and
told one of the guards to bring forward the principal witness.
Adele closed her eyes and cursed as the Boy sloped out of the
darkness to her left. At the judge's insistence, the Boy stood
on the dais facing her and the jurors sitting so silently on their
benches.

'Well, Boy?' The judge's voice grated. 'Tell us again what
you have seen and heard.'

The Boy did so in a loud, carrying voice. He gave his account.
The church echoed to his words as he described Adele's depre-
dations. The plunder seized from houses, the killing of victims
with a blow to the head, the flaying of their corpses and the
preservation of their skins. Adele could only sit and listen.
She tried to interrupt but a vicious blow to her mouth by one
of the guards silenced her. Once the Boy had finished, she
protested again, only to receive a second blow which bloodied
her nose and lips. Adele strained against the bonds. She stared
around at what was now her judgement chamber: a place of
rippling light and dancing shadows. She recognized who the
jurors truly were, the ghosts of her victims come for vengeance!
She was cold, lonely, but above all she was trapped, and there
was nothing she could do.

'Adele Puddlicot,' the judge declared, 'do you have any answer or defence to the dreadful accusations levelled against you?' The judge paused as someone came into the church, stepped onto the dais and whispered heatedly into the judge's ear.

'It is as we thought.' The judge signalled for the messenger to withdraw. 'We have ransacked your chamber, Adele Puddlicot. We have discovered more evidence of theft, as well as hideous cruelty to your victims.' The judge turned. 'Members of the jury, how do you say?'

'Guilty.' The full-throated response of the jurors rang through the church.

'And worthy of death?'

One of the jurors now rose. 'We find Adele Puddlicot guilty of heinous crimes but of one especially. She is a witch, a practitioner of the Black Arts, a woman who sacrifices to demons. She is not worthy to live on God's earth or receive his redeeming grace.'

Adele just slumped on the stool. It was useless to protest so she gave vent to the fear and anger seething within her. She staggered to her feet cursing and shouting, crashing against the guards trying to restrain her. Eventually Adele, bruised and weary, was forced back down onto the stool to hear the horrifying sentence passed against her.

'She was guilty of many crimes against God and man but, above all, she was a witch,' the judge declared. Sentence was then pronounced – she would be buried alive. Adele screamed and ranted but she was seized and bundled out through the corpse door and escorted across the cemetery. A group of torchbearers went before her, the light from their fiery brands revealing the way along the winding coffin paths. Adele continued in her protests as they dragged her through the brambles and gorse into an open space at the far end of God's Acre: a desolate place, called Haceldema, the Field of Blood, where those who died on the scaffolds and gibbets of Southwark lay buried. They approached an ancient yew tree, its branches stretching down to form a chamber within. The jurors carrying the torches paused. Adele was forced to witness the cabinet in which she kept her collection of skins being doused in oil and set alight: a furnace of leaping fire, which soon consumed everything thrown on it. Once the flames had died, two of the jurors pushed their way through the branches of the yew tree. In the light of sconce torches thrust into the ground, they began to dig and hack at the rain-drenched earth. The noise of their picks and mattocks, the gasps and grunts of the workmen being the only sound.

Adele fought to keep her composure. The Boy she had taken in and called her son had betrayed her. He had forsaken her as others had during her long life. Adele, however, was determined to escape the full rigour of her punishment. She had always secretly conceded that one day her life, and what she did, would be abruptly checked. Once she had learnt that warrants were out for her arrest along with proclamations demanding her seizure had been posted, Adele made certain preparations. She had raided an apothecary's house only a walk away from this church. She had discovered a miniature casket crammed with hard pellets. A skull painted on the lid of this casket gave a warning to all to be careful with the noxious substance within. She had tested two of the pellets on the cats and rats which infested her tenement. She didn't have to wait long, death had been very swift.

Adele had placed some of these pellets into the pocket of her velvet smock and she was now determined to use these rather than await the horrors planned for her. Adele's arms were bound tight, the ropes around her chest bit into her flesh, but she could still move her hands. She moaned and fell to her knees, her captors let her crouch on the ground. She moved her right hand and scrabbled her fingers into the shallow pocket. She could do that and manage to pluck out two of the pellets. Sitting back on her heels, Adele lowered her head and, straining against the ropes, thrust the pellets into her mouth; they immediately began to crumble. Adele swallowed hard and took a deep gasp of air as she was pulled to her feet and pushed towards the freshly dug grave. She was roughly forced in and made to kneel. One of the captors shoved a leather gag into her mouth, tying it at the back of her head to make it secure. Adele did not care. She could already feel a harsh dryness in her mouth, fiery shooting pains in her belly and chest. She was pushed over to lie on her side and bruised her face. Nevertheless, the pain inflicted by her captors was swept up by the fire raging through her entire body, making her jerk and tremble even as the dirt was piled down over her. She could hear voices shouting but she was beyond that now. She closed her eyes and welcomed the engulfing darkness.

From the shadow of a nearby yew tree, the Boy watched the woman he called 'Mother' be committed to the grave. He realized what was happening but, like the street-swallow he was, felt no emotion, no sadness, no regret, only relief that he had survived. The Boy had sheltered with Adele for almost two years. He had helped in her work, as she called it, but the Boy was sharp enough to realize when her time was drawing to an end. The chaos and darkness Adele could exploit was beginning to fade. The parish of St Erconwald's was awakening from its nightmare sleep. The law was being enforced. Those deemed 'utlegatum – beyond the law' would be proclaimed as wolfs-heads and hunted down. Justice was swift and terrible. The Boy could not read the proclamations nailed to the door of St Erconwald's, such documents meant nothing to him. However, the Boy had listened to the chatter of other street-swallows. How Adele Puddlicot had been proclaimed 'beyond the law and not included in the King's peace.' A jury had been empanelled and they wished to question Adele on serious charges. More importantly, or so the Boy was informed, anyone consorting with her, protecting her, hiding and supporting her, would also be indicted, whilst anyone providing information leading to her arrest would be rewarded. The Boy had made his decision. One morning he had slipped into the church and informed the Judge, as he called him. The Boy had blurted out all that he knew, everything he could remember about Adele. In return he had been given a reward which he now clutched close to his chest. A heavy purse of coins which would join the others collected by the Boy and buried in a secret place in this cemetery.

The Boy watched the jurors pat the soil over the freshly dug mound. In accordance with the ritual for the execution of a witch, the jurors sprinkled ashes and poured a little wine above the mound. The jurors then talked amongst themselves, preparing to leave: torches were doused, lanterns raised and the execution party moved away into the darkness. The Boy waited until they had gone, then he stole across, forcing his way through the yew branches to squat before the freshly dug mound of earth. He thrust his hand into the wet soil and recalled what the judge had told him. How Adele came of rotten stock, a malignant to be hunted down, and so she had been.

The Boy listened carefully for any sound but there was nothing except the distant chatter of birds and the crackling of the gorse bending under the quickening breeze. The Boy wondered what he should do next. He had some coins hidden away but perhaps it was best if he changed. He could apprentice himself or present himself as a foundling of the parish? He could take another name, a family who lived here in Southwark? 'Or I'll be a mercenary,' he whispered. 'I'll be a soldier's boy and follow the trumpets. Yes?'

The Boy patted the mound. He would never forget those nights with Adele in their garishly decorated cellar with a corpse sprawled against the wall. Adele would begin to peel the skin expertly then, when she tired, she'd pick up a fife to play a reedy tune to which she'd dance. He would sit smiling and clap his hands for more. Oh no, he'd never forget such evenings . . .

London. June 1381.

The Day of Judgement had dawned. The one foretold by Holy Scripture. A Day of Wrath, a Day of Mourning! Heaven and Earth in ashes burning! This was the day set aside by Heaven. The Day of the Great Slaughter when the strongholds fall and judgement takes place. The Upright Men, the leaders of the Great Community of the Realm and the captains of their dreaded street warriors, the Earthworms, truly believed their hour had come. They had sown the seed. They had protected the flame. They had plotted and planned, now harvest time was here. A bloody reaping. The time and place to settle ancient scores. Once this was done, they would build a new Jerusalem on the banks of the Thames. After the bloodshed, Justice! A new Heaven and a new Earth! The rebels passionately believed in this. The peasant armies would be victorious. London would be razed. The Temples of Mammon torched and purified with fire. The great and the powerful would be removed in a surge of bloodletting; indeed this had already happened. A thicket of decapitated heads decorated long poles above the gates of the city whilst the cadavers were left to pour their life blood into the sewers. No one would be safe. No one would be excused or pardoned, be it prince, prelate or priest.

The Upright Men would have loved to have swept through London and captured the hated John of Gaunt, uncle of the boy King Richard and self-proclaimed regent for his nephew. However, Gaunt had realized the storm was breaking. Oh, he could have visions of grandeur. He could, as common report had it, visit Westminster Abbey to refurbish the great English throne so he himself could sit there and pretend his day had come. Gossips reported how Gaunt had visited Westminster. The regent's henchman Thibault, his Master of Secrets, had emptied the church so Gaunt could pray for divine protection. It never came. Gaunt realized it was time to leave and, like the fox he was, had swiftly slipped the coop. He had travelled north to the Scottish March to treat secretly with King Robert. One thing Gaunt had dreaded was a war in the north when he was already deeply involved in one to the south. He could not, he would not fight a war on two fronts. He would concede anything to the Scots as long as he could do this without attracting the attention of his enemies in both the city and the court. In a word, Gaunt had fled, leaving London open to the rebels.

The Upright Men soon realized that Gaunt had eluded them, but his magnificent palace of the Savoy was another matter. The rebels had surged like a swollen river up into Cheapside before turning south to attack, plunder, and ruthlessly raze Gaunt's opulent residence. Any guards disappeared as the rebels swept in. Destruction soon followed. Parks, herb plots and flower beds were brutally ravaged. Gaunt's hated insignia and colourful heraldic devices were utterly erased. Buildings were set alight. Outhouses torched and livestock slaughtered. The Savoy which, according to one London chronicle, 'was unrivalled in splendour within England' was ruthlessly sacked. That same chronicler was amazed at how the rebels, their black and scarlet war banners placed around the entire palace, did not seize Gaunt's possessions but simply destroyed them. They burnt all the clothes, coverlets and beds, as well as the precious headboards. One of these decorated with heraldic shields was said to be worth almost a thousand pounds. Nevertheless, that too joined the napery, silverware, valuable pottery and expensive kitchenware all brought into the main hall where a great bonfire raged. Gold and silver, priceless jewels and precious stones could not be burnt so they were crammed down the palace sewers or into jakes pots. Since they couldn't lay their hands on Gaunt, the rebels had to make do with abusing a representation of him. They found one of Gaunt's most expensive quilted jerkins, fashioned out of costly cloth laced with precious gold and decorated with ivory buttons. The Upright Men fastened this jerkin to a lance and used it as an archery target; afterwards they pulled it down and ripped it open with sword and axe.

Only one place still remained safe. Gaunt's chancery chamber at the far end of the palace had been cleared and commandeered by two self-proclaimed Upright Men, captains of the Earthworms, Halpen and Mildew. This precious pair had already forced their way in, locking and bolting the door behind them. Once inside, Halpen and Mildew had removed the turkey carpets from the floor, pulling these aside until they found the hidden trapdoor. They broke through this, lifted up the heavy treasure chest and placed it on a waiting barrow. They unlocked and unbolted the chamber door, threw it open then abruptly paused. The noise of devastation had now receded, though Halpen and Mildew could see the glow of fire further down the gallery. However, their view was almost blocked by a sinister visitor, his cowl pulled forward, his face all masked. This dreadful apparition lifted the primed crossbow and gestured at both of them.

'Leave the barrow,' he ordered. 'Go back into the chamber. Go back,' he repeated threateningly. 'Bolt the door but first give me the key. Now!' he shouted. Halpen hastened to obey. The two Upright Men had no choice but to comply. They only carried sword and dagger; both of these were sheathed whilst their opponent's crossbow was powerful and deadly. They scrambled back into the chamber, slammed the door and bolted it: their opponent swiftly inserted the key, turned it and threw it away. He then placed the crossbow into the barrow, grabbed its handles and pushed the small handcart out through the palace, going down a narrow, hidden path to a barely known garden gate. Once through, the masked man trundled the barrow along the streets and runnels which lay ominously silent.

The rebels had yet to spill out and, like some deadly mist, move along the city lanes and trackways. The masked stranger, sporting a heavy mail jerkin beneath his cloak, reached a now deserted Queenhithe. Most captains and masters had taken their craft and disappeared. The masked stranger desperately searched for a more seaworthy boat. However, in the end he had to be satisfied with the small skiff he'd hidden away at the far end of the quayside beneath spikey, sharp gorse. Praying and sweating, for the summer sun was strong, the stranger managed to place the chest in the stern of the boat. He took great comfort at the sound of clinking metal though he realized he could not open it. The chest had a number of clasps with three locks along the rim. These would take some considerable time to force so it was best left for a better day. The masked stranger clambered into the boat and cast off. Bending over the oars, he pulled hard and quietly thanked God the river lanes were completely deserted. Indeed, the Thames was like a sea of glass moving serenely beneath him. The man pressed on the oars. Now and again he'd glance over his shoulder, satisfied that he was aiming for that desolate quayside close to St Mary Overy, only a short walk away from his chosen destination, St Erconwald's cemetery. He reached the quayside, dragged the chest off and pulled it up the shallow steps. He caught his breath and went to find the street barrow, spade and mattock he had hidden earlier. He loaded the chest onto the cart and pushed the barrow along the narrow lanes and into the runnel leading up to St Erconwald's. He passed The Piebald tavern, which lay locked, shuttered and eerily silent. The masked stranger, however, recalled strange rumours that the Upright Men of this parish had mysteriously vanished during this Season of the Knife. The parish cemetery lay peacefully enough, though the masked man sensed this was only the calm before the storm. The northern levies of the peasant army had arrived in London but the Kentish horde had not, though they were moving swiftly, determined to seize the bridge, cross it and so join their allies in the City.

The masked stranger reached the cemetery, which was

basking peacefully under the warm summer sun. Here and there
spring sparrows fluttered and chirped while a blackbird sang
its heart out amongst the tombstones. The masked stranger
glanced around and felt a sense of desolation. He took a deep
breath, rose and pushed through the lychgate onto one of the
narrow twisting coffin paths until he reached the family grave.
He did not delay but, grabbing the spade, he began to hack,
digging deep to create a hiding place for the treasure chest. So
immersed in his task, and comforted by the silence which
seemed to cover the place like a cloak, the masked stranger
failed to glimpse the figure squatting under an ancient yew tree
watching his every move.

Westminster. November 1381.

Murder, shepherd and leader of the Night Wraiths, had certainly
set up camp in London and no more so than around Westminster.
The royal enclosure included the kings' great abbey of St
Edward, home of the Blackrobes, the Benedictines, a veritable
cohort of monks, priests and lay brothers. The abbey buildings
soared to the skies, their towers, cornices, walls and sills intri-
cately decorated and carved with eerie symbols and signs. All
of these were guarded by a host of gargoyles, *babewyns* and
other grotesques etched out of stone. During the day these
carved monsters glared down but at night, or so legend had it,
these carved monkeys, apes, demons and griffins came alive to
crawl down the walls and gather in ghastly revelry amongst the
decaying plinths and memorials of the abbey's sombre cemetery: a broad stretch of God's Acre which housed the decaying
remains of thousands of Blackrobes who'd occupied the site
long before William the Norman had swept in with fire and
sword. He had built the great Tower of London to overawe the
capital and so bring both the city and Westminster under
the iron control of the Crown.

William and successive kings, however, soon discovered that
those human Night Wraiths, the assassins, killers, slayers and
murderers – the entire brood of their homicidal father Cain –
were no respecter of place or season. Murder, as the chroniclers
and scribes remarked time and time again, was a constant

presence in the royal precincts of Westminster. A 'murderous maze' is how they described the needle-thin runnels which coursed through the royal enclosure. Westminster was a truly ancient place where lofty three-storey mansions, now much decayed, leaned over as if eager to touch each other. So close were these heavy-storeyed, crumbling mansions that one could pass from house to house through their upper windows. Naturally, many of the wolfsheads, the legion of outlaws and miscreants who prowled the darkness of Westminster, used such decaying dwelling places to defeat the law. In doing so they could challenge that veritable embodiment of royal justice, the scourge of London's underworld, the portly yet very shrewd Sir John Cranston, Lord High Coroner of the city. Cranston's power and status had been recently enhanced over Westminster, both the majestic abbey, its grounds, as well as the royal precincts, which included the palace and the great offices of state such as the Exchequer, Chancery and Wardrobe. Indeed, if murder nested in the dark and dirt it was also no stranger to the great ones of the land. Ambitious clerks conspired against each other, as did their masters, and these vicious rivalries often led to bloodshed and sudden death, be it by the dagger, the garrotte or the cup of poison.

However, early on the morning of the first Sunday of Advent, the year of our Lord 1381, Murder swept into the very heart of the King's own chapel at Westminster, along the nave, across the sanctuary and up amongst the choir stalls. This exquisitely beautiful part of the church was bathed in the light from a host of fragrant, beeswax candles. The Blackrobes had gathered to sing and chant the Divine Office. Brother Sylvester, the sacristan, had begun Lauds, the dawn hymn of the church.

'Arise and come great King . . .'

The sacristan intoned and the community replied with one voice. The plain-chant swept on, rising to fill the great open space of the abbey church as the first light of dawn began to prick then dazzle through the brilliantly painted windows above the stalls. Shadows shifted and curled. Incense plumed from smoking thuribles, drifting in clouds to bathe and dampen the stone-carved faces of angels and demons which decorated the soaring white walls of the nearby sanctuary. The psalm

ended. Brother Sylvester, principal sacristan, stepped back on to
the lectern to read from the Prophet Daniel, a dire, sombre passage
about looking into the visions of the night to see the Abomination
of the Desolation standing in the Holy Place. He had hardly
finished this chilling prophecy when the Abomination, lurking
in that sacred shrine, struck like a well-aimed arrow or falling
blade. A chilling cry of the deepest pain cut like a spear
hissing through the chill air of the sanctuary. Another cry echoed,
followed by a hideous crashing in the stalls. Lauds abruptly
ended. Brother Sylvester left the lectern and hurried up to where
monks were gathered around one of their comrades, who lay
half wedged against the choir stall, retching and jerking like a
man possessed. Sylvester asked the brothers to withdraw. Once
they had, Sylvester crouched down. The fallen monk now lay
still and silent, his body strangely rigid, his white skeletal face
half turned to show one glassy dead eye, whilst a dark mucus
seeped between the stricken monk's half-open, bloodless lips.

'It's your sacristan!'

Sylvester turned at a tap on his shoulder and stared up at the
pale-faced Prior Norbert, infirmarian, leech and apothecary of
the great Abbey.

'It's Robert,' the infirmarian said. 'Let me look.'

Sylvester rose and stepped away to allow Norbert to kneel
beside the now silent Robert. The infirmarian pressed his hands
against the fallen monk's throat then both sides of the neck. He
leaned down, his sharp, beak-like nose sniffed at the victim's
mouth.

'Undoubtedly,' he hissed over his shoulder, 'poison! Brother
Sylvester, your assistant has been cruelly poisoned.'

PART TWO

'Behold the body is laid in the box.'

Later that same Sunday morning, so bitterly cold that the iron-hard frost which had crept through London still held fast, Brother Athelstan, who wished he felt warmer, crossed himself and murmured his usual prayer for patience. Parish priest of St Erconwald's, the Dominican friar regarded his parish as a token of reparation for what he now called 'sins of his youth'.

'Sometimes,' Athelstan whispered to himself, 'I do think I have repaid in full!'

'What was that, Father?' Watkin the dung collector and self-appointed leader of the parish council, rose to his feet. He beat his leather jerkin, so gusts of smelly dust rose to mingle with the incense, candle smoke and kissing bread coated with sweet wine. Such fragrances always lingered after Athelstan had celebrated his Jesus Mass, usually – but apparently not today – a time of quiet reflection.

'What was that, Father?' Watkin repeated.

Athelstan simply sketched a blessing in the air. He then smiled at his parish council seated along three benches, positioned to face the celebrant's chair that had been brought especially from the sanctuary so Athelstan could preside over this meeting. The friar stared around, as if to ensure all was well. Mauger the bell clerk was sitting at his chancery table, now covered with sheets of vellum, inkpots, sander and quill pens. All the parish documents had been taken from their great coffer along with the parish seal. These included the Blood Book, which nestled close to the Register of Parish Proceedings and the Requiem Book; this listed the names of the dead whose relatives had paid for chantry Masses to be sung for their souls.

'Everything is ready, Father.'

'Is it now, Watkin?' Athelstan murmured. 'Is it now?'

Athelstan gestured at the dung collector. 'Sit down and wait for a while. And that goes for you too.' Athelstan pointed at Pike the ditcher, Watkin's henchman and close associate in all the mischief his parishioners planned and perpetrated. 'I am waiting . . .' Athelstan raised his voice so it rang around the ancient, cavernous church. 'I am waiting for a certain individual to arrive.' Athelstan paused. 'No less a person than Remart the relic seller who, I believe, is touting a powerful relic . . .' Athelstan's declaration provoked a profound silence. The friar smiled at himself. He had given the wandering relic seller permission to set up home in the deserted old death house which stood at the centre of God's Acre, that broad, unkempt cemetery which surrounded St Erconwald's. Remart had hardly settled in before he was drawn into mischief, conspiring with the others in the dimly lit taproom of The Piebald tavern, a place Athelstan considered to be the parish's second church. The taproom was a veritable cauldron, where all kinds of deceitful mischief were cooked, garnished and prepared. The matter in hand was no different. Remart would eventually arrive and, until then, Athelstan would remain silent. He was certainly determined not to be drawn into the furious debate now bubbling beneath the surface over who should play whom in the parish's planned Nativity play. There was more pressing business. Long before Mass, Tiptoft, Cranston's red-haired courier, had roused Athelstan with a cryptic message from the Lord High Coroner that Sir John would visit his secretarius Brother Athelstan shortly after the Jesus Mass. Cranston's courier, clothed in his usual Lincoln green, could offer no further information, except that Sir John hoped to bring a visitor.

'Father.' Athelstan glanced up. Watkin sat with his hand raised. 'Father, can I play Herod?'

'I told you, Watkin, that must wait. So talk amongst yourselves.'

Athelstan rose and walked over to the rather battered baptismal font which stood in the shadows close to the main door. Athelstan crouched down as if studying the delicate paintings that the parish artist had begun to create there, filling the cracks and tears in the stone with brilliant colours to highlight the different scenes. Athelstan hoped that his absorption with the font would distract his parishioners, who were now heatedly whispering amongst themselves. Athelstan continued to crouch and study the miniature images celebrating the Sacrament of Baptism: jugs of flowing water; the Christ Child surrounded by heavenly cherubs; fiery demons being pressed back by the water of Baptism into a sea of flaring charcoal. Athelstan felt something brush his sandaled foot. He turned and smiled at Bonaventure, the great one-eyed tomcat who finished his morning circuit of the church to hunt and kill any mice who dared to nest there.

'Good morrow, my friend,' Athelstan murmured. Bonaventure simply meowed and stretched, the usual sign that he was impatient for his morning milk. 'We are all waiting, Bonaventure . . .'

The corpse door suddenly crashed open. Athelstan rose as Bonaventure raced to investigate.

'Remart!' Athelstan exclaimed. 'Where have you been?'

The lank-haired relic seller, a tall beanpole of a man, simply raised a hand then went back outside. He returned pushing a battered wheelbarrow carrying a long arrow chest. At Athelstan's direction, Remart, muttering his apologies, pushed the barrow into the space between Athelstan's sanctuary chair and Mauger's chancery table. He then removed the lid and Athelstan stared down at what he always suspected.

'This!' Athelstan declared, pointing down at the corpse of a mummified monkey, 'this,' he repeated, 'is definitely not the body of the pygmy who reportedly accompanied the Three Wise Men to Bethlehem. He certainly was not captured by Herod's soldiers and executed. Let me make it very clear, these are not the mortal remains of a martyr, like those of the Holy Innocents who suffered and died in the cause of Christ's birth.' Athelstan wiped the spittle from his lips. 'I am furious,' he bellowed, 'furious at such sacrilege and stupidity, if any of you know what that means.' Athelstan paused. His parish council now cowered on their benches, heads down, not staring at this little friar garbed in the black and white robe and mantle of the Dominican Order. In the main, Athelstan was always gentle and kind, reflected in his smooth, olive-skinned face, full mouth and expressive deep-set eyes. However, his parishioners also knew how Athelstan battled against a furious hot temper. On the rare occasion this was unleashed, his flock was only too willing to scatter. This was such an occasion.

The ominous silence deepened. Mauger became interested in the sharp nib of his quill pen, his fellow parishioners stared down at the floor. Eventually Watkin leaned forward to catch the gaze of Benedicta, the widow woman, her lovely face and long, raven-black hair framed by a dark-blue hood edged with squirrel fur. The widow woman who had a special place in Athelstan's heart, nodded understandingly at Watkin. Benedicta rose and walked over to where Athelstan stood, glaring down at the grotesque sprawled in the arrow chest.

'Father,' she murmured, 'how did you get to know about all this mummery?'

Athelstan took a deep breath and half grinned at this woman whom he secretly described as 'lovely of form, lovely of face and lovely of soul.'

'Sit down, Benedicta. Don't worry.' Athelstan's grin widened. 'I will keep calm and composed.'

Benedicta returned to her seat whilst Athelstan sat down in the throne-like sanctuary chair.

'Let me begin,' he declared. 'Westminster Abbey houses the Blackrobes, the Benedictines. Their sacristan is not only in charge of the sanctuary and all its precious objects, but indeed the security of the abbey as well, be it door or gate. Now the sacristan, a Brother Sylvester, a formidable man, or so I understood, nourished a pet monkey.' Athelstan raised a hand to quell the clamour from his parishioners. 'He called the creature Barak and was very attached to it. Some days ago, the monkey escaped. God knows how, but it did. Now, late yesterday evening I was visited by the Sanctus Man who,' Athelstan again raised his hand to quell the chatter of his parishioners, 'as you know, is a self-appointed authority on relics. Well he should be, shouldn't he, he sells such rubbish himself. The sanctuary man apparently visited The Piebald tavern.' Athelstan turned in his chair to glare at Joscelyn, the one-armed former river pirate and now the proud owner of The Piebald. The taverner lounged disconsolately between two of his henchmen, Crispin the carpenter and Ranulf the rat-catcher, who sat nursing his cages containing his beloved and ever noisy ferrets, Audax and Ferox.

'On display in the taproom,' Athelstan continued, 'was this mummified corpse. You, Remart, supported by others who really should have known better, claimed it to be the naked corpse of a pygmy. In truth, these are the gruesome remains of Barak the monkey. I can see its neck has been savaged.' Athelstan rose and walked over to the arrow box, staring down at Barak's mortal remains. Athelstan peered at the monkey's right wrist. He was searching for an injury which, according to the Sanctus Man, was one of the creature's distinguishing marks. However, the recent mummification process, as well as the ripening of dead skin and muscle, seemed to have disguised this. Athelstan crossed himself and silently conceded that the black-haired monkey with its tight, crumpled face, long legs and arms could be presented as a pygmy to those who'd never seen such a monkey, never mind a pygmy. He could make out the wounds in the throat, probably the work of one of the savage wild dogs which prowled Westminster. These mongrels were so ferocious, Gaunt had ordered them to be killed on sight. Undoubtedly the corpse had later been found and recently embalmed, using every artifice to make the monkey more human by pinning its ears back and other subtle changes.

'The Sanctus Man,' Athelstan continued, returning to his chair, 'established that Barak's corpse was plucked from the Thames by the Fisher of Men. Apparently he'd found it bobbing along the waters, close to the deserted quayside of La Reole, a mere walk from the Fisher's Chapel of the Drowned Men.' Athelstan paused. The Fisher of Men was a black-garbed recluse who stayed in the shadows along with his legion of helpers, a coven of grotesques who rejoiced in such names as Hackum, Soulsham, Fleabite, and others who served under the command of their master's henchman, that human fish Icthus. 'Well,' Athelstan clapped his hands softly, though he could see that he had every-one's attention, 'the Sanctus Man informed me that Barak's corpse was sold to a mysterious stranger with a wheelbarrow. At the time, no one knew the monkey's name or origins. Only when the Sanctus Man heard about the pygmy being exposed to view, for a charge, in the taproom at The Piebald, did he investigate.'

'Did he know what he was looking for?' Benedicta asked.
'One distinctive aspect was an injury to the right paw.'
'Does this Brother Sylvester now know?'
Athelstan shook his head. He doubted that Sacristan
Sylvester would want the corpse back; the animal was dead
and that was the end of the matter. The Sanctus Man claimed
he had informed Athelstan about what he'd seen to protect the
parish from any repercussions. Athelstan understood this, though
he also suspected that the Sanctus Man was only too pleased
to oust another rival relic seller from the market place.

'Father,' Benedicta declared, 'do you really think people
would accept such a story?' She stifled a laugh behind her hand.
'I mean, an embalmed monkey?'

'Remart,' Athelstan pointed at the relic seller, 'you of all
people can answer that. What do you and your fellow guildsmen
peddle as sacred? A swan feather touted as fallen from the wing
of the Holy Ghost? A sweat cloth used by St Joseph? A hair
brooch allegedly used by the Virgin? Goliath's toenail? I know
of at least six heads of St John the Baptist, a stone kissed by
Delilah, not to mention those foreskins taken by Samson from
the Philistines.'

'I have only got one of them, Father,' Remart interjected.

'In heaven's name!' the friar bellowed back, but then fell
silent as Benedicta began to laugh. Others joined in. Athelstan
relaxed as the tension swiftly eased. He smiled his thanks at
Benedicta and sat down, watching Remart being playfully
pushed and poked by the others. Athelstan murmured a prayer
as he listened to the good-natured teasing. In truth, St
Erconwald's was crammed with the likes of Remart: souls
who floated along the river of life, being swept up and left
forsaken by a world they could not control. Even veteran
parishioners such as Watkin, Pike, Crispin and Ranulf, not to
forget the fair Benedicta, had a history which, in some cases,
they'd prefer to keep well hidden.

Remart was certainly one of these. He had appeared in the
parish around the Feast of All Souls, last armed with a letter
of commendation from Prior Anselm at Blackfriars, the
Dominican motherhouse across the river. Apparently Remart
had once trained to be a Dominican lay brother but, on his own

request, he had left his friary close to Warwick Castle and journeyed south. He had gone to Blackfriars, and Prior Anselm had begged Athelstan to give Remart every help, both shelter and sustenance. Athelstan had done what he could. Godbless, the beggar man, had died earlier in the year along with his pet goat Thaddeus. Athelstan needed someone to occupy the old death house, to look after the cemetery and drive away the warlocks and wizards who liked nothing better than to gather at midnight beneath a rich full moon to practise their black arts and make sacrifice to the demon lords of the air.

'Father?'

Athelstan broke from his meditations and stared into the lean, bony face of the Hangman of Rochester. His true baptismal name, Giles of Sempringham, was now only a part of the hangman's tangled, haunted past. A strange, eerie creature, though highly talented, the hangman, with his long, straw-coloured hair, glass-like eyes and death-like pallor, was a well-known figure across the city. The hangman exercised his special skill on execution days, be it outside Newgate, on the broad, smooth meadow of Smithfield, above Tyburn stream or even on the gallows along the approaches to London Bridge.

'Father, you are staring at me strangely. Are you pleased?' The hangman gestured at the fresh paintings on the baptismal font. 'Are you happy with these? It's the best I could do.' The hangman fingered the hempen threads which hung either side of his black leather jerkin. The strings had been especially selected to bind and hold the noose around the hands, feet and neck of some condemned felon.

'I am very pleased.' Athelstan touched the hangman's black, gauntleted hand. 'Giles, your skill as a hangman is only surpassed by your talent to depict the most eye-catching paintings.'

'Are you waiting for Sir John?' The hangman's voice faltered. 'It's just that I met Tiptoft crossing London Bridge . . .'

'I am waiting . . .'

'Is it the Flayer?' The hangman crouched before Athelstan like a penitent waiting to be shrived.

'Oh yes, I have heard that name, hideous crimes . . .'

'Hideous indeed, Father! A soul definitely bound for hell. The Flayer abducts streetwalkers, the lowest of the low who have no prancing pimp to protect them. The Flayer takes his victims to some dark, reeking dungeon. As you know, Father, so many of these cesspits stretch across the city. Once alone, the Flayer slaughters his victim and peels her skin. God knows what he does with it.'

'But why?'

'Some hellish reason, Father. No one knows and so far nothing is done.' The hangman played with his cords. 'Ah well, Father,' he smiled, 'I have come to tell you of more dangers to your peace of mind. Our miracle play for the Nativity – you are building a crib for it?' Athelstan nodded. 'Well, Father, be warned. Judith the mummer wants a living crib. She wants to stage the Nativity story along the streets of the parish. Can you imagine it, Father? Benedicta's house could be where the Virgin lived. Watkin's, Herod's palace. The Piebald inn, with Joscelyn offering his own stable for the Christ Child. So . . .' The hangman whirled round as the Devil's door in the north transept crashed open and Crim the altar boy came hurtling along the nave.

'Father! Father!' He cried. 'Fat Jack,' Crim abruptly stopped, fingers going to his lips. 'I shouldn't have said that, should I? Anyway, Father, Sir John Cranston, the Lord High Coroner, together with a stranger, a Blackrobe, sweeps towards us.' Crim's shouted declaration carried through the church, silencing the chatter amongst the parish council. Athelstan whispered his thanks to the hangman and got to his feet just as the postern gate in the main door of the church was flung back.

'Jack Cranston, my little friar, I have come to see you and,' the coroner strode out of the shadows, 'and, of course, your most worthy parish council. I rejoice at seeing them here rather than being dispersed, busy about their different mischiefs. Including, I understand, the embalmed corpse of some poor, benighted monkey.'

'*Pax et bonum*, Sir John, to you and your companion.' Athelstan walked over to clasp the hands of the Blackrobe standing behind Cranston. The monk pulled back his deep cowl to greet Athelstan and exchange the kiss of peace.

'Good morrow, Brother Athelstan.' The Blackrobe spread his hands. 'I have heard so much about you. I am Austin Sinclair,

Prior of Melrose Abbey in Scotland.' The Blackrobe turned and looked quickly around. 'An ancient church,' he declared. 'A place of worship for many a year. And the same goes for Melrose.'

Athelstan caught the soft lilt of the visitor's accent. A learned, cultured scholar, Athelstan reckoned. Sinclair would be well-trained in the diplomatic niceties of both his order and the Scottish court. Cranston had informed him earlier in the week about the imminent arrival of envoys from the north who had come to treat on the usual issues along the Scottish March. Apparently, Prior Austin Sinclair led that delegation. Athelstan glanced quickly towards his parishioners, who had become restless.

'Sir John,' he declared, 'we should adjourn to my house. Some wine, some oatmeal?'

'No, no.' Sinclair had now crouched to stroke the ever-inquisitive Bonaventure, who adored Sir John and never missed an opportunity to brush himself against the coroner's stout legs or even, if the opportunity would present itself, leap into Cranston's lap. Athelstan watched the prior fondle the great tomcat.

'I have one of my own.' Sinclair glanced up smiling. 'A good companion, yes, in our lonely life?' Athelstan nodded, even as he studied his visitor more closely. Sinclair had a long, smooth face with a jutting chin. He was sharp-eyed and inquisitive. A monk but also a man who enjoyed the finer things in life. Sinclair's black robe was of the finest wool, rings adorned his fingers, bracelets circled his wrists, whilst a glittering silver medal chain hung around his neck. The prior's rubicund face was close-shaven and oiled with perfumed nard, whilst his teeth were firm and white. The Blackrobe was most composed. He seemed to have made the journey from the city without even staining either his sandals or his robe.

'My little monk, you seem lost?'

'I am a friar, Sir John, and I am not lost.'

'But we do need to talk,' the coroner insisted.

'And the sooner the better, yes?' Athelstan replied.

'Mauger?' Cranston bellowed at the bell clerk. 'You keep order here for Father because I need him, as I shall,' Cranston beamed at Athelstan, 'explain to your patient parish priest.'

'Brother Athelstan,' Sinclair shooed Bonaventure away and rose to his feet, 'I am sorry to intrude but I do need your advice and counsel.'

'Should we adjourn to my humble abode?'

'No.' Cranston gestured further down the nave. 'St Erconwald's chantry chapel will be refuge enough. In the meantime . . .' Cranston walked over to the arrow chest. He pushed the lid off with the toe of his boot. 'Satan's tits.' He breathed. 'Athelstan, is this . . .?'

'Yes, Sir John. What you earlier described as the benighted monkey, its corpse mummified, desecrated to make it appear something else. Which is why,' Athelstan raised his voice so his parishioners could hear, 'which is why,' he repeated, 'the monkey is to be given honourable burial in God's Acre. Yes, Watkin?'

'Certainly, Father.'

'Benedicta,' Athelstan beckoned at the widow woman to draw closer, 'please ensure that the burial quickly takes place. Try and keep order until we return.'

'And we need good order,' Cranston insisted. 'Our honoured guest Prior Sinclair wants to have words with certain members of this parish.'

Athelstan again told his flock to be patient and wait before leading his visitors along the nave to St Erconwald's chantry chapel. He opened the door built into the oaken trellis partition and waved his visitors in.

'Sweet heaven,' Prior Sinclair murmured. 'Brother Athelstan, this is truly beautiful.' The Blackrobe stood gazing around the chapel. He crouched to feel the thick turkey cloth which covered the floor, whispering his admiration at the elegant oaken chantry furniture, the ivory-white cloth covering the altar, as well as the bejewelled reliquary, containing a piece of St Erconwald's cloak, hanging on its silver chain. Finally, as Athelstan described it, 'the true glory of the chapel', a delicately painted glass window depicting scenes from the life of St Erconwald. Athelstan smiled with pleasure at the compliments, waving the prior and Sir John, still swathed in his bottle-green military cloak, to the cushioned wall bench beneath the window. Athelstan offered to fetch refreshments from his house but the prior shook his head whilst Sir John let his cloak slip so Athelstan could glimpse the miraculous wineskin which Cranston carried everywhere.

'So here we are and so let us begin,' Athelstan declared. 'Prior Sinclair?'

'I am Prior Sinclair of Melrose Abbey. I have journeyed to London to treat with your young King . . .'

'But still King . . .'

'Whatever, Sir John, that does not concern me. I am here, sent by the Scottish Crown to treat with the King and his council. We hope to establish a lasting peace along the Scottish March.'

'A noble aspiration,' Cranston retorted. 'Something both kingdoms have striven for since time immemorial.'

'Be that as it may, I am meeting King Richard and members of the royal council; Arundel, Howard and their ilk. But,' the prior leaned forward, his black-mittened hands going out towards Athelstan, 'I also need you, Brother.'

'For what?'

'Well, you have already solved the mystery of the missing monkey. In doing so, you have also quashed the rumour that certain of your parishioners had stumbled over the corpse of a pygmy, a member of the retinue of the Three Kings when they visited Christ in Bethlehem.' The prior clapped his hands, light-blue eyes twinkling in amusement as he rocked himself gently backwards and forwards on the wall bench. Cranston simply grinned, took a slurp from the miraculous wineskin and winked at Athelstan.

'Don't worry, Brother,' Sinclair sketched a blessing in the air, 'I will inform Sylvester the sacristan that his monkey died peacefully and now lies buried in hallowed ground.'

'Thank you.' Athelstan scratched the side of his chin. 'But you have other business here besides a dead monkey?'

'We certainly do,' Cranston retorted. 'Early today, Brother Robert, the sub-sacristan, confidant and close friend of his superior, collapsed in the choir stalls whilst chanting Lauds. There is an allegation that he was poisoned.' Cranston drew a deep breath. 'The abbey is also a royal chapel in the domain of the Crown. I have authority there. The King himself has asked me,' Cranston gave a lopsided smile, 'has asked us to investigate. Now strange things have happened in the abbey recently. Apparently last Wednesday, on the eve of the Feast of the Blessed Andrew, Sub-Sacristan Robert closed the entire abbey down after compline . . .'

'I am sorry,' Athelstan raised a hand, 'I don't understand.'

'The sacristan,' Prior Sinclair declared, 'as you may know, is to make all things secure. He holds the keys and clasps to all openings from a narrow postern door to the great gates of the abbey. Sacristan Sylvester always delegates this to Sacristan Robert. Now, on that particular evening, Robert locked every door and hatch. Apparently, he did this once Compline had been sung and all the good brothers had adjourned for the night. Nobody would have discovered what had happened if it had not been for the anchorite who lives in a cell in the north transept of the abbey. He began to scream and yell at the dead of night. He left his anker-hold and hurried into the nave. Now the Devil's door in the north transept is always left on the latch, not bolted or locked, just in case someone like the anchorite or a sanctuary man might have to leave the abbey, be it due to a fire or some other accident. According to what we know, the anchorite, however, found this door securely locked. Terrified out of his wits, he hurried into the bell tower and began to peal the tocsin.'

'Apparently,' Cranston intervened, 'this anchorite, and there's a story about him, claimed the church was deserted except for a demon.'

'A demon?'

'Yes, Brother, a demon, garbed and belled, sliding up the pillars or racing like a shadow across the flagstones of the nave.'

'Garbed and belled?'

'So the anchorite claimed. This demon wore the habit and cowl of a monk and pealed a handbell as if proclaiming itself to the world.'

'And so what's the cause and reason for all this?'

'Brother Athelstan,' Prior Sinclair replied, 'all this happened on the day after I arrived. My Lord Abbot instituted the most rigorous investigation but nothing was discovered. Nothing was stolen or damaged and, apart from the claims of the anchorite, there was no cause or reason for the tocsin.'

'And the sub-sacristan?'

'Oh, he admitted he had made a mistake and simply locked a door he shouldn't have. He claimed to be tired.' Prior Sinclair smiled thinly. 'There are stories about how Brother Robert had more than a liking for English mead. Anyway,' he sighed, 'by the time I had settled in, the investigation had produced nothing except the rantings of a lunatic anchorite.'

'Sir John, you said there was a story about this anchorite?'

The coroner took out the miraculous wineskin, drank a generous mouthful and offered it to both of his companions who politely refused. Athelstan seized the opportunity. He held up a hand, murmured his excuses and opened the chantry chapel door. He stood listening for a while then closed the door and returned to his seat.

'Nothing,' he smiled, 'except fierce discussion over the blessing of animals and pets on the Feast of St Nicholas. Ursula the pig woman wants her sow to be thrice blessed. Ranulf intends to bring his entire family of ferrets. Crispin the carpenter says he has built a new house for Herbert the hedgehog and wants both sanctified, whilst I,' Athelstan tapped his chest, 'will bring Philomel my old warhorse and, of course, Bonaventure, if I can keep him still for a short while. Anyway, to return to the anchorite.'

'The Magician of Melrose,' Cranston murmured.

'Why that?'

'Brother Athelstan,' Prior Sinclair took up the story, 'the abbey anchorite used to be a Benedictine monk, a member of our community at Melrose. He was baptized Ricard and entered our order at an early age. He proved to be a truly brilliant scholar. Ricard studied the sciences, a true observer of nature, especially the skies and all the mysteries of the heavens. A scientist like your friar Roger Bacon, a man after your own heart, Brother Athelstan. I understand that – when the weather permits – you climb to the top of your church tower to study the skies.'

'I do study the stars,' Athelstan laughed, 'but I am no scholar. Just an observer of the way our world is charged with the glory of God.'

'Brother Ricard was the same but his constant studies affected his mind, his soul and his vocation. He became infected, if I can use that term, with the new learning seeping in from Hainault and Flanders, theories about the commonality of man and the true purpose of government. Ricard argued that society should follow the rhythms of nature and allow full freedom for all souls to flower, equal in everything irrespective of their birth. Now this did not sit well with his superiors in the order or those outside. Ricard was investigated. An indictment was presented to the Holy Inquisition. Eventually Ricard was accused of a list of crimes including a most deadly one, the practising of the black arts, hence his nickname the Magician of Melrose. He was ill-treated, imprisoned and forced to live on hard bread and filthy water. This did not break him. Indeed, he became more zealous and, in the eyes of his accusers, more manic. Some would have rejoiced to see him burn at the stake.' Prior Sinclair crossed himself. 'God be thanked, the Benedictines of Scotland decided that Ricard should end his days as a recluse, an anchorite in the great Benedictine abbey of St Edward's at Westminster.'

'And how long has he been there?'

'About seven years. One of my tasks as a delegate is to visit Ricard and wish him well.'

Athelstan heard a gentle snore and glanced quickly at the coroner. Cranston, comfortably muffled, was leaning back against the wall, eyes half closed. Athelstan smiled. Unknown to the stout coroner, the paintings on either side of Cranston's head depicted a horde of black and red demons, armoured like hobelars, spears pointed at an angel hovering just above Cranston's head. Prior Sinclair seemed equally tired, leaning forward, hands clasped, staring down at the floor. Athelstan rose quietly. He walked to the door, opened it, and stood there listening. He closed his eyes as he heard Imelda, Pike's bitter-tongued wife, clashing yet again with Clarissa and Cecily, the two parish courtesans, over who should take the role of the Virgin Mary in the planned Nativity play. Athelstan groaned loudly and returned to his seat.

'Never mind.' He shook his head as Cranston broke from his dozing to ask him what was the matter?

'What is happening out there,' Athelstan pointed at the door, 'happens whatever the weather, the season or the hour. Let us concentrate on the matter in hand. On Wednesday, the eve of the feast of St Andrew, we have the noble abbey of Westminster disturbed by the tocsin. The good brothers are roused and hurry down to their abbey church. This is long after Compline, the last service of the day, so every good monk should be tucked up in bed. They find the church completely locked and bolted from outside. Once they do gain entry, the anchorite complains about seeing a demon dancing through the abbey, which terrified him so much that he tried to escape. However, no door was left open so he sounded the tocsin. Despite all this, after a thorough search is made, nothing amiss is discovered. Father Abbot initiates a full investigation but its only conclusion is that Sub-Sacristan Robert made a mistake by locking a door he shouldn't have done. However,' Athelstan raised a hand, 'first there is the question of the demon, cloaked and cowled, ringing a bell glimpsed by the anchorite. Was this a phantasm, a figment of the anchorite's imagination, or something else? The recluse certainly believes he saw something and, correct me if I am wrong, he has never created such a disturbance before, otherwise this would be dismissed as one of many such occasions. Prior Sinclair, would you agree with that?'

'Yes, yes I would.'

'More seriously,' Athelstan continued, 'a few days after this, Brother Robert the sub-sacristan collapses and dies of poisoning while singing in his choir stall. Now again, correct me if I am wrong, Prior Sinclair, but, during the sacred season of Advent, Benedictine monks observe the great fast, just one meal a day, usually in the evening, though they are allowed to drink water whenever they wish. So how was Robert poisoned? How did the assassin carry out his dreadful design? Brother Robert ate nothing and, I suspect, he only drank water from a common source, yes?'

'You must ask Sacristan Sylvester the same,' Sinclair replied. 'But, from what I have learnt, no one saw Brother Robert drink or eat anything as they processed to the choir stalls whilst a thorough search of his body, his clothing, as well as the contents of his cell, revealed nothing suspicious. No cup or goblet, plate or platter, not a trace of any food or drink tainted or untainted. So,' Prior Sinclair added wryly, 'you must also speak to

Prior Norbert, our infirmarian, who conducted our abbot's investigation into the strange events which, of course, ended with Brother Robert's death.'

'Murder,' Athelstan intervened. 'It's important that we define a death and Brother Robert's was certainly an unlawful slaying. Indeed, malicious homicide and, I suppose, Sir John, we are to investigate this?'

The coroner pulled a face, nodded, then rose to his feet, shaking his great cloak out. 'There is other business as well, Brother, the reason for Prior Sinclair's visit to your parish. Quite singular.' Cranston sat down and gestured at the Blackrobe. 'Perhaps it is best if you tell our good friar here.'

'Brother Athelstan, I am prior of Melrose and, as you may know, my abbey houses a great chronicle which records all the notable happenings, be it at Melrose itself or London, Paris, Rome, Avignon and elsewhere. The honourable office of chronicler is one conferred on successive monks in our illustrious order. We have always been the recorders of happenings, be it the Venerable Bede who wrote long before William the Norman or the *Anglo-Saxon Chronicle*, its different versions being compiled in various Benedictine monasteries across England.' Prior Sinclair cleared his throat. 'I have been honoured with such high office. I am a *peritus*, skilled in the drawing up of annals and histories. I am well-versed in the great chronicles, be it Higden's *Polychronicon* or Thomas of Walsingham's *History*. Now I am fascinated by the Great Revolt which broke out in London and across the southern shires earlier this year. I understand that, due to a miracle, many of your parishioners, deeply involved with the rebels and their council, the Great Community of the Realm, survived the bloodletting both during and after the revolt. I call it a miracle because I understand a number of your parishioners were in fact rebel leaders, Upright Men who commanded and led their ferocious street warriors the Earthworms. I . . .'

'I think I know what you are going to say my friend,' Athelstan intervened. 'So let us say it for you. Yes, Sir John?'

'Brother Athelstan's parishioners,' Cranston declared, 'were taken into royal custody for their own safety and security. Few if any suffered because of the revolt or the way it was brutally crushed. Nevertheless, Prior Sinclair, I also concede that our noble parish council, so busy blathering and fighting amongst themselves, ranked high in the councils of the Upright Men, whilst the Earthworms were recruited from the many rogues who infest St Erconwald's. Of course this is all in the past now.' Cranston shrugged. 'Brother Athelstan's parishioners were granted a full and free pardon, signed and guaranteed by Master Thibault himself.'

'Prior Sinclair,' Brother Athelstan asked, 'let us cut to the quick. What do you want?'

'I would dearly love to meet with, indeed, reside in this community.' He shrugged. 'I need to find out as much as I can about the Great Revolt.' He leaned forward. 'Can you imagine how important such evidence would be when I write my chronicle? I can declare that my history is not hearsay but drawn on the real experiences of those who plotted and planned the Great Revolt. Brother Athelstan, I would love to become a member of your parish . . .'

'You wish to lodge with me?'

'No, Brother Athelstan, many thanks for your kindness, but I do not wish to impose. Moreover, I know all about The Piebald. I will take lodgings there. I understand,' he lowered his voice, 'so Sir John has informed me, that The Piebald itself was a prime meeting place for those plotting and leading the revolt.'

'Too true, too true,' Cranston murmured. 'There were those in the royal council who would have loved to have seen The Piebald reduced to ashes. Oh, they were all there, the leaders and captains but,' Cranston got to his feet, 'Brother Athelstan, Prior Sinclair, let us share this good news with our beloveds.'

'The beloveds,' as Cranston described them, fell silent when Athelstan approached the lectern. He blessed them and then announced what Prior Sinclair had told him. At first the news was received in stunned silence, then the council erupted in cheering and shouted assurances that Prior Sinclair could not have chosen a better place. Joscelyn the taverner, who could smell a profit from a mile away, fair danced with joy. Merrylegs the cook clapped his hands in glee, for his pastry shop would do good business. Even Cecily the courtesan and Clarissa her sister sensed that good times were coming. Athelstan and his two companions let the elation run its course. The friar, standing close to Prior Sinclair, listened carefully to what his visitor would like. Once the clamour began to peter out, Athelstan again stepped up to the lectern whilst Mauger rang his bell as if demented. Once silence was imposed, Athelstan smiled around at his parishioners.

'Prior Sinclair,' he declared, 'will reside at The Piebald. He has politely refused any help from me. He insists on paying for everything, including your time and your help. He would also like to talk to others who served in the Great Community of the Realm, be it Upright Men or captains of the Earthworms.' Athelstan paused. The most vociferous of the parish council, the likes of Watkin, Pike, Crispin and others, now sat silent. Moleskin the boatman leaned over and whispered heatedly at Watkin. Others became involved. Athelstan strained to hear, only to realize that these former Upright Men were now gabbling in their own tongue, the coarse patois of the alleyways, a habit they invoked whenever they wished to exclude Athelstan from their conversation. After a while, he'd had enough. He clapped his hands, glaring at Watkin.

'What is this about?' he demanded.

'Nothing really, Father. We were simply discussing whom we could invite to The Piebald, former Upright Men who secured a pardon and cheated the gallows.' Watkin turned and bowed towards the hangman. 'I say this with all due respect.'

'And?'

'Well, Father, we couldn't choose better than Halpen the Hare and his henchman Mildew.'

'Oh yes,' Athelstan murmured, 'I have heard their names and know about their sins.'

'Two mischief makers,' Cranston declared, 'more fit for both the gallows and hell than many of their companions.'

'What did they do?' Prior Sinclair queried.

'Halpen and Mildew were couriers and scurriers, envoys and messengers of the Great Community of the Realm, highly trusted by the Upright Men such as Tyler, Straw, and others of that canting crew. Those two, that precious pair, two cheeks of the same arse, escaped the hangman's noose by a jump and a whistle.'

Athelstan nodded. 'Oh I see! Once the revolt looked to be doomed, Halpen and Mildew turned King's evidence.'

'In a word, yes – like so many others.'

'And now?'

'Oh,' Cranston pulled a face, 'they are protected and rewarded. No one dares go against them. It's a good choice, Prior Sinclair. Halpen and Mildew still dine out on what they know. I wish you well with them. Oh yes,' Cranston continued, legs apart, cloak thrown back, 'as I said, a good choice. What Halpen and Mildew know about the Great Revolt would be of great interest. However, I think I am done here.' Cranston glanced swiftly at Athelstan, a pleading look. 'Brother, I need you now. It is time to go.'

Athelstan agreed. He left Prior Sinclair in the care of Benedicta, asking Watkin and Pike to watch over their visitor and ensure both he and any baggage were safely lodged at The Piebald. The leaders of the parish council cheerfully agreed, even as Athelstan wondered about why they seemed so deeply excited by their visitor. Nevertheless, as Cranston whispered in his ear, time was passing and he needed to show Athelstan something before they reached Westminster. Athelstan hastily donned his cloak, pulling up its deep capuchon to protect his head and face. He tugged on his mittens, snatched his chancery satchel, made hasty farewells of his parish council and followed Cranston out of St Erconwald's.

The broad, open precinct before the church was now busy with traders, hucksters and chapmen setting up their makeshift stalls. They loudly advertised their tawdry goods to entice potential customers, the shabbily dressed residents of the parish as well as travellers leaving the city for the main thoroughfare into Kent. Here, Cranston was joined by his chief bailiff Flaxwith, and the latter's constant companion, his ugly-faced mastiff Samson, along with a small cohort of Guildhall bailiffs who went before the coroner to clear the way. Such assistance was desperately needed as they went along the narrow, reeking runnels leading down to London Bridge.

Despite the biting cold, the ice-strewn cobbles and the threat of snow, the streets were frenetically busy. The approaches to the bridge were thronged by makeshift markets, with traders selling everything from buttons to pig trotters, boiled and roasted, spiced and ready to eat. The air reeked with different smells and odours, some sweet and delicate, others so foul they made passers-by gag and splutter. Food and drink traders, hot-pot girls and platter-boys tried to entice customers into ale booths and wine tents. Cooks, pastry sellers and spicers offered delicacies – fresh, they claimed – from carcasses where the blood had readily spilled and the offal hooked out. Athelstan took a pomander from his satchel to cover both nose and mouth. He faithfully plodded after Cranston, who pushed his way through the throng, ignoring the curses and foul insults from the sharp-eyed naps and foists as they promptly disappeared, eager to hide from the keen-eyed coroner.

Justice was also busy along the thoroughfare. The stock and pillories were in full use, with petty criminals held fast by neck, wrist or ankle, so they could be insulted and pelted with filth by passers-by. Market beadles, city bully-boys, made their presence felt. These 'rogues in livery', as Cranston described them, lashed out with sharp, white wands to drive away the legion of urchins desperate to filch and steal from the stalls. The beadles also beat and whipped the dogs and cats hunting both the vermin and scraps of food on the steaming midden heaps. Early morning hangings had just taken place on the soaring, three-branched gibbet where the naked corpses of two housebreakers caught red-handed hung next to that of a ballad seller. This unfortunate had been found guilty of composing a story that the real John of Gaunt had been accidentally smothered as a baby and replaced with a butcher's son. Cranston read the proclamation pinned on the hanged man's naked chest. The coroner laughed sharply, crossed himself and passed on.

At last, they approached the bridge. Athelstan murmured a prayer for protection. He always felt panic stricken, anxious, in a throng of surging people, and never more so than on London Bridge. Athelstan fought to compose himself. True, he was passing between heaven and earth, but he would soon be across. The friar tried to ignore the fast-flowing river beneath thundering against the starlings. He could also hear the clacking of the mills and the screams and shouts of those in boats and barges as different craft threaded their way through the gaps under the bridge where the Thames roared like some savage beast. Shops and houses lined either side of the thoroughfare: these only deepened the feeling that this narrow crossing was not of this world but an eerie passageway between heaven and earth.

Athelstan whispered a prayer and kept his eye on Cranston, surging through the press like some war barge along the waters below. Athelstan was fully aware of the different sights and sounds, even though he kept his hooded head down. They passed the small bridge church of Saint Thomas a Becket. A choir of altar boys stood outside its door singing an Advent hymn to the Virgin. A group of Friars of the Sack occupied the lower steps, listening attentively to the words and joining in when the choir reached the antiphon. Funeral parties barged their way through, the coffins they carried bobbing on the shoulders of mourners like corks on water. Dung collectors were emptying the lay stalls between the houses, hurling the steaming, stinking filth into high-sided carts. What they couldn't, including the decaying corpses of cats and dogs, they cast into the river below. Beadles played the bagpipes so their wail could drown the sounds of the cries and curses of those locked in the finger stocks close to St Thomas's.

They passed the house of Robert Burdon, Keeper of the Gates and a leading member of the Fraternity of the Knife, London's Guild of Executioners. The keeper was busy on the top step of the gatehouse; a trestle table had been set up and along this stood a line of severed heads. Each of these was receiving what Burdon always called 'his loving ministrations'. Before the heads were poled, they were washed, pickled and dried; the hair, if there was any, neatly combed. Garbed in his usual blood-red taffeta, Burdon was, as always, ripe for gossip. Athelstan, however, sighed with relief. The beggar man, the frenetic lunatic toad-eater, garbed in horse-skin from head to toe, had taken up position on the lowest step of the gatehouse. This madman, who haunted the bridge from dawn to dusk, was loudly proclaiming how a severed head always housed the soul of the executed felon. So, for a coin, the toad-eater would chant a lament, a song of mourning.

Cranston and Athelstan hurried on. They reached the end of the bridge and turned right into what Cranston called 'a true

den of darkness', the rows of derelict tenements which lined
the alleyways under the shadow of the Tower. The decaying
and dilapidated houses squatted like old, slimy toads; fat, ugly
buildings, their bloated walls coated with a thick sheen of filth.
These dwellings of the damned couldn't even stand straight but
leaned across, blocking the light along the twisted alleyways
below. 'The meadows of hell', as people described this collection of streets and alleys. No light shone here, only the occasional
fitful glow of lantern, candle or fire flame. Sometimes, very
rarely, a shaft of daylight would pierce the murk but, as Athelstan
quietly conceded to himself, this only emphasized the gathering
murk through which indistinct shapes moved swiftly and
furtively. Here and there, a door, gate or window slammed shut.
Voices called, strident and carrying, proclaiming how the King's
coroner was passing with Athelstan of Southwark. The friar
recognized that such declarations kept them safe. No one would
dare accost them. The only people allowed through this filthy
labyrinth were either soldiers or bailiffs armoured, ready for a
fight or a priest such as himself.

They turned a corner. A bonfire blazed before the battered
doors of a derelict house; this was guarded by more of Cranston's
bailiffs who stood, swords drawn, cudgels at the ready. Cranston
had words with one of these who kicked open the door and,
taking two cresset torches, led Cranston and his party down a
stinking, shabby passageway. The ground underfoot was covered
in crackling, grey dirt: rats, long, black sloping shapes, scamp-
ered and squeaked. The vermin brushed cobwebs which spread
thick and full like fishnets across every corner, ledge and shelf.
They entered a narrow chamber. Athelstan glimpsed the abomination laid out along the floor, vividly illuminated by the leaping
flames of the fire dishes carefully placed around the skinned
corpse. Athelstan, covering his mouth and nose, closed his eyes
and whispered a prayer for help. He then crouched down by
the corpse, Cranston standing behind him.

'The mortal remains of some poor wench,' Cranston
lugubriously declared. 'Look at her forehead, Brother.'

Athelstan did and noticed the hole, an ugly, black wound in
the centre of the forehead.

'A butcher's blow,' Flaxwith muttered. The chief bailiff had wisely left his mastiff outside. 'Felled like some cow or sheep,' Flaxwith continued. 'I have seen the likes done many a time in the shambles outside Newgate and the slaughter sheds of Smithfield. The bastard stunned her then skinned the corpse.'

Athelstan nodded in agreement before taking a generous mouthful from the miraculous wineskin Cranston thrust at him.

'This is not the first?'

'No, Brother, it certainly isn't. This must be about the tenth victim.'

'When did it begin?'

'Around the beginning of autumn.'

'The Eve of the Feast of St Matthew,' Flaxwith interjected. 'Twentieth of September.'

'God preserve us,' Cranston breathed, 'that's my marriage day. Anyway,' the coroner continued, 'I thought it was just one of those grotesque slayings perpetrated by some passing madcap. I was wrong. The killer is a lunatic who hastens from slaughter to slaughter.'

'And his victims?'

'Always female, the lowest streetwalkers, the cheapest of whores, women raddled with disease, desperate for a penny. The killer, we now know as the Flayer, brings them to a benighted place like this and, well, you can see what happens.'

'Yes, yes I can.' Athelstan's stomach was now more settled. He blessed the corpse and murmured a requiem then returned to his study of the remains of some poor creature created by God and despatched back to Him in such a gruesome fashion. He stared, hiding his horror at the mass of red and blue flayed flesh, which still had a human form, an impression helped by the fact that the reddish hair and eyebrows had not been touched. Athelstan wondered what could compel one human being to inflict this on another. Was Prior Anselm correct, he wondered? Was there a darkness in the human soul? Some malignant growth which, when it reached full flower, could spill into a savagery even a demon in hell would weep at?

'Why?'

'God knows why, Brother.'

'No, that's not my question. Sir John, this is a dreadful death, a truly hideous slaying as the others must have been. However,

murder prowls London and its name is legion. So why is the
Lord High Coroner and his secretarius being drawn into this
hideous litany of killings?'

'Oh, quite simple, Brother. The remains of all the Flayer's
victims have been removed for burial to the Minoresses, close
to the Tower and . . .'

'Oh yes. Mother Abbess is a powerful woman, much revered
and respected by our young King. The abbess is well-known
for her care and compassion towards the poorest streetwalkers
of the city. I am sure that, disgusted and angry, she has made
her views known very clearly to our noble Prince.'

'Your arrow has hit the target, Brother. I am . . . we are to
investigate these killings, trap the Flayer and hang him.'

'I have seen enough. Oh, before you go, let me anoint the
remains.'

Athelstan swiftly unstrapped his chancery satchel and took
out the phials of sacred oil. He murmured a benediction then
quickly intoned the 'De Profundis', ending with the requiem.
Once he had finished, Athelstan drew a deep breath and
brusquely anointed the gruesome remains of a woman the friar
had never met or known. He tried to ignore the grisly feel of
the skinned flesh beneath his fingers as he thumbed a cross
on the forehead, eyes and sagging mouth.

'I've done all I can,' he whispered. He blessed himself and
got to his feet. 'Sir John, I would be grateful if you could see
that this unfortunate corpse be gently removed and given
honourable burial.'

Cranston said he would. They left the rotting tenement,
Cranston striding quickly along the street, which twisted like
a snake until they reached a broader thoroughfare leading
to the quayside. Cranston shouted that they had to go to
Westminster. Athelstan quietly groaned but followed the
coroner and his retinue down to the icy-cold quayside, which
reeked of smoke, brine and rotting fish. Cranston commandeered a six-oared barge for himself and Athelstan, yelling at
Flaxwith to have the corpse removed then go back to the
Guildhall where Cranston would meet him.

The barge pulled away. Athelstan resigned himself to sitting
in the canopied stern, wiping the river spray from his face as

he watched the oarsmen, their captain sitting in the prow, bending in unison over the oars. Next to the captain sat a boy with a tambour which he beat to establish a rhythm for the crew. Now and again the boy would pick up a hunting horn and blow lustily upon it, a warning to other craft, which responded with their own trumpet blast. Lanterns glowed, tongues of glowing flame in the mist, which shifted and danced above the racing, turbulent river. Athelstan, to distract himself from the constant pitching, stared around the edge of the canopy.

The river was certainly busy. A magnificent Venetian galley, its paintwork a brilliant hue of colours, thrust its way through, scattering the herring boats, fishing smacks and other small craft crawling across the river like water beetles. The galley was escorted by two royal war cogs; massive, fat-bellied vessels with soaring masts, raised sterns and jutting bowsprits. Behind these, an even more compelling sight: a majestic, formidable barge; a towering high-prowed craft, painted blood-red from stern to poop. Six oarsmen on either side, all cowled in deep capuchons and dressed in inky-black garb. Athelstan immediately recognized the vessel and its owner standing in the high stern, the Fisher of Men, cloaked in the robes of a Benedictine monk. The Fisher wore a stiffened velvet mask over his face, whilst metal-studded gauntlets protected his hands. The funeral barge was leaving some quayside heading back to the Chapel of the Drowned Men on a deserted quayside just past La Réole.

For a while, this ghostly craft ploughed the river alongside Athelstan's boat. The friar shouted his greeting to the eerie midnight figure standing in the stern, who turned and raised a hand in greeting before shouting at his oarsmen. The funeral barge surged forward like a greyhound from the slips and disappeared into a bank of rolling mist. Athelstan leaned back in his cushioned seat and wondered if the Fisher's henchman was on board, that eerie figure who called himself Icthus, the Greek word for fish. In fact, that's what Icthus looked like, with his webbed hands and feet, his completely hairless face and head, sloping brow and cod-like mouth. Icthus was in fact a human fish, a born swimmer, impervious to the cold, always dressed, both within and without, in a simple linen tunic. In a twinkling of an eye, Icthus could strip, slip into the river and swim like a darting salmon or a twisting porpoise.

Athelstan stole a glance at Cranston but the coroner was fast asleep, slouched sideways cradling his wineskin, as a mother would her baby. Athelstan wondered if the coroner had questioned the Fisher and his henchmen about the atrocity they had just visited? Had these mysterious river people fished out skinned corpses from the river? Athelstan chewed the corner of his lip. The Flayer who had perpetrated such an abomination must have a reason for it. Why murder a woman, skin her corpse then leave that for public view? Athelstan closed his eyes as he realized he had made one mistake in viewing that corpse. The Flayer had left mangled remains but what had happened to the skin? Athelstan was sure he had not seen that. He leaned over and shook Cranston awake.

'Sir John, my apologies.'

The coroner forced a smile. 'What, my little friend?'

'The victim we've just viewed. Where's the skin?'

'The bastard took it with him – always does – he must collect them – probably stored them in a treasure chest, though heaven knows why.' The coroner went back to sleep and Athelstan to his reflections. Did the killer rejoice in shocking others with such a disgusting sight? Or did the Flayer take a deep pleasure in the act itself? A foul deed, which poured some sort of balm over his tortured soul. If so, did the killer get rid of some of the corpses, hide them away, and what better place than the river where a corpse could lie undetected until it rotted into nothingness? Athelstan recited a verse from the psalms and steadied himself as the boat lurched. Were philosophers like Augustine correct, he wondered? Augustine argued that all human beings are a mixture of what they inherit, where they come from and how they are formed. How malignant diseases of the spirit can take root in childhood and then, dependent on circumstances, shrivel and die or even be replaced by good, healthy roots. On the other hand, such malignancy could be encouraged to grow like some pernicious weed in a garden. Did the corruption spread out to choke the good seed, destroying harmony and integrity, binding the soul to nothing except itself? But why now? Why had this Flayer emerged in these last few months? Athelstan opened his eyes at a sickening lurch of the barge and a splash of ice-cold spray across his face.

'There it goes!' A now-awakened Cranston nudged Athelstan. The friar stared around the edge of the canvas canopy and followed Cranston's direction. The barge had shot along the rapid flow of the Thames as it beat against the starlings protecting the struts and pillars supporting London Bridge. Athelstan murmured a prayer of thanks. He had been so immersed in his own thoughts, he'd become oblivious to the barge surging through the narrow galleries beneath the bridge, that veritable forest of wood, a tangle of timbers. The roar of the river and the clatter of the barge now receded. Cranston, who seemed to be totally unperturbed by the violence of the river, was jabbing a finger at a huge two-masted war cog displaying the royal arms of Scotland. The warship's gaily coloured banners flapping in the wind proclaimed the Crown of Scotland with its silver saltires and rampant red lions.

'*The Bannockburn*!' Cranston exclaimed. 'Scotland's greatest battle cog.' Cranston turned back and grinned as he wiped the spray from his face. 'It's moving from Queenhithe quayside to the one near the stews of Southwark. From what I gather, *The Bannockburn* brought Prior Sinclair from Edinburgh. He must have informed the captain about his plans to stay at The Piebald, so it has moved station.' Cranston gently nudged his companion. 'My little monk . . .'

'Friar, Sir John.'

'Your parish is becoming important?'

'That's what worries me, Sir John. Why has it become so important and what will the consequences be?'

Cranston snorted with laughter, took a gulp from the wineskin and returned to his dozing. Athelstan pulled his deep hood closer about him as he wondered about Prior Sinclair. He had learnt from friends at Blackfriars how the Scottish Benedictines were becoming keen and accurate chroniclers. John of Fordun was well-known, whilst the great historian Jean Froissart, who'd chronicled all the great achievements of Edward III and his son the Black Prince, had been invited into Scotland and given royal licence to wander wherever he wished. Athelstan also understood any chronicler's interest in the Great Revolt, which had broken out so abruptly and spread so swiftly to engulf London and the southern shires. A rebellion which, for a brief moment in time, almost brought King, council, Parliament and Church crashing down. Now the revolt was dead, its leaders either rotting on some lonely gallows or shivering in exile. A few of the Upright Men, captains of the Earthworms, still lurked deep in the shadows. They called themselves 'The Reapers' but, in truth, their hour had come and gone.

Athelstan was more intrigued by the strange elation shown by his parishioners over the invitation to Halpen the Hare and Mildew. Athelstan was acquainted with both of these worthies and he'd wryly conceded to himself that Watkin and his merry crew were simply looking forward to being reunited with old comrades. Athelstan half dozed, trying to close his mind to the pitching of the boats, the blare of horns and the cries of the oarsmen. The barge had now passed the great quaysides of Dowgate, Queenhithe and Castle Baynard. Keeping close to the shoreline, the barge moved swiftly on. Athelstan glimpsed buildings along the Strand, in particular the blackened ruins of the Savoy Palace, still being cleaned and cleared after it had been burnt and pillaged during the Great Revolt.

'I wonder,' Athelstan murmured to himself, 'if Watkin and his coven will take Sinclair there? Ah well.' Still reflecting on the doings of his ever-mischievous parishioners, Athelstan closed his eyes and intoned a psalm. He'd barely finished when Cranston shook him by the arm. They were now approaching King's Steps, close to the abbey. Athelstan disembarked, leaning heavily on Cranston's arm, for the friar felt slightly giddy after the cramped river journey.

Athelstan followed the coroner up the steps into Westminster, a small city in itself dominated by the majestic, soaring abbey with its precincts, stone-paved corridors and passageways, over which harsh-faced gargoyles, *babewyns*, saints and angels gazed unseeingly down. A place of worship where smoke and incense from beeswax candles constantly fragranced the air. The abbey was also a place of study and learning with its carrel-lined cloisters, the smell of leather, scrubbed parchment, ink and wax providing a permanent perfume. Such pleasant smells reminded Athelstan of the great scriptorium at Blackfriars where he had spent so many pleasant days immersed in his studies. Clutching his satchel, Athelstan followed the coroner as they swept along galleries, Cranston's high-heeled riding boots rapping the pavement like the beat of a drum.

Athelstan found it hard to keep up as they passed gardens, herb plots and raised flower beds. A host of different sounds echoed through the chilling, cold air: bells ringing, doors closing, choirs chanting, the constant murmuring of the brothers they passed. At last, they reached the great abbey itself, entering the nave by the narrow south door. Here they waited whilst a lay brother went searching for both Sacristan Sylvester and Prior Norbert, the infirmarian. The lay brother returned, his red-cheeked face wreathed in a fixed smile. He led Cranston and Athelstan up into the choir then left into the sacristy, a long, ill-lit chamber with aumbries on either side for vestments. More albs and surplices hung from pegs on the wall, whilst stacks of coffers, caskets and chests filled every available space. Two Benedictines sat behind a table at the far end. They rose as Cranston and Athelstan approached, waving their guests to chairs before the table.

'Sir John Cranston, Brother Athelstan, you are most welcome.'

One of the Blackrobes came around the table to clasp hands and exchange the kiss of peace, his companion, moving a little slower, did the same. Cranston and Athelstan then took their seats. Two more candles were lit, bathing the table in a pool of light.

'There.' The Benedictine leaned forward. 'Let there be light, eh Sir John, Brother Athelstan? I am Sylvester, principal sacristan of this abbey, and this is our infirmarian Prior Norbert. I understand you have questions to ask. Please accept our assurance that we will help as much as we can. But now,' Sylvester waved to a tray bearing silver-chased goblets, 'some refreshments, sweetmeats, a cup of Rhenish to refresh the mouth? I am afraid we cannot join you. The great Advent fast has begun.'

'A time for discipline and penitence?'

'Of course, Brother Athelstan, all to prepare for the Holy Season and the great feast of Christ's birth. Please?'

Cranston and Athelstan accepted a cup and one of the delicious sweetmeats; a mixture of honey, no bigger than a coin,

it simply melted in Athelstan's mouth. So delicate, he took
another. The friar used the occasion, whilst the usual courtesies
were being exchanged, to study the two Benedictines. Sylvester
was a youngish man, the image of the perfect monk with his
smooth, well-oiled, clean-shaven face, expressive eyes and full
lips. His eyebrows were neatly clipped, his tonsure perfectly
cut. Sylvester's robes were of sheer, black wool, his cincture
snow-white. Rings adorned his fingers and a silver brooch
circled his left wrist. Sylvester was well-spoken though with a
slight accent. Athelstan queried him on this and the sacristan
explained how he had been raised in Scotland and educated at
Melrose.

'So you know Prior Sinclair?'

'Of course and, before you ask, our anchorite as well, he
must have seen your arrival.'

'Ah, Brother Ricard, the so-called Magician of Melrose?'

'Mad as a march hare,' Brother Norbert intervened.

'Why?' Cranston demanded.

'Because, my Lord Coroner, his humours are greatly disturbed
caused by speculation on truth he should have left well alone.
There are certain paths scholars should not even dream of
walking, for they are fraught with danger. Oh yes . . .'

The infirmarian lapsed into silence as the sacristan gripped
him gently by the arm. Prior Norbert was a complete contrast
to his companion. He had an almost skeletal face with deep-set
dark eyes and white, wispy streaks of hair. Sharp-nosed and
thin-lipped, the infirmarian, with his claw-like fingers and dusty
robe, reminded Athelstan of some black-feathered bird of prey.

'Well, well.' Athelstan put his goblet firmly back on the table.
'We are here about the sudden death, or should I say murder,
of your sub-sacristan, Brother Robert, earlier today. He collapsed
and died during Lauds?'

'He did, Brother Athelstan.'

'Well at the moment there's not much to discuss,' Athelstan
remarked. 'So it's best if we view the corpse immediately.'

'Is that necessary?'

'I am afraid so, Prior Norbert. No one wants to disturb the
dead, but I need – we need – to view that corpse.'

The prior glanced at his companion, who simply shrugged

and nodded. Both Benedictines rose and led Cranston and Athelstan back into the choir, across the sanctuary and down into the nave. They were making their way across to the north door when a voice rang out, strong and strident.

'Greetings, my Lord High Coroner! Greetings, Brother Athelstan, Dominican friar and parish priest of that nest of sinners at St Erconwald's.'

Athelstan paused, glancing to his left and right.

'Over here,' Sylvester murmured. 'The anchorite cell.'

Sylvester led them deep into the shadows of the transept. The anker-hold was simply a wooden box, an oaken enclosure built against the outside wall of the abbey. It was cleverly constructed, with a pentile roof, three sides of polished wood with a door in the centre panel. Above this was a grille, a squint through which the anchorite could view what was going on around him. Athelstan tried the handle on the narrow door but it was locked from within. Standing on tiptoe, Athelstan peered through the grille at the eyes glaring back at him.

'Greetings indeed, Brother Athelstan,' the anchorite proclaimed. 'You want to question me? Then come in, but only you. Not the others. Not Fat Jack. Certainly not my brethren from the abbey.' Athelstan glanced at Cranston who merely shrugged.

'Do what you have to,' Sylvester murmured.

Athelstan knocked on the door to the anker-hold. It swung open, creaking on its hinges. Athelstan glanced at these; they were of the hardest leather, and yellowing with age. The friar stepped into the cell and looked around. The chamber was neat and clean, the air fresh with the scent of burning incense snaking up from a thurible in the corner. There was a cot bed, a stool, a chest, a table and a lavarium. The anchorite pulled back his hood. Athelstan clasped his hand and pulled him close to exchange the kiss of peace. The anchorite's hands and face were freezing even though a brazier, crackling with fiery charcoal, more than warmed the room. The impression of iciness was heightened by the anchorite's face and watery, sad eyes. Nevertheless, he was personable enough, patting his bald pate and tapping his shaven cheeks.

'No hair, Brother Athelstan, because I am really no longer a

Blackrobe, so no tonsure.' The man's voice, thickened by a strong northern burr, faded away as he glanced quickly to his right and left as if something was distracting him. He stood scratching his chin, lost in thought, then glanced slyly at Athelstan. 'Brother,' he waved the friar to a stool, 'you can sit there whilst I perch, like a scholar, on the edge of my bed. Now,' he leaned forward as Athelstan settled himself, 'you have questions to ask me?'

'I certainly have, my good anchorite. What happened on the night you tolled the tocsin? Well?'

The anchorite grinned slyly, whispered to himself, and Athelstan wondered if the man was fully in his wits yet, just as abruptly, the grin faded, being replaced by a knowing, cunning look.

'This abbey is a strange place, Brother Athelstan.'

'Why?'

'A hall of ghosts, a place of flitting shadows. The dead throng here. I can hear them whispering as they ride the air.'

'And on that particular night?'

'Oh, the abbey was locked and shuttered. The night lanterns had been lit and placed along the nave. I am glad they do, Brother Athelstan; they keep the darkness at bay even though the shadows still dance. They dance and they dance. I am sure they call my name then they go. You see, once this abbey is locked, silence descends. That night was different. I am sure I heard voices and the sound of grating.'

'Grating?'

'Yes, Athelstan, grating as if a piece of timber was being dragged along the nave, but that also faded. I thought it was my imagination until I heard noises again. I peered through the squint,' the anchorite pointed to the grille high in the door, 'I saw them. Honestly, Brother Athelstan. I saw the demons dance. I thought I saw the flap of their jerkins and heard their demonic bells.'

'Demons? Bells?'

'Oh yes, Friar, they were long and tall, at least a child's height, sliding and twisting around the pillars. Up and down, up and down, climbing here, climbing there! Then,' the anchorite made a face, 'more noise! God knows what that was, then there was silence. I sat straining for any sound but there was none. I became nervous, frightened. I,' he paused, 'the Advent fast had begun.' He moaned. 'It started this Sunday morning and now it is Sunday evening. Oh Brother, what I would love is a plate of those honeyed comfits I saw being taken into the sacristy.'

'Perhaps Prior Norbert might . . .'

'No, Brother, not now! The prior and sacristan are strict, obedient to the letter and the spirit of our rule, even though I am no longer a Blackrobe.'

'So, to return to that night here in the abbey church. Silence descends: did this make you more nervous, agitated?'

'Yes, Brother, so I decided to investigate. There is a narrow postern in the north transept, the Devil's door, the only door to be left unlocked and unbolted just in case something happens here during the night. Sometimes there are vigils or a man may take sanctuary or, of course, there is myself. Anyway, I thought that whatever had troubled me would have left through that postern. So I hurried across, only to find it firmly locked. I became even more concerned,' the anchorite babbled on, 'I tried every single door. They were all locked. I felt as if I was a prisoner. I wondered if some malignant was hiding in the church. Brother Athelstan, I shelter here in my anker-hold. I am not a prisoner, a captive, but that's what I felt that night, trapped in a dark church with heavens knows what.'

'So you sounded the tocsin?'

'Of course.'

'And?'

'Oh, the brothers came hurrying down. The doors were unlocked. The church searched, but nothing was discovered, nothing at all.'

'And Brother Robert?'

'He claimed to have made a simple mistake, it must have been. The only Blackrobes who hold the keys are Brother Robert and, of course, Sacristan Sylvester. They are responsible for all the doors, windows and entrances. They are the ones who lock and unlock. Of course, Father Abbot has his keys and so has Prior Norbert, but they only act when necessary, and certainly not that night.' The anchorite took a deep breath. 'So, you have no food for a poor, famished anchorite?'

'None.' Athelstan smiled apologetically. But,' Athelstan got to his feet, 'I will have a word with Prior Norbert, who knows . . .'

Athelstan left the anker-hold and rejoined Cranston and the two Blackrobes. They were studying a freshly executed wall fresco depicting a scene from Revelation which celebrates the victory of the Lamb of God over the powers of darkness.

'Brilliant,' Athelstan murmured, moving closer to study the hellish scene beneath God's throne. He pointed to a group of gluttons being led away by a cohort of fiery, fat-bellied demons. 'I talked to the anchorite. Amongst other things he mentioned that he was very hungry, already feeling the effects of the great fast. I wonder . . .'

'Later,' Prior Norbert snapped. 'The anchorite must observe the rules and the rituals whilst we, Brother Athelstan, need to show you a corpse.'

PART THREE

'The Devil carry him to his place.'

Brother Fergal Clifford was also wondering about the sub-sacristan's corpse. A fellow Scotsman, Robert had hailed from Arbroath, Fergal's own birthplace. Indeed, they were both, along with the others, as Brother Robert used to style them, 'Guardians of the Stone', the famous Stone of Destiny now resting beneath the great coronation throne which dominated the abbey sanctuary. Brother Fergal was wondering what was the true cause of Robert's death. Was it really murder? Yet, as Fergal had confessed to Prior Norbert, he and Robert had gone down to the choir together. The sub-sacristan, like himself, had eaten and drunk nothing but stoups of clear water; these were ladled out from a bucket used by others of the community without any ill-effects whatsoever.

Fergal returned to his calligraphy. He dipped his quill pen into a pot of gold-coloured ink, embellishing the letters of the script he had just finished. The words, 'In Principio – in the Beginning,' now began to glow with the golden light of the rising sun. Fergal, still distracted by Brother Robert's death, quickly read what he had written. Fergal was certain that something had been troubling Robert, he was sure of it. Before his sad and untimely death, the sub-sacristan had become taciturn and withdrawn, as if distracted by some hidden worry. But what? Had Robert grown homesick for Scotland? The allegiance of the Blackrobes was not to any king or prince but to 'The Sancta Regula – the Holy Rule of St Benedict', as laid down by father abbots in monasteries, priories and abbeys across Europe. These leaders of the Blackrobes, dedicated Benedictines, were very keen to break down barriers between one kingdom and another. Where you came from didn't matter. Who you were, a Benedictine, was the only truth. Accordingly, Englishmen were despatched to Scottish houses whilst the subjects of King Robert II were sent south to abbeys such as Westminster.

Fergal was glad he'd been commissioned to come here. He and the other Guardians of the Stone were close to the very heart of Scottish kingship, whatever the English might proclaim. The Stone of Destiny was very sacred, they knew its every inch. This was the stone Jacob had used as a pillow at Bethel. Pharaoh had later seized it, only to be drowned when Moses closed the sea over the Egyptian army. Above all, this was the stone on which Scottish princes sat, knelt or stood, to be anointed and crowned king.

Fergal stared around the cavernous scriptorium with its polished elmwood carrels, lecterns, desks, shelves and aumbries. Lanterns glowed where they hung from silver hooks driven into the ceiling beams. Capped candles exuded their own scented smoke and light. Fergal swallowed hard. He felt a twinge in his stomach. He wondered if this was God's judgement on him during this holy fast of Advent. He rose and crossed to the small recess where the almoner had laid out pewter jugs of water. Fergal filled a goblet and sipped at the cold freshness. The discomfort in his belly had now turned to a nasty pain, bile coated his throat and shooting pains pierced his chest. He had difficulty in breathing. Fergal staggered back towards his carrel only to crash into desks and chairs. Other monks, now alarmed, jumped up to assist him but Fergal was beyond human help. Mouth frothing, eyes rolling back, choking on his own vomit, Fergal collapsed to the floor.

Athelstan was just finishing his examination of the sub-sacristan's corpse, laid out beneath a white cloth on the mortuary table in the abbey's bleak death house, when a lay brother threw open the door and hurried in to announce 'a horrid death in the scriptorium.' Prior Norbert whispered to the sacristan, gesturing at Cranston and Athelstan to follow him out, back across the small cloisters and into the monastic precincts.

They found the scriptorium in uproar. Chairs and tables had been pushed away or overturned. Some of the brothers crouched together, fingers to their lips like a huddle of frightened children. Others were gathered around the body of a white-haired monk sprawled out on the floor. Prior Norbert immediately imposed order. He and the sacristan cleared the monks away from the victim, allowing Athelstan to kneel down beside the stricken man. The friar immediately searched for the blood pulse in the monk's neck, but there was none, and the same was true when Athelstan felt both wrists. He turned the twisted corpse over and flinched at the dead man's grotesque face. The skin had turned a liverish hue, the parted lips were slightly purple, a thick, dirty mucus seeping out to stain the dead man's bewhiskered chin.

'You'd best give him the requiem blessing,' Prior Norbert advised, coming to crouch on the other side of the corpse with Sacristan Sylvester standing just behind him. Cranston handed Athelstan his chancery satchel. The friar hastily donned the purple stole and undid the metal clasps of the anointing pots. He dipped his finger and daubed a cross on the dead man's forehead, eyes, mouth and chest before murmuring the prayer of absolution. Once finished, assisted by Prior Norbert, Athelstan prised open the dead man's mouth, running his fingers around the shrunken gums and peg-like teeth. Nevertheless, apart from the mucus, there was no trace of any other substance. Athelstan rose and crossed to the lavarium and washed his hands. When he came back, Cranston was questioning both monks about the dead man, his name and duties in the abbey.

'You think Fergal was poisoned, Brother Athelstan?'

'I know so. Wouldn't you agree?'

The sour-faced prior nodded in agreement. 'But how?' he queried. 'When and by whom? Brother Fergal, like the rest of us, had to observe the great fast. He abstained from food and drink.'

'Except for water?'

'But the brothers have informed me,' Norbert replied, 'that Fergal drank from the common jug. Moreover,' the prior stepped closer, lowering his voice, 'Fergal was murdered with some noxious poison. Brother Athelstan, our herb plots, spice and flower gardens contain an array of poisons, as do my coffers, chests and aumbries. Moreover, poisons of every source can be bought along the narrow streets of Westminster, be it in the houses of warlocks and wizards or the apothecary shops which sell without question to anyone who has the means to buy.'

'True, true,' Cranston agreed. 'Westminster is a place where poisoning is common along with other deep-dyed, mortal sins. We know the poison came from somewhere. More pressing is: how was it administered?'

'I have searched his mouth,' Athelstan murmured, staring down at the corpse. 'Nothing. And there is nothing here?'

'Nothing,' Prior Norbert declared. 'Nothing that has not been shared by others.'

'And Fergal's cell?'

Norbert shrugged. 'Let me show you.'

They left the scriptorium, going along a stone-paved corridor to a gallery and a row of individual cells. These were nothing more than narrow chambers, each with a lancet window, lavarium, cot bed, table and stool, a chest beneath a row of pegs and a stark crucifix nailed in some prominent place. Many of the cells had been left wide open, their doors pushed back, most of the brothers being busy on different tasks across the abbey.

They entered Fergal's cell, no different from the rest with its simple furniture and few personal possessions. Athelstan thoroughly searched for any food or drink that might have been recently taken, but couldn't find even a trace of a crumb or a drop. Murmuring his thanks, Athelstan let the two monks escort both him and Cranston back to the abbey church. Prior Norbert asked if there was anything else the coroner or Athelstan wanted to see or do? Cranston responded by saying they were ready to leave. Athelstan was about to say the same but paused at a crashing sound which echoed through the nave.

'Building work,' Athelstan queried, 'on a Sunday?'

'No,' Sacristan Sylvester retorted. 'I will show you.'

He led them back across the sanctuary, into the nave and down to an outside door. Athelstan expected the anchorite to shout a greeting but the nave lay deathly silent. Sylvester opened the door and Athelstan gazed out at a cart where workmen were unloading stone slabs. 'Brother Sylvester wants,' Prior Norbert smiled, 'to create a small paved area where we can stand when the weather is poor and our feet don't become clogged in thick mud. The work has just recently started and I hope it continues tomorrow. Now Brother Athelstan, Sir John, is there anything else?'

Cranston glanced at Athelstan who just shook his head. They made their farewells of the two Benedictines and walked quickly back to King's Steps and the waiting barge. They clambered in for a turbulent yet safe crossing, landing at Southwark side, tramping the narrow streets winding up to St Erconwald's.

Even though it was only late afternoon, darkness was falling. The cold had grown more bitter, driving people indoors, away from the constantly buffeting breeze. Good-hearted bailiffs had created bonfires so the poor and dispossessed, as well as the usual dark-dwellers, could congregate. They could warm themselves before the fires as well as cook the scraps of meat and vegetables they'd either filched or picked up from beneath the market stalls. Many of these nightmare figures were well-known to Athelstan: Toad-Face, No-Teeth, Spotted Simon, Lawrence the Lunatic, Mulkin the Mad. These congregated with other members of their tribe; moon people, troubadours, chanteurs, riddle-makers, chapmen and tinkers, they all greeted Athelstan with cries for help. He distributed what few coins he had and they passed on. They reached the precinct of St Erconwald's, that great paved expanse stretching before the church. Athelstan paused and stared around. The church seemed empty, no light glowed, and the doors were undoubtedly locked. God's Acre lay eerily quiet. Cranston, who'd decided to accompany his little friar to ensure all was well, pointed back down the alleyway.

'Brother, you heard them. Your beloved parishioners are in the rival church. If you want to see what mischief they are up to, we'd best go back.'

'Yes, yes, Sir John, you are correct. Let us join them in The Piebald.'

Cranston was correct, the tavern taproom was packed with parishioners. They sat cradling tankards of blackjacks, listening rapturously to a speaker standing on a crate. Beside him, another stranger nodded in agreement to everything the chanteur was relating. Athelstan held a finger to his lips as a sign for Sir John to remain silent. Cranston, however, leaned down.

'Halpen the Hare,' he whispered, 'and his henchman Mildew. Both cheeks of same filthy arse. Both fit for hell as any unrepentant sinner.'

Athelstan simply shook his head as he peered through the poor light at both visitors. He had certainly heard about the precious pair. Envoys, leading couriers of the Upright Men, trusted representatives of the Great Community of the Realm, well protected by the Earthworms. Athelstan had learnt how these twins of terror, like so many rebel leaders, had earned a royal pardon by voluntarily surrendering to the King's peace. Both men certainly deserved their names. Halpen was slim and wiry with brown, greasy, spiky hair, flat twitching nose, large pointed ears, pursed lips and protuberant front teeth. Halpen looked like a hare. Mildew, on the other hand, was squat and fat, greasy hair plastered flat over his balding head. He had pouches for cheeks, his plump face blotched and spotty. Nevertheless, despite appearances, Halpen and Mildew had their audience in thrall. Halpen was a born chanteur, a storyteller, a spinner of words, and he used this to describe Wat Tyler's march on London, the plundering of the city and, above all, the attack on John of Gaunt's palace, the Savoy. Watkin, Pike and the rest sat in the front row, either side of their guest of honour, Prior Sinclair, who seemed totally absorbed by the story. Athelstan, standing next to Cranston in the shadows of the doorway, carefully peered through the murk at a stranger standing to the friar's left, leaning against the taproom wall. Athelstan had never seen him before. The newcomer was garbed in dark leather jerkin and leggings, his military cloak and well-furnished warbelt thrown casually over his shoulder. The stranger had night-black hair, his sour face was clean-shaven. He seemed interested in Halpen's tale, yet kept looking around as if searching for someone else. At last, Halpen finished with a vivid description of the confrontation between the young King and the rebel leader Wat Tyler at Smithfield. He then pointed dramatically at Cranston.

'In which,' Halpen trumpeted, 'our noble Sir John, the Lord High Coroner of London, played a most dramatic role. No less than executing Tyler. Sir John valiantly dragged the rebel leader from St Bartholomew's and brought him to the proper place for execution.'

All the customers in the taproom now turned, staring at Cranston. A few smiled; others just gave dark, glowering looks. Athelstan caught the smouldering resentments of some of those present. After all, it was only a few months since the rebellion had petered out, wounds still festered, grievances and grudges still nursed. The friar sensed the tensions gathering in the taproom. He walked forward, pushing his way through, clapping his hands while proclaiming how both he and the Lord High Coroner needed a little refreshment. At the appearance of their beloved parish priest, the tensions dissipated. The crowd broke up, surging towards the buttery table, eager for Joscelyn and his minions to fill their empty blackjacks. Halpen and Mildew approached Cranston, hands extended, but the coroner ignored them. Athelstan, noting how truly ugly both men were, simply sketched a blessing in their direction. He then followed Cranston over to where Prior Sinclair stood in deep conversation with Watkin, Pike and Benedicta. Athelstan saluted all four.

'Well?' he demanded, putting his hand on their visitor's shoulder. 'You have learnt a lot?'

'I certainly have.'

'Prior Sinclair wishes to stay longer,' Benedicta declared.

'I certainly do. I look forward to it. I am very happy to be here. I give glory and thanks to the Lord High God.'

The prior's accent was now more pronounced. He was red-faced, slightly fumbled, and Athelstan realized that their visitor had drunk deep on Joscelyn's specially brewed ale.

'Prior Sinclair has been given the bridal chamber,' Watkin, equally flushed, announced dramatically. 'It will be next to the one Joscelyn has reserved for Halpen and Mildew.'

'Why did you choose those two?' Athelstan asked.

Watkin simply stared back, eyes blinking. 'We chose them, Father, because they know more than most people.'

'I have offered to reward them,' Prior Sinclair intervened, 'and I have asked them to stay here. I will pay their bills. They can have good lodging and hearty meals. Your parishioners fully agree, Halpen and Mildew will be lavishly entertained.'

Athelstan nodded as Pike began to describe some of the tavern's favourite dishes. Athelstan half listened but he was truly intrigued at how swiftly matters were proceeding. Sinclair was a Scottish friar yet he had seemed to ease his way in here without any trouble, and why Halpen and Mildew?

'Why Halpen and Mildew?' Athelstan spoke the question before he could stop himself. 'I am sorry, I know I have asked this but I am truly intrigued.'

'Father, as I said,' Watkin retorted, 'they are knowledgeable, they are old comrades. They feel safe coming to our parish with you, Prior Sinclair and, of course, Sir John.'

'Did you ask for them?' Athelstan turned to Sinclair.

'We recited a list,' Pike slurred.

'Your parishioners recommended Halpen and Mildew, so they were chosen.' Prior Sinclair raised his blackjack. 'I am so very pleased.'

Athelstan smiled understandingly but he was still intrigued. He felt as if he and his parish were being swept along on a wave of events they couldn't control. So many things coming together at the same time. The disturbance at Westminster, the murder of the two brothers, Sinclair's presence at St Erconwald's and the emergence of Halpen and Mildew.

'Father?' Watkin demanded.

'Ah yes, ah yes.' Athelstan nodded across the taproom. 'Who's the stranger, the gentleman leaning against the wall?'

Cranston stared hard at the newcomer. 'A former soldier,' he murmured. 'Perhaps a mercenary, now turned bounty hunter. I have seen the likes before.'

'He calls himself Paltoc,' Watkin blurted out.

'Does he now?' Cranston retorted. 'Then it's best, before I go, that we have words with Master Paltoc. Gentlemen, Lady Benedicta,' Cranston bowed, 'I bid you goodnight.'

Cranston, accompanied by an equally curious Athelstan, pushed his way through the merry throng, ignoring the good-natured catcalls and jokes. Paltoc, who'd sat down on a stool, now rose to greet them, putting his cloak and warbelt on the floor beside him. He bowed at Cranston and Athelstan.

'What an honour indeed. A meeting with the famous Sir Jack and his equally illustrious secretarius Athelstan.'

'Forget the flattery.' Cranston poked the man gently in the chest.

Paltoc simply smiled. 'No flattery, Sir John, simply the truth.'

'And the truth about you, sir?'

'I am Paltoc . . .'

'Was this the name given to you over the baptismal font? I mean, if you were ever baptized?'

'I certainly was, Sir John. If Brother Athelstan scrutinizes the baptismal records of his ancient church, you will find an entry on the second of February – the feast of the Purification of the Virgin – the year of our Lord 1351. I was baptized Hugh Jonathan Paltoc. If you then search amongst the funeral entries, you will find the burials of my mother and father as well as my younger brother Raoul.' Paltoc's accent became more noticeable as he stumbled over certain words.

'You are Hispanic?'

'My father was, Sir John. He hailed from Castile. My mother was English.'

'Ah yes.' Cranston took a step forward, peering close at Paltoc. 'Yes, you are Hispanic. Your father must have joined the retinue of John of Gaunt when our noble regent journeyed to Castile. He had a personal guard of Hispanics though many of them . . .'

'Have left.' Paltoc finished his sentence.

'As did you.' Cranston stepped back. 'And now you are a mercenary. You hunt for reward. You are ready to take the heads of those who are declared wolfsheads, utlegatum – beyond the law? Yes?'

Paltoc, slanted eyes all wary, nodded. 'You have it, Sir John.'

'So whom do you hunt?'

'Why you, Sir John.'

'I beg your pardon?'

'Sir John, I joke. I went to the Guildhall. Simon your scrivener informed me that if you were not lodged at The Lamb of God, you would be here at St Erconwald's.' Paltoc smiled. 'I was only too pleased to return to my own parish. I have heard a great deal about you, Brother Athelstan.'

'Never mind that,' Cranston barked. 'You haven't answered my question and I am getting impatient.'

'Sir John, *pax et bonum*. I meant no offence. I came searching for you because I am looking for employment.' Paltoc picked up his warbelt and strapped it on. 'I have learnt about a sinister assassin prowling the slums who likes to skin his victims.' Paltoc cleared his throat abruptly. 'The dark-dwellers are calling him "The Flayer". I understand there are proclamations against him posted on the Cross at St Paul's, the Standard in Cheapside and elsewhere. A princely sum for his head.'

'And what makes you think you can catch him?'

'Because that's what I am good at, hunting and trapping killers. Yes, I served with my Lord of Gaunt. I left his service. I stayed in Scotland for a while then I journeyed south. London provides the best hunting ground. So, to answer your question, Sir John, I am a hunter.'

'In which case,' Cranston patted Athelstan gently on the shoulder, 'you have a great deal in common with my bosom comrade here, but look, Master Paltoc, early tomorrow come to my chambers at the Guildhall. We will seal indentures, agree to expenses and discuss the reward you will receive if you trap this killer. I want, I need, the Flayer to be hanged, and the sooner the better. Do you understand?'

'Yes, Sir John.'

The coroner and Paltoc clasped hands; the mercenary then picked up his cloak and bade them goodnight.

'Any port in the storm, Brother Athelstan,' Cranston murmured, watching Paltoc shoulder his way through to the buttery table. The mercenary then abruptly turned and came back, but this time he approached Athelstan.

'Brother, I have a favour to ask. I need to search out the graves of my parents and brother. I walked your cemetery – crosses, plinths, memorial stones, even bushes, have either disappeared or been moved?'

'Yes, yes they have,' Athelstan replied. 'Terrible damage was done during the Great Revolt. The rebels from the south swept through here on their way to London Bridge. I could lock and bar my church but not my cemetery. Many rebels camped in God's Acre. They had very little respect for the living, never mind the dead. But, if I can help in any way . . .'

Paltoc thanked him and rejoined the throng milling around the buttery table.

'Brother Athelstan,' Cranston declared, 'I must be gone. The shadows lengthen and the day is done. Pray God for a quiet night.'

Cranston and Athelstan exchanged the kiss of peace and the coroner left. Athelstan stared around the noisy taproom.

'And I must go too,' he murmured. 'It's time for prayer then for bed.'

If Athelstan had hoped for a quiet night, he was disappointed. The friar was roused at first light by a pounding on the door. He hurriedly dressed and went down to where a breathless Benedicta, accompanied by Crim the altar boy, were waiting in the freezing cold. Crim lifted his lantern.

'Follow us, Father,' he explained, 'but watch your footing. There's been a hard frost.'

'Brother Athelstan,' Benedicta grasped Athelstan's wrist, 'you'd best come to The Piebald, something's very wrong. Joscelyn went up to the chamber where Halpen and Mildew were sleeping. In a word, Brother, they cannot be roused. The door was locked and bolted from within.' Benedicta pulled at his wrist. 'You must come, you must come!'

Athelstan hastily donned his robe and cloak, fastened on his sandals, and followed the bobbing pool of light from Crim's lanternhorn. They crossed God's Acre into the precinct then along the alleyway leading to The Piebald. A cold, sombre dawn. Merrylegs' cook shop had just opened. The pastry cook, assisted by his host of children, were firing the ovens, braziers and half stoves.

Outside the shop, the youngest of the family stood with a tray of sweetmeats. Crim took one, as did Benedicta, absentmindedly popping them into their mouths. Athelstan almost followed suit but then didn't. Merrylegs shouted a greeting, followed by a question about what was happening, but Athelstan and his escort hurried on. They reached The Piebald; its taproom was still busy. Customers from the night before had slept either on benches or makeshift mattresses. Athelstan followed Benedicta across the taproom and up a broad set of stairs. Athelstan always quietly marvelled at The Piebald. Despite its rather dingy

exterior, its galleries and stairs were broad, sturdy and fairly
well lit. They reached the top. Joscelyn, together with Watkin,
Pike, Crispin, and others of their coven, were gathered outside
a chamber at the far end of the gallery. The room next to this
was occupied by Prior Sinclair. The bleary-eyed Scottish monk
had come out to discover the cause of the tumult. Benedicta
stood aside to allow Athelstan through.

'I heard the banging.' Prior Sinclair, face heavy with sleep,
caught at Athelstan's arm. 'A noise to wake the dead!'

'Sorry,' Watkin rasped, 'but Halpen and Mildew asked to be
roused at daybreak. I and my,' Watkin jabbed a finger towards
Pike, 'I and my comrades were sleeping the sleep of the just
downstairs. Yes, Joscelyn?'

'I knocked and I knocked.' The one-armed taverner shook
his head. 'But nothing.'

'Right.' Athelstan turned and pointed at Crim. 'We will need
you and a ladder. How big is the chamber window?'

'Not very big, Father.' Joscelyn scratched his chin.
'Certainly not big enough for a man to crawl through. Anyway,
it is shuttered from inside.'

'Though you can squint through the gap,' Crim blurted out,
then covered his mouth with his hand.

'Can you now?' Athelstan leaned down. 'Crim, is it true?' The
altar boy just stared back. 'Is it true,' the friar repeated, 'that you
and other boys climb up a ladder to peer into the chambers when
Cecily and her sister are entertaining some passing traveller?
Well, that's not for now. Joscelyn, you have a ladder, yes? Crim,
you will go up. On second thoughts,' Athelstan unclasped his
cloak, 'I will do it myself.'

'Father!'

'Don't worry, Benedicta, these worthies will hold the ladder
secure.'

They went down through the taproom and into the tavern
yard. Joscelyn ordered the ladder to be brought and leaned it
just beneath the chamber window. For a while, there was some
confusion, then Athelstan, gripping the ladder by its sides, began
the ascent. He reached the top trying to ignore the cold, buffeting
breeze. He pulled at both shutters but they were clasped fast.
He pushed each one slightly to the side and created a narrow

gap. Athelstan, balancing himself carefully, stared through the slit he'd created and groaned at what he glimpsed. Halpen the Hare and Mildew, garbed in their nightshirts, hung by their necks from stout hooks driven into the beams which spanned the ceiling. Turning his head, Athelstan could clearly see the two corpses twirling slightly to the eerie creak of the ceiling beam. Athelstan scrabbled down the ladder.

'Force the door,' he rasped. 'Both men are dead, murdered, hanging by their necks.'

'In heaven's name,' Benedicta exclaimed.

'How can that be?' Watkin murmured. 'Last night was most enjoyable, an evening of merry roistering, and now this?'

'And how?' Joscelyn exclaimed. 'My tavern enjoys a good reputation. Both men were hale and hearty when they adjourned to their chamber.'

'Force the door,' Athelstan interrupted. 'Force it now. The chamber has a lock?'

'Yes, Father, a good stout one. The key still hangs on the inside. The door is bolted at top and bottom from within.'

'Come, it is time.'

Athelstan strode back into the taproom and up to the chamber. Watkin and his companions, at Athelstan's insistence, followed, carrying a yule log from the store. Athelstan crouched down and peered through the keyhole. The key was still there. Athelstan then pressed at the top and bottom of the door until he was satisfied that both bolts had been pulled fully across. He then studied the hinges; thick, dust-laid, leather clasps pressed in and glued to connect the door to the lintel. Athelstan turned to his parishioners. They just stood silently, watching him intently. Athelstan repressed a slight shiver. There was something very, very wrong here. True, two men had been hanged and yet . . .

'Father?'

'The door hangs secure, it must be forced.'

'It's best if we aim for the hinges.' Crispin the carpenter shouldered his way through. 'Father, the lock and bolts will be harder to smash.'

Athelstan agreed. The yule log was lifted by six parishioners and, under their priest's direction, they began to pound the door, smashing the wood close to both hinges. The battering continued. The men paused now and again to catch their breath and ease the soreness of muscle and limb. Joscelyn's minions brought up stoups of ale then the crashing continued. The ruined door sagged, hanging off its tattered hinges so it could be forced back to create an entry. Athelstan ordered everyone to stay outside then squeezed into the chamber. The room smelt foul. A still burning taper candle afforded some light to illuminate the horror of those two corpses swinging gently by their necks. A truly silent, sombre place, just those corpses moving, the rope and beam creaking.

Athelstan, warning others not to cross the threshold, swiftly scrutinized the chamber. He picked up an almost empty wine jug and goblets, sniffing at their contents, swilling the wine around, yet he could detect nothing amiss. He quickly emptied the remains of food left on a platter into the jug followed by the dregs from the goblets. Ignoring the rising murmur at the doorway, Athelstan carefully continued his scrutiny. The window was nothing more than a small square of wood carefully fixed into the stonework and filled with stiffened parchment still intact. The shutters were firmly barred; even if they had been open, no one could have used such a narrow gap to get in and out of the room. The floor and ceiling were sound, as were the plastered walls. There was certainly no trace or indication of a secret entrance.

Athelstan turned to the two corpses. He gave both a blessing then glanced around. The clothing and warbelts of both victims lay heaped on top of a chamber chest. Both sword and dagger were firmly sheathed, nor did the room betray any sign of violence. Athelstan examined the ice-cold wrists and fingers of the murder victims. He could detect no sign of resistance, no mark or ligature around the wrists to indicate they had been bound, no wisps of rope in their fingernails. Athelstan could only conclude that both men had been hanged, offering no resistance to the ropes choking them to death.

'It looks like suicide,' Athelstan whispered to himself. 'But that's ridiculous. Two men in the same chamber, hanging themselves at the same time. Utter nonsense! Moreover, if they did hang themselves, what did they stand on? Where is the stool, the ladder, the table which they would have used then kicked away to begin their death struggle? And the why.' Athelstan went between the swinging corpses and glimpsed the small scraps of parchment pinned to the sleeve of each nightshirt. A square piece of well-scrubbed parchment. He loosened both, crossed to the candle and peered down at the two words scrawled in red ink. 'Justica Fiat – let justice be done,' and underneath a crudely drawn sickle which Athelstan recognized as the insignia of the Reapers. Still ignoring the clamour at the doorway, Athelstan stared down at the scraps of parchment. The Reapers were truly a menacing threat. They were the most ardent of the Upright Men, ruthless leaders of the Earthworms. Both before and during the revolt they had imposed order to protect the purity of their dogma, summed up in that doggerel verse:

'When Adam dug and Eve span

Who was then the gentleman?'

After the revolt had been crushed, the Reapers became a coven dealing out summary punishment to those they considered deserved it. But how and why now? Athelstan turned and snapped his fingers at Pike and the rest thronging in the doorway.

'Cut the corpses down.' The leading members of the parish council edged nervously in.

'Come, come,' Athelstan urged, 'we have seen enough corpses in our day.'

Encouraged by their priest, the parishioners pulled across a chest. Pike climbed on, dagger drawn, and severed both hanging ropes, whilst the rest, joined by others including Benedicta and Mauger, caught the corpses and laid them out on the floor. Athelstan, holding the phials of sacred oils that Crim had hastily fetched from the priest's house, administered the requiem. Moving swiftly, he tried to ignore the twisted, purple faces and swollen tongues caught between rotting teeth, the dried spit coating the stubbled chins of both dead men. Once he had finished, Athelstan examined the corpses for any sign of recent violence. Pike whispered how both men had once served in the royal array. Athelstan nodded as he inspected old scars and long healed wounds. Satisfied that he could find nothing amiss,

Athelstan administered the final blessing. He then ordered the two corpses to be taken to the parish death house, adding that he would meet the full parish council immediately after the Jesus Mass.

Athelstan tried to keep his mind closed to the rush of thoughts threatening to distract him completely. He had returned to the priest's house, shaved, washed and dressed properly. Once ready, he had hurried down to the church and, as reverentially as he could, celebrated the divine mysteries. The friar now heaved a sigh of relief as he sat down in the throne-like sanctuary chair. Mauger and others had arranged this as well as benches for this important meeting of the parish council. Athelstan could certainly sense the excitement and tension over the two killings. His parishioners being as keen as he was to discover the truth behind the murderous mystery.

'No formal record will be kept,' Athelstan declared, turning to Mauger, 'a simple memorandum to my own satisfaction and that of Sir John Cranston.' The Lord High Coroner's name stilled the murmuring and whispering.

'Oh yes.' Athelstan rose to his feet and crossed to the lectern; he paused as Paltoc, cloaked and hooded, came sauntering in. The mercenary pulled back his hood, nodded at Athelstan then went and sat down with his back to the baptismal font. 'There is no doubt,' Athelstan continued, 'that two hideous murders have been perpetrated at The Piebald. I cannot accept that Halpen and Mildew both committed suicide at the same time. They seemed contented enough, whilst there is no evidence that they brought about their own deaths. So,' Athelstan moved back to sit in his chair, 'Watkin, what happened last night?'

'A very enjoyable evening,' Prior Sinclair declared as he swept into the church, strode around the parish council and stopped to bow to Athelstan. 'Brother, my apologies. I decided to return to my own chamber. I hope sooner rather than later I can celebrate my own Mass. In the meantime, may I join you?'

'Of course.' Athelstan smiled and gestured to an empty space next to Benedicta. 'Prior Sinclair, you are most welcome. I would appreciate any contribution you make.'

'Father, how long will we be here?' Remart the relic seller, sitting on the edge of a bench, shuffled to his feet.

'Were you there last night?' Athelstan asked. Remart shook his head.

'Father, I went out to sell items and returned long after the chimes of midnight.'

'Is that so?' Athelstan asked, staring around. A chorus of agreement answered his question.

'In which case, Remart, you and any others not involved may go.' Athelstan was quietly amused that the relic seller was the only one to leave; the rest, wherever they had actually been on that fateful evening, were riveted by the unfolding mystery. 'Very good. So, Watkin, what happened?'

'A night of revelry, Father, that's all. Halpen and Mildew drank deep, very deep, and then adjourned to their chamber.'

'One of the best,' Joscelyn interrupted, 'one of the very best rooms in my tavern.'

'Quite, quite,' Athelstan retorted. 'More importantly, did anyone visit them?'

Watkin shuffled his mud-caked boots and grinned slyly.

'Watkin?'

'We did.' Cecily the courtesan and her sister Clarissa leapt to their feet, both young women glaring defiantly around. The temper of these two ladies was legendary. No one dared even snigger or whisper. Members of the council just stared down at the floor or up at the cobwebbed ceiling. Athelstan followed their gaze and quietly promised himself to arrange a thorough clean once winter had passed.

'As I said, we did,' Cecily repeated.

'Very well. And when you ladies left the chamber, Halpen and Mildew were very much alive?'

'A little tired,' Cecily replied, ignoring a snigger from behind her. 'They were mawmsy with drink.'

'They certainly were,' Watkin agreed.

'So Cecily and Clarissa leave the chamber. Nobody else went up and no one saw, glimpsed or heard anything amiss?'

'No one, Father, no one at all.' The Hangman of Rochester, who'd been standing in the shadow of the door, walked forward. 'Father, I have scrutinized both corpses, the nooses and the knots which tied them.' He laughed abruptly. 'Certainly not my handiwork, but undoubtedly that of a professional, someone who has carried out hangings. A simple knot, Father, which would slip and tighten the noose. Both men would have choked to death in a most frightful way.' The hangman's words created a deep silence amongst the parishioners.

'And the Reapers?' Athelstan demanded. 'Do you know any of them, I mean personally?' Again, silence. 'Any strangers seen around here last night?'

'I saw four men hooded and visored,' Benedicta called out. 'Crispin, you also saw them?'

'I went out into the alleyway,' the carpenter declared, 'I glimpsed a group of strangers further down. I caught the glint of steel. I went back in. Benedicta was just inside the doorway. I told her what I'd seen. We both slipped out into the alleyway. The strangers looked as if they were going to approach, even confront us, but then they turned and disappeared into the dark.'

'Anything else?' Athelstan insisted. 'Anything amiss, out of the ordinary? Anything?' Athelstan struggled to remain calm. He stared hard at his parishioners. He did not know what was the most challenging: the mystery of what had happened in that chamber, or the baffling silence which now confronted him. 'I am searching,' Athelstan's voice turned harsh and carrying, 'I am searching for an explanation as to how two men, guests of this parish who offered to help Prior Sinclair, another guest, could end up being choked to death at the very heart of our community. Halpen and Mildew were murdered in that chamber, but how the assassin could enter and perpetrate such a crime and then, just as quietly, disappear is a true mystery. Moreover, there is no sign of violence or resistance from these two men, former soldiers. Equally baffling is how the murderer could escape from that chamber when its one and only entrance remained locked and bolted from within.' Athelstan drew a deep breath. 'For the moment we can do nothing, except give those two victims honourable burial in God's Acre. God have mercy on them and on this community.'

Athelstan rose and collected his belongings. He swept out of the church and went up through God's Acre to the priest's house.

Unlocking the door, he went in. Everything was in order; Benedicta must have visited it after Mass. The bedloft was orderly and neat. The great kitchen table scrubbed to a cleanness, whilst oatmeal bubbled in a pot over a carefully banked fire glowing in the narrow, mantled hearth. Herbert the hedgehog had rolled itself up into a ball in the far corner. Bonaventure, who had faithfully followed Athelstan from the church, sniffed at the hedgehog then stretched out in front of the fire. Athelstan always prayed, as he did now, that both tomcat and hedgehog would live amicably. Herbert really should live out in the garden, but Benedicta insisted he did great work in cleaning the floor of flies, insects and other vermin.

Athelstan sketched a blessing in Herbert's direction and poured Bonaventure a dish of fresh milk then served himself a bowl of steaming oatmeal. He ate slowly, stopping now and again to sip at his blackjack of morning ale. He thought about the great fast at Westminster now that the season of Advent had begun. Athelstan put his horn spoon down and closed his eyes. He reflected on those two monks, the victims of poisoning, leaving their chambers. The first was intent on chanting Divine Office, the second to work in his scriptorium. Both had no means to get food or drink except a stoup of water used by the community. No trace of any other food or drink was available to them. He had examined their corpses, the mouths of both dead monks were clean and clear. The abbey refectory and buttery would be locked and vigilant. Abbey officials such as the strict-faced Norbert would ensure that the fast was observed, in both the letter and the spirit of the rule. So how had those men been poisoned? What was the common link here?

Athelstan opened his eyes. Brothers Robert and Fergal were from Scotland, as were Prior Norbert, Sacristan Sylvester and, of course, Prior Sinclair. Secondly, did the poisonings have anything to do with the strange events earlier in the week, when the now slain sub-sacristan Brother Robert made a mistake in locking all the doors of the abbey? Yet this posed another mystery. The anchorite, the so-called 'Magician of Melrose', claimed something or someone remained in the deserted abbey church after it had been locked. The anchorite talked of glimpsing a flapping cloth, of hearing bells and seeing a dark shape or shadow flitting about the church. Indeed, the recluse had become so terrified, he had left his anker-hold. He saw nothing, but grew even more fearful when he realized he might be trapped in the abbey church with whatever sinister presence lurked there.

'What,' Athelstan whispered to himself, 'was all that about?' And, to return to St Erconwald's. What was the truth behind Halpen and Mildew's death in that locked chamber? Why and how were they killed? Had the Reapers, somehow, truly struck in such a mysterious way? Then there was that grisly, gruesome assassin, 'The Flayer'. Athelstan felt a deep revulsion at what he'd seen in that filthy cellar. A true experience of evil, of cruelty and degradation inflicted on one of God's poor innocents; a wretched end to a wretched life. Athelstan crossed himself. He was about to open his chancery satchel when he heard a sharp knocking at the door.

'Come in!' Athelstan shouted. Prior Sinclair and Paltoc, bitterly complaining about the cold, came in rubbing their hands and stamping their feet against the chill. Athelstan insisted that both his visitors sit on stools on the other side of the table. Both gratefully accepted the bowls of hot oatmeal and blackjacks of morning ale. Cloaks thrown aside, Athelstan's two visitors attacked the food and drink with gusto, complaining between mouthfuls about how it was so cold, snow must be imminent. As they ate and talked, Athelstan studied his visitors carefully. He sensed there was something wrong yet he could not express it. He wondered if it was only a coincidence that both men had arrived in his parish at the same time?

'Father.' Paltoc put his spoon down. 'Can I look at the baptismal records of St Erconwald's and, of course, its funeral register? I need to know where my parents are actually buried. God's Acre at St Erconwald's is broader and more tangled than I ever imagined.'

'Of course.' Athelstan pointed at a metal-studded coffer beneath the bedloft. 'The parish chest over there is a veritable treasure of information. There are more in the arca kept in the sacristy. Some records are missing but the *Book of Tombs*, as we call it, will provide their names. You say Raoul was your brother . . .'

'Edward and Edith were my parents. Their day of death was 16 December 1371 for my father and 15 May 1374 for my mother. I believe I am going to have some trouble locating their graves. I was present at their funerals. Crosses and plinths were set up, but when I returned to that part of the cemetery, a great deal has disappeared.'

'The passage of time, my friend.' Athelstan gestured at the hour candle on its stand in the corner. 'Time is like a flame, it burns. Shortly after your mother's death, the parish was taken over – and I use that phrase wisely – by a priest who didn't give a fig either for God or man. The church was neglected and the cemetery even more so. Worse was to happen. When the Great Revolt broke out, rebel armies from the southern shires swept through Southwark to seize London Bridge and passage into the city.'

'They camped in your cemetery,' Prior Sinclair spoke up. 'You told us that.'

'They certainly did. Anyway, I will try to help you, Master Paltoc, as much as I can. Is there anything else?'

'We were in The Piebald last night.' Prior Sinclair shook his head. 'All I saw in the taproom was revelry and all I heard were enthralling stories about the revolt. I confess,' he struck his breast, 'that I ate and drank to my heart's content but, there again, I was among friends. I retired to my chamber where I slept deeply and well. I could hardly keep my eyes open. As far as I am concerned, it was the most peaceful night. I saw or heard nothing amiss.'

'And I, too, drank in the taproom.' Paltoc grinned. 'Brother Athelstan, you certainly have an array of interesting parishioners.'

'That's one way of describing them,' Athelstan retorted.

'I stayed to watch and listen. I recall Ranulf the rat-catcher boasting about the recent festivities of the honourable guild of rat-catchers, only for Watkin to proclaim the glories of the worshipful guild of dung collectors – that is what the evening was like, Brother Athelstan. I, too, saw nothing out of place.'

'Did you learn much Prior Sinclair?'

'I certainly did. Your parishioners, along with Halpen and Mildew, gave accounts any chronicler would envy.' The Benedictine sighed noisily. 'We ate and drank to our fill, but now,' he smiled at Athelstan, 'a day's work beckons. I must write up what I learnt. However, first, I offered to help Master Paltoc find his father's grave. What was it? Your father, Edward, Michael Paltoc, died on 16 December the year of our Lord 1371, and Edith Mary, your mother, 15 May 1374. Is that correct?' Paltoc nodded. 'Brother Athelstan,' Prior Sinclair made to rise, 'can we begin?'

Athelstan agreed. He crossed to the parish chest, pulled it out, pushing back the lid. Prior Sinclair and Paltoc spent most of the afternoon sifting through the documents although they found it nigh impossible to place the Paltoc graves. Now and again, they would leave to tour God's Acre, only to return, freezing and disappointed.

Darkness fell. Athelstan's visitors left for the night. The friar completed some tasks in the house then visited the church to ensure that it was safe and locked. He felt tempted to climb to the top of the tower and study the stars, but the skies had clouded over and a thickening mist had boiled up, spreading its tendrils around St Erconwald's, small clouds of it even drifting ghost-like along the nave. Athelstan locked the Devil's door behind him and walked back through the cemetery. He paused at the old death house but no light glowed, and Athelstan wondered what Remart would be doing out on a night like this? He just hoped the relic seller had not supped too deep and was lying unconscious in some filthy runnel. So preoccupied with his own thoughts, Athelstan started violently at the shadows which seemed to rise from the tombstones either side of him. The mysterious visitors, hooded and visored, were made even more sinister by the fading light. Athelstan stood stock still, trying to curb his own panic. He stared around, at least six in all, garbed like Night Wraiths.

'What is it?' Athelstan drew a deep breath and took a step towards the dark-dweller directly confronting him; he paused at the sound of a crossbow being clicked.

'We mean you no harm, Brother Athelstan. *Pax et bonum* at all times.'

'You certainly have a macabre way of displaying your goodwill and benevolence towards me.'

'We mean you no harm.' The voice was low and grating. 'We bring you and Sir John Cranston a message from the Reapers. Halpen the Hare and his henchman richly deserved their hanging.' Listening intently, Athelstan gauged the speaker was cleverly disguising his voice and speech, imitating the clipped tone and slurred words of the street-dwellers.

'Why do you say that and why tell me now?'

'Because . . .' The speaker paused at the hooting of an owl nesting in a nearby stunted cypress tree.

'A herald of death,' the friar exclaimed. 'Fitting enough for a midnight meeting such as ours.'

'True, true,' the Night Wraith replied, 'now listen. Halpen and Mildew were traitors from the start. They sent many innocent souls to the gallows. They took their Judas coins from the Crown, even though they acted like the staunchest Upright Men and the most fervent amongst the Earthworms. You may have heard the stories, the suspicions about their true role in the revolt – although it was a case of "much suspected, nothing proved", as with so many of their kind. Now they have paid for their treachery and treason against the common good. Sentence has been passed, judgement given, punishment carried out. Tell Sir John,' the speaker stumbled over his words and Athelstan wondered if this was a carefully prepared declaration, 'tell our Lord Coroner,' the voice insisted, 'to let it be. We, the Reapers, have gone into the field and harvested what had to be scythed. Fare ye well, Brother Athelstan.'

'So you carried out judgement?' Athelstan queried. 'But tell me. How did you enter and leave such a secure chamber? How did you kill so silently? Indeed,' Athelstan added, 'so cleanly?'

'We are the Reapers, Brother Athelstan. Our reach is long, our scythes sharp. Nothing can protect those we wish to harm. Not the law nor the likes of Sir John, and certainly not locked doors and sealed windows. The message has now gone out to others we hunt, a proclamation of intent which is meant to chill

their souls and freeze their treacherous minds. Tonight we have
come to tell you this and so we are finished. Again I say to
you, fare ye well.'

The Night Wraiths simply withdrew as silently as they had
appeared. Athelstan stood listening to the darkness, straining
eye and ear for any danger, but all he heard was the mocking
cry of a night bird.

Athelstan reached his house, unlocked the door and stepped
into the warmth and light of the fire still crackling in the hearth.
Trying to shake off the blood-chilling meeting in God's Acre,
Athelstan opened his psalter and, despite the distraction, recited
Compline, the last part of Divine Office. He repeated the verses
of the psalm which cried for God's protection, pleading with
God to keep a watch and set a guard against those who wished
him ill. 'They worship demons,' Athelstan whispered, 'they set
up false gods, they break your commandments, let these be the
very snare which entraps them.'

For a while, Athelstan sat reflecting on the psalm. He then
patted a dozing Bonaventure and made himself ready for bed,
taking off cloak and linen undershirt, pulling on his woollen
night vest. He gratefully climbed into his bedloft and fell fast
asleep.

Athelstan slept well but woke early before dawn. He
hurriedly dressed and went down to celebrate the Jesus Mass
before a small group of parishioners, led by Benedicta, Ursula
the pig woman, Hilda her sow and, of course, a heavy-eyed
Crim. Athelstan hoped to meet his parishioners but, just as he
lifted his hand for the final blessing, he glimpsed the green-
garbed Tiptoft, Sir John's courier, slip through the corpse door
to stand beside a squat, fat pillar. Immediately Athelstan
finished Mass, he despatched Crim to fetch Tiptoft. The
messenger was, as usual, terse and blunt: Sir John was waiting
for Athelstan at Westminster Abbey, where two more poisonings had occurred.

After a turbulent passage across the Thames in Moleskin's
barge, Athelstan, accompanied by Tiptoft, entered the soaring,
cavernous nave of Westminster Abbey. Sir John was waiting in
St Edward's chantry chapel, deep in discussion with Prior
Norbert and Sylvester the sacrist. Both monks rose to greet

Athelstan, Norbert insisting the friar sit, relax and recover from his hurried journey through the damp darkness. A platter of toasted cheese-bread and a pot of hot broth were hastily brought from a nearby buttery, together with a jug of morning ale.

Athelstan, breathless, sweaty, and yet chilled by the freezing journey, forced himself to relax. He ate, drank and basked in the warmth of the nearby braziers.

'Well.' Sir John Cranston who looked as fresh as a springtime daisy, leaned forward, rubbing his hands together, his light-blue eyes hard and unsmiling. 'His Grace the King,' he began, 'is not pleased, nor is Father Abbot who, as you know, is a very close friend of our sovereign.'

'More poisonings?'

'More poisonings,' Cranston agreed. 'Athelstan, this abbey is the King's own chapel, the place of coronation and royal anointing. Yet it's been turned into a place of slaughter, murder and blasphemy. I was roused in the early hours and told to hasten here.'

'Why?' Athelstan retorted. 'Please, Sir John, why am I here?'

'Two deaths. More poisonings. I've waited for you to view the corpses first.'

'Who? Where? How? When?'

'I am here as the Lord Abbot's representative,' Norbert declared sonorously, getting to his feet. 'So let's view the corpses.'

Athelstan expected to be taken to the death house close to the abbey infirmary; instead they were led up the nave to the anker-hold. Norbert opened the door and ushered them in to the bleak, stark chamber, now well-lit by lanternhorns placed around the two corpses laid out on the stone floor. The anchorite's thin, scrawny body lay next to that of a short, fat man, his bald head gleaming in the light, his fat cheeks now hideously suffused with a deep pallor, eyes bulging, lips coated with a dried, dirty-white froth. The shock of death was the same on the anchorite's thin, narrow face.

'In God's name, what happened here?' Athelstan murmured, kneeling down beside the corpses, trying to ignore the horror of those two faces, two men snatched away by violent, sudden death. The friar murmured a prayer.

'We will take care of the anointing,' Sylvester whispered, 'that's the least we can do for our brothers.'

'How did it happen?' Cranston demanded. He had sat down on a stool, cradling the miraculous wineskin.

'I came down here,' Sylvester declared, 'to ensure the high altar was properly prepared for the dawn Mass. I found Brother Malachy,' he gestured to the corpse, 'close to the throne chair. He just lay there, body all twisted, face contorted. Then I realized our anchorite was also strangely silent.'

'What do you mean?'

'Well, usually he rises and sings a morning hymn, but not today. I hurried over, calling his name, but there was no reply. So I came to the anker-hold. Its door was already open.' He gestured at the corpse. 'I found the same. I decided to house both corpses here.'

'I have scrupulously examined them,' Prior Norbert spoke up. 'I examined their mouths. I found nothing because they must have eaten and drank nothing except water from the common jar.'

'And the poison – its source?'

'God knows, Brother Athelstan. I have been through my medicine cabinets and coffers – nothing is missing.'

'But you've mentioned before how the abbey has its own herb and shrub plots. There must be enough noxious plants there.'

'Ah yes.' Norbert crouched down to face Athelstan directly. 'But listen, Brother, you have to carefully prepare such potions; shredding, grinding, mixing and milling. You need water, milk, or some other juice to create a paste or cream. It takes quite a considerable time, and even more considerable patience.' Norbert rose and sat on the edge of the bed. 'Then you have to administer it, as well as disguise it as cleverly as you can. That too takes time and is fraught with difficulties.'

'Yet,' Cranston interrupted, 'we are here in Westminster. Beyond the abbey walls there's a warren of narrow, ill-smelling streets which house apothecary shops, not to mention the dens of warlocks and wizards where you can buy any poison under God's sun.'

'True,' Sylvester retorted, 'but we Benedictines do not have such ready monies, whilst we can hardly go into some apothecary's garbed in our monkish robes demanding a phial of poison.' Sylvester gestured at his colleague. 'You have definitely checked your own store, compared them with the ledger book?'

'Of course, all is in order. What you refer to is kept under lock and key and it hasn't been disturbed.'

Athelstan got to his feet. 'Listen,' he declared, 'four members of this community have been poisoned in the royal chapel of Westminster. One of these was an anchorite, the other three were Blackrobes, Benedictines.' Athelstan pointed down to Malachy's corpse. 'God bless him, but who was he?'

'A Scotsman. Oh yes,' Norbert rubbed his hands together, 'Malachy and the others called themselves Guardians of the Stone. There were four of them: Sub-Sacristan Robert, Brother Fergal, Brother Malachy, and the fourth is Brother Donal.'

'Malachy,' Athelstan observed, 'was found poisoned close to the coronation chair of England. I believe the Stone of Destiny is lodged beneath that throne. Why should he come down here so early in the morning?'

'Oh, Malachy always did. He would like to touch the stone and say a prayer for his kingdom and its Prince. He and the others viewed the stone as a very precious relic. They were devoted to it and to each other.'

'Were they resentful?' Cranston asked. 'Were they hostile to English claims over Scotland? Did they see themselves as strangers in a foreign land? Did they resent the stone being held captive here?'

'No, no.' Sylvester shook his head. 'They were, first and foremost, Benedictine monks, Blackrobes loyal to our order and its rule. They would hold small ceremonies to honour the stone. Like Malachy, they would come to pray beside it. To be perfectly honest, I think they liked being close to something so precious.'

'Look,' Prior Norbert intervened, 'let us show you the stone.'

He and Sylvester first covered the corpses, saying that lay brothers were on their way to take the remains to the death house. Athelstan blessed both bodies. He knew it would be a waste of time to examine them himself. The murderous pattern had been clearly established. The assassin, whoever he may be, was hiding deep in the shifting shadows of his own wicked soul. All four victims had been cunningly poisoned, the murderer leaving no clue to his deadly handiwork. He glanced at Cranston who also looked baffled, standing chewing the corner of his lip. Brother Norbert declared they were ready. Athelstan and Cranston followed the two Benedictines out of the anker-hold, going along the hollow, empty, cavernous nave.

'A place of treasure,' Athelstan whispered to Cranston as he gazed around this magnificent building with its soaring pillars, enamelled precious metals and eye-catching murals depicted in a sweep of brilliant colours. The ever-fragrant perfume of incense sweetened the cold, misty air. The gleaming embossed wooden screens dividing the different chantry chapels reflected candlelight and the glow of lanternhorn. An array of stone statues, saints, angels, gave the impression that they were being closely watched by a presence they couldn't see. The abbey was beginning to stir, though this was only the distant sounds of kitchens and butteries. They went through the magnificent rood screen, dominated by life-sized statues commemorating Christ's passion, and into the exquisitely furnished sanctuary, a place of deep glory and profound prayer. A line of magnificent stained-glass windows coloured the light streaming through them, so it looked as if God's own grace was pouring into this sacred place. Golden sanctuary lamps with blood-red glass glowed fulsomely around the pure gold pyx, hanging on its silver filigree chain to the right of the majestic high altar. This holiest of holy was covered by a cloth of gold and illuminated by a host of pure beeswax candles. Athelstan and Cranston followed the two Benedictines as they genuflected towards the altar before moving across around the back, to where England's great coronation chair stood covered by a thick, purple pall edged with the finest lace. The two Benedictines removed this covering to reveal the resplendent gilt-wood throne, its high legs, armrests and newel posts sheathed in gold, the seat covered by a red-gold cushion displaying the snarling leopards, the personal insignia of English kings. Athelstan gazed in wonderment and then knelt to peer into the open shelf beneath the seat.

'The "Stone of Destiny",' he whispered.

'It is too heavy for us to pull out,' Sylvester hastily explained as he came to kneel by Athelstan. 'But by turning the throne, you can glimpse it.'

'It doesn't look much,' Athelstan declared. 'And yet this stone is sacred for Scotland and its royal house.'

Athelstan peered in at the stone and, at his request, the two monks, helped by Cranston, moved the throne so Athelstan could see more of this famous icon. Athelstan thought it was a roughly rectangular mass of coarse-grained, reddish sandstone. Using the lanternhorn that Prior Norbert had put down beside him, Athelstan carefully circled the chair, examining the stone. He noted the iron staples in the sides, probably used to push poles through so it could be lifted and moved. On the back edge of the stone he also noticed the crudely carved crosses and other symbols.

'I know something of the stone,' Athelstan remarked over his shoulder, 'but little about its origins.'

'They claimed it's ancient and very sacred.'

Athelstan turned swiftly, clambering to his feet to meet and greet Prior Sinclair who, together with Paltoc, had slipped quietly into the sanctuary. The prior bowed to Cranston and exchanged the kiss of peace with Athelstan and the two Blackrobes. 'They claim,' Sinclair went to kneel before the throne, 'that the Stone of Destiny was the stone mentioned in the Old Testament, on which the patriarch of Jacob used to rest his head at Bethel. You know the story? Jacob had a famous dream where he saw angels going up and down a ladder which spanned heaven and earth. Accordingly, the stone was judged as holy. It passed into the hands of Scota, the only daughter of the pharaoh, whom Moses drowned in the Red Sea. The stone had a fairly adventurous history, being passed from hand to hand. At last it was entrusted to the abbey of Scone in Scotland and became the coronation chair of a line of Scottish kings.'

'Until the English seized it?'

'Yes, Sir John.' Sinclair walked a little closer, almost as if to hide from the light pouring through the window, keeping carefully to the shadows. 'Oh yes,' Sinclair repeated, 'the stone was removed. On his march through Scotland in the year of our Lord 1296, Edward I, great grandfather of the present King, occupied Scone Abbey. He seized the stone and brought it south. It has remained here ever since. According to the Treaty of Northampton, enacted by the present King's grandfather in 1328, the stone was to be returned to Scotland.'

'And why wasn't it?'

'Oh, Brother Athelstan, the London mob refused to allow it to be taken even though the English Crown had solemnly sworn that this stone would be returned.' Prior Sinclair spread his hands. 'And there you have it. Brother Norbert,' Sinclair turned to the prior, 'I understand there have been more murders? The anchorite and poor Malachy, both poisoned like the others.'

'True,' Norbert grated, 'and little progress has been made . . .'

'But we will,' Athelstan exclaimed, stung by the barbed remark. 'Always remember,' Athelstan smiled around, 'God's mill does grind exceedingly slow, but it also grinds exceedingly small. Now,' Athelstan pointed at Paltoc, 'why are you here?'

'At my request, Brother Athelstan.' Sinclair patted Paltoc on the shoulder. 'Remember I am a visitor and a stranger to London. Such a great city with its busy, bustling streets, surging crowds and constant stream of visitors. Paltoc is my sword man.'

'A wise choice,' Cranston agreed. 'A very wise choice. It's not safe being a stranger in London. And your pursuit of the Flayer?'

'Another reason for my being here, Sir John. I need to talk to you.'

'Do you now?'

'Yes, Sir John.'

'And your parents' grave?' Athelstan asked.

'I can't find it. Tombstones, plinths and crosses have either been removed or flattened. I may need your permission to dig a little.'

'I will agree as long as it's done appropriately. Watkin and Pike can help.' Athelstan pointed at Prior Sinclair. 'Have you enjoyed your stay at St Erconwald's?'

'I certainly have, Brother. I only hastened here to do business of my order but I hope to return to St Erconwald's very shortly.'

'You have brought the royal cog, *The Bannockburn*, to Southwark side?'

'A logical decision, Brother Athelstan. I am Scotland's leading envoy.' He smiled. 'I like to keep the cog close. After all, as you will agree, I must have a respite from The Piebald; it's necessary for the humours.'

'Too true, too true,' Athelstan retorted. 'So now . . .' He turned back to Prior Norbert. 'Before we leave . . .' Athelstan paused at a crashing and a screaming beyond the rood screen, the patter of sandalled feet, shouts and exclamations, then a figure, garbed in the black robe of a Benedictine, hurried through the rood screen to slump beside the high altar. The monk crouched, gasping and spluttering, waving his hands at other brothers who hastened into the sanctuary after him.

'What is this?' Prior Norbert roared. 'What in God's name – and I mean that – is happening here?'

The monk, who had thrown himself down by the high altar, staggered to his feet.

'Brother Donal.' Norbert grasped the hapless man by the arm and made him sit on the stool that Sylvester hurriedly brought across.

'I claim sanctuary,' Donal gasped. 'I claim sanctuary, here in my own abbey.'

The monks who'd pursued Donal made to intervene, saying that Donal had become fey in his wits.

'No, I am not!' Donal screamed back. 'Three of my brothers, Guardians of the Stone of Destiny, as we call ourselves, have been cruelly slaughtered, poisoned like rats in a barrel. You,' Donal pointed across at Athelstan and Cranston, who now stood separate from the Benedictines, 'you, Sir John,' Donal trumpeted, 'are the King's own coroner. These deaths,' he gasped, 'these deaths must be investigated, the killer trapped.'

Donal then put his face in his hands and burst into tears. Athelstan watched carefully. Donal was genuinely terrified. The friar could clearly understand why. Three Benedictines, not to mention the poor anchorite, had been slain so swiftly, so silently, as if the Angel of Death had simply spread its wings over this abbey. Athelstan glanced at Sir John, who was taking refreshment from his wineskin. He then turned as Prior Sinclair plucked at his sleeve.

'Brother Athelstan, before I forget, I bring messages from the lovely Benedicta. The food and drink taken from Halpen's chamber were fed to the rats which prowl the tavern's cellars.'

'And?'

'No mishap, Brother, nothing at all. Benedicta also said that Ursula the pig woman wanted to see you urgently on a most important matter.'

'I am sure she does,' Athelstan smiled his thanks, 'but for now . . .'

Prior Norbert had imposed order, removing the brothers from the sanctuary. Once this was done, Athelstan demanded that the sanctuary be cleared of everyone, as he and Sir John wished to have private words with Brother Donal. Prior Norbert reluctantly agreed, then he and Sylvester left.

Donal, who had moved to the mercy enclave built into the wall of the apse behind the high altar, was now more composed. Despite the fast, he eagerly accepted the coroner's wineskin, drank noisily, and would have continued to do so if Cranston had not seized it back. Athelstan, sitting on a stool facing Donal, patted Cranston on the arm, a gentle reminder that Donal was not being greedy, he was just frightened.

'So sorry, so sorry. Brother Athelstan, Sir John,' Donal mumbled, yet loud enough for Athelstan to catch the strong Scottish burr in his voice, 'I am so sorry,' he repeated. 'I have panicked, caused a tumult amongst my brothers and,' he pointed at Sir John, 'I have broken my fast and done so joyously as my belly exults with the taste of the finest Bordeaux.'

'Never mind that,' Athelstan demanded, 'why are you here? Why seek sanctuary in your own abbey church?'

'Because of the slaughter of Robert, Fergal, Malachy and, so I understand, the anchorite, though God knows, I, or we, had little to do with him.'

'But you and your three brothers, now dead, styled yourselves Guardians of the Stone of Destiny?'

'Yes, yes we did. All four of us are Scottish. Indeed, both myself and Fergal served in the King of Scotland's array before we joined the order. Now the Benedictines, as I am sure you have been informed, love to set aside barriers, borders, anything which cuts one kingdom off from another. There are Englishmen in Scotland along with French, Gascon, Hainault . . .' Donal's voice gave way as he gazed anxiously around. 'I am troubled,' he said, 'I am afeared.'

'Donal, do you know of any reason why your brethren and the anchorite were poisoned?'

'No, Brother,' Donal wailed. 'I do not know why, how or who. I am just frightened.'

'So you and the others were Guardians of the Stone of Destiny?' Cranston pulled his stool a little closer to the enclave. 'What does that actually mean?'

'Oh, we pray before the stone through which we touch the very heart of Scotland, its King, princes and people. We pay homage to the stone. We honour it. We mourn that it is kept prisoner in exile like ourselves, locked away in this majestic though forbidding abbey. Oh yes, and,' Donal lowered his voice, glaring furtively around, 'at crowning times or crown days, you know, when kings formally wear their crown and sit on their throne of glory, we would honour the stone on which Scottish kings would stand with sword and sceptre to proclaim their power. We would festoon it with flowers. Such a day is fast approaching, the third Sunday of Advent.' Donal wiped his lips on the back of his sleeve. 'We, the Guardians, using a slide of polished oak, would lever the stone out, light candles and pray for the honour of the King of Scotland.' Donal paused, blinking furiously. Athelstan wondered if the man was fully in his wits, and yet what he told them seemed to be harmless enough, more play-acting than anything else.

'So you can tell us nothing more, nothing to shed light on this murderous mystery?'

'Nothing, Brother, nothing at all.'

Cranston and Athelstan left the abbey church. Sacristan Sylvester, urbane and smooth as ever, was waiting for them in the gallery porch. He informed them that Master Paltoc was in the guesthouse buttery. When Cranston and Athelstan entered that long chamber with its jet-black beams and brilliant white plaster, Paltoc was sitting at the head of the long buttery table supping on a blackjack of ale. He lifted his head as they entered and continued to drink, staring into the middle distance, lost in his own thoughts. Cranston and Athelstan slid onto the benches either side. Athelstan was wary, becoming increasingly suspicious at the way this stranger had slipped so quietly into his parish.

'Well, my friend?' Cranston demanded briskly. 'You asked to see us, well, me in particular. Do you have news, fresh intelligence about the Flayer?'

'No, Sir John, though I wish to God I did. However, as you said I could, I visited your chambers in the Guildhall. The clerks informed me that there have been no further murders, none whatsoever, which means,' Paltoc added grimly, 'that the Flayer must be preparing a fresh outrage.'

'He may have already struck time and again,' Athelstan declared. 'I mean just because a fresh corpse hasn't been discovered doesn't mean a murder, or even more than one, hasn't taken place. Some poor pathetic whore sprawled in a place no one visits.'

'I would agree. The one thing I have established is that the Flayer prowls, hunts and seizes his victims in the most squalid parts of the city.'

'True.' Cranston slurped from his wineskin. 'Though what you say is not new. The Flayer pounces on his victims, or rather, in the first instance, entices them into some God-forsaken cellar or derelict pit to perpetrate his abominations.' Cranston drove the stopper back into his wineskin. 'Easy enough, eh? Some poor wench, raddled with disease; hungry, thirsty, freezing cold. Believe me, their name is legion. The prospect of a coin would certainly draw them into the most forsaken spot.'

'Sir John, fresh proclamations against the Flayer have been issued. The council are offering great rewards for his arrest or for providing information which would lead to him being seized and successfully convicted. These proclamations have been posted on the Standard at Cheapside, the great Cross at St Paul's and elsewhere. Do you think they will be successful?'

'What do you mean?'

'Well, the Flayer will keep his abomination secret, well away from public view or anyone sharp-eyed to notice anything amiss.

The Flayer probably hunts his victims under the cover of darkness and Sir John, as you know, at night parts of this city are pitch-black.'

'It will work,' Cranston retorted, 'in a most wondrous way. For a start, it will concentrate the minds – not to mention the pockets – of the legion of informers which swarm through this city. I have also made it known, as my clerks must have informed you, that a most renowned man-hunter – you, Master Paltoc – has been hired to hunt this gruesome assassin.'

'Sir John, I am flattered, but why?'

Athelstan narrowed his eyes. Paltoc seemed agitated. Any bounty hunter would be delighted at such renown, and the prospect of securing a very generous reward. Was Paltoc truly interested in hunting the Flayer, or was it a pretence for something else? If so, what? Cranston, who'd risen to loosen his warbelt, now sat down as he sighed in relief. He poked Paltoc gently on the shoulder.

'You asked me why, so let me tell you. First, the Flayer, our nasty killer, now realizes we know of him and his filthy ways and that we are prepared to spend good money to trap him. Secondly, it demonstrates to the citizens of this great city that the Crown and its officers, namely myself, take such crimes, such sins against the common good, most seriously.' Cranston simply pulled a face at Paltoc's sarcastic burst of laughter. 'Thirdly,' the coroner blithely continued, 'we have certainly stirred the pot of all this wickedness. The informers and spies, those hungry for reward, will now join the hunt and make the Flayer's dreadful life even more dreadful.'

'And fourthly, Sir John?' Athelstan asked, intrigued by what was being said.

'Well, as you know, Brother Athelstan, the sons and daughters of Cain, those branded as assassins by God himself, exude an arrogance, a deep belief in their own superiority. Now,' Cranston licked his lips, 'we have publicly challenged the Flayer. We have dared to confront him. We are knights in the lists. We have entered the tourney ground. Or,' he shrugged, 'it's like a hunt. We have issued a fresh challenge, a wager that we can bring the Flayer down. I just pray that the Flayer is arrogant enough to recognize all this and so rise to the bait.'

'Dangerous, Sir John?' Paltoc replied.

'True, but life is dangerous. Much more sinister is that rare assassin, cold and devious, who will not be provoked.' Cranston got back to his feet, gesturing at Athelstan to do the same. 'Every time I step into the street danger threatens. But, there again,' Cranston fastened the snaps of his cloak and grinned at Paltoc, 'I can be more dangerous than any skulker in the dark.'

Cranston and Athelstan left Westminster, the coroner loudly declaring over his shoulder that he'd had enough of the abbey, it was time to seek the comfort and consolation of his own private chapel, The Lamb of God in Cheapside. Athelstan recognized that the large coroner was full of life and, as Cranston himself had conceded, ripe for mischief.

They went along Fleet Street, heading for Farringdon ward, and so down into Cheapside. Athelstan faithfully trudged behind the coroner who swaggered ahead, one gauntleted hand hanging loose, the other firmly grasping the hilt of his long sword. Cranston was immediately recognized. Dark shapes slunk away from doorways. Gates and shutters were banged shut. The street-swallows, the young sons and daughters of the dark-dwellers, those midnight folk who feared the coroner, shouted insults in a tongue that Athelstan couldn't fully understand. Instead, to calm his own unease, the friar broke from his meditations, gazing around for something to distract his attention.

London was certainly busy. The hard, cold weather made walking easier as the filth-strewn runnels and alleyways were frozen hard. The harsh frost also covered the midden heaps in its icy embrace so their reeking odours were not so powerful. They passed the dung carts and wheelbarrows of the street sweepers, and Athelstan wondered what mischief Pike and Watkin would now be brewing. He had sent an urgent message to Sir John about the murders at The Piebald, whilst he needed to question the coroner about his sinister midnight visitors, the Reapers. As he pushed his way through the throng, Athelstan wondered how many of these now flocking along the city streets were secretly Upright Men or even former Earthworms who had tried to ransack and burn the very shops and stalls they were passing. Athelstan always thought that the Great Revolt was dead and those involved fleeing for their lives. Nevertheless, the events at The Piebald disproved it. Halpen and Mildew had been under the protection of Master Thibault, Gaunt's henchman, yet they'd been seized and executed like common felons. The Reapers, if they were responsible, seemed to move wherever they wished, be it a busy tavern or a lonely graveyard in the dead of the night. Yet Athelstan felt deeply suspicious about what was happening. He just hoped that Sir John would be able to help.

Clutching his ave beads, Athelstan glanced to his left and right. The city certainly drew in both the weird and the wondrous. Advent had begun, so the moon people – who staged different masques and other mummery – now flooded into London, waiting to be hired by this parish or that ward for one of the season's mystery plays. These colourful, noisy itinerants, their necks and wrists festooned with ribbons, were accompanied by all the other road wanderers. Tinkers with cups clattering on chains around their necks. Chapmen in their drab fustian. Fire-eaters, their faces garishly painted. Witches, warlocks and fortune tellers who hid their appearance behind dusty robes, hoods and visors. Dancers, chanteurs, minstrels and troubadours also touted for business; all of these were eager to celebrate the different festivals of Advent, Christmas and Twelfth Night, the Feast of the Asses, the Annunciation to the Virgin, the Journey of the Three Wise Men and the Palace of Herod.

The air resounded with the cries of what these mummers could do and how much they would charge. A colourful, noisy throng, carefully watched by the sharp-eyed street foists eager to pick a purse or empty the pockets of these seasonal visitors. The bailiffs and beadles, the self-proclaimed defenders of the streets, were busy in their usual brutal way, lashing out with their splintered white wands against any troublemakers. These petty officials were city bully boys, with drinkers' bellies and ale-soaked faces, watchmen who imposed harsh and summary justice with their portable finger screws, stocks and clasps. Wandering whores were lashed. Tinkers trading without licence thrashed. Ale-sellers guilty of trickery were soaked in the freezing horse troughs, or shoved into lay stalls crammed with every kind of disgusting filth, be it human or animal.

Cranston pushed his way through, going under the dark mass

of St Paul's and past the soaring, iron gates of Newgate, where the hanging carts waited to take condemned felons to the gallows overlooking Tyburn stream. Cranston called this the filthiest part of the city, because of the reeking stench from the slaughter sheds where fleshers, soaked in blood, cut the throats of chickens, rabbits, calves and cattle before loading the fresh bloody mess onto their gore-strewn stalls. Athelstan detested having to walk through such a slaughter yard. He felt slightly sick, agitated and sweat-soaked. But then Cranston turned and grinned.

'Courage, little friar – The Lamb of God eagerly awaits your arrival!'

PART FOUR

'No one goes over it without dying.'

Brother Donal sat on the mercy stool behind the high altar in the sanctuary of Westminster Abbey. He felt calmer now, though his hot sweat had turned cold. Donal, however, shrugged this off. He had been born in the Highlands and been tested and not found wanting by the harsh frosts and soaking icy winds of the glens. He was Scottish, yet here he was in the royal chapel of Westminster. Donal leaned over and fingered the morsels on the platter before him. Some kind soul had left them as a comfort. Donal picked up the pewter beaker and sipped the cold water. He was a gardener here in the abbey. He loved nothing better than to tend the herb plots, flower beds and vegetable gardens. The only enemy he'd ever encountered were the weeds, yet Donal even enjoyed his constant battle against them. He knew the flowers by name and their seasons, when they should be pruned and when they would come to full flower. He lived a quiet, prayerful life. Sometimes he would visit the library or the scriptorium to read about the properties of certain flowers, or the potency of different herbs. He and Prior Norbert would often confer on what remedies and potions needed to be distilled. What herbs were to be plucked, what part of each plant should be crushed and preserved. Of course Donal would join his brothers for meetings in the chapter house or file into the choir stalls to sing Divine Office.

Donal the gardener had lived a serene, harmonious life of work, prayer and study, the true calling of a Benedictine monk, a Blackrobe. Of course he sought out the company of his fellow countrymen. He, Robert, Fergal and Malachy had always been proud of their Scottish heritage and took even greater pride in styling themselves 'Guardians of the Stone'. In a way, Donal and the rest, although they would never admit this in public, were secretly pleased that the Stone of Scone, the Stone of

Destiny, was kept here in the abbey. True, the sacred slab was pushed beneath the great throne of England, a symbol, or so they said, of England's sovereignty over Scotland. Be that as it may, the stone was there to be reverenced, honoured and paid homage to, especially on those occasions when, according to custom and ritual, the kings of Scotland would stage their formal Crown-wearing ceremonies.

Donal had become used to this life of quiet harmony. The devastating revolt had come and gone. Nothing had really changed. Oh, the rebels had threatened the abbey, but no real harm or damage was done. Indeed, he felt sorry for those swept up in the Great Revolt because nothing had really changed. John of Gaunt was still in power and the great Lords of the Soil openly boasted about their power and status.

Donal abruptly felt a nasty cramp in his belly. He moved to the side and, as he did, glimpsed the great English throne and, just beneath the seat, the Stone of Destiny. Donal recalled how, last May, Gaunt had come to Westminster and the entire church had to be emptied for a while. Master Thibault, the regent's henchman, had proclaimed that his master wished to pray before the statue of the Virgin and make careful devotion in the chantry chapel of St Edward the Confessor. Naturally no one opposed him. Indeed, Father Abbot was pleased because Gaunt brought gifts for the royal chapel and laid them on the high altar; pounds of pure beeswax candles and large chests crammed with rolls of snow-white linen, Gaunt's gift to the different shrines in the abbey church.

Naturally his visit provoked speculation and comment. Some of the brothers maintained Gaunt had come out of sheer desperation to pray for divine help with the sea of troubles confronting him. Others whispered that Gaunt was preparing for an important meeting with Robert of Scotland; after all, hadn't all the documents and manuscripts appertaining to Scotland been removed from the library and sent to Master Thibault? Such manuscripts were only returned on the afternoon of Gaunt's visit last May. A few of the brothers, who allegedly knew more than they should, maintained Gaunt simply wished to sit on the throne to measure himself up for kingship, in the event of his young nephew Richard dying of some sudden sickness or fatal fall.

Donal paused, wincing with pain as he gripped his belly. He had drunk a great deal of cold water and eaten those morsels. Perhaps that was the cause. Donal startled at a strange, eerie cry then realized he was responsible. He was losing control like a man in a fever. Donal leaned back against the wall. Oh, the harmony of Westminster had been disturbed ever since that Wednesday evening. Afterwards Brother Roberts had become so withdrawn, talking to himself, then loudly protesting to Donal that he was sure he had not locked that door. So what was all the commotion about? Donal gagged on the bitter bile forming at the back of his throat. He had been a Blackrobe for decades, a young novice then a fully fledged monk, taking his solemn vows to the Benedictine Order. Now all that had been shattered. Donal clutched his stomach. Perhaps he shouldn't have panicked, yet he had become frightened. He'd been tending the garden yet he was sure he was being watched. A deep sense of chilling foreboding had seized him. He'd turned and saw that dreadful creature, Barak the monkey, scampering amongst the foliage. Donal was certain he had glimpsed the nuisance in his coloured cape. Yet how could that be? Sacristan Sylvester had loudly proclaimed the creature had escaped. Some even maintained the monkey was dead . . .

Donal abruptly leaned forward at the ferocious pain which jabbed his belly like a knife wound. He stared around, he tried to open his mouth to scream but he couldn't. He realized what he had done wrong but it was too late. He tried to speak but then collapsed, sprawling out onto the cold hard floor of the sanctuary.

John of Gaunt, self-styled regent, was closeted with his Master of Secrets, the innocent-looking Thibault. Gaunt was clearly worried. He sat plucking at his exquisitely woven blue and gold jerkin or fingering the silver SS collar, the Lancastrian insignia, displayed so prominently around his throat. He blinked his ice-cold blue eyes and ran a hand though his blond hair, tugging at its strands as he stared down the table.

'Your Grace?'

'Master Thibault.' Gaunt moved his chair, turning slightly to face the only man he trusted. 'I am concerned about this business at Westminster.'

'The business at Westminster, your Grace, does not concern us. Cranston and Athelstan have become involved because a monk was poisoned. As you know, your nephew the King already displays signs of imperiousness. He regards Westminster Abbey as his personal chapel. Cranston and Athelstan were commissioned not by us but by your nephew the King to investigate. All we can do is "keep silent and watch". Whatever happens, your Grace, we must not be drawn, we must not become involved.'

Gaunt's head went down as he slumped in the chair. Thibault, however, stared across at the triptych on the far wall celebrating the story of the flight of the Holy Family into Egypt. Thibault hid his smile. He and his master must flee from what was happening at the abbey. They must not be drawn in. Gaunt had wished to discuss the matter but Thibault had insisted that they should only talk here in their secret chamber in the Tower, close to the chapel of St John the Evangelist. Outside their troops massed, Gaunt's personal bodyguard ready to act when their master gave the sign. Gaunt was impetuous; he would charge when it was more prudent to walk slowly and quietly. Thibault rose and crossed to the chamber door. He opened it and smiled. The soldiers guarding the stairwell were Spanish, mercenaries from Castile. Even if they could eavesdrop, they would not understand. The Master of Secrets closed the door, locked it and walked back to his chair.

'Remember,' he whispered, sitting down and leaning close, 'this business does not concern us. Your Grace, a few months ago you commissioned me to have the throne in Westminster Abbey re-gilded and refurbished. That took place after Easter last. I supervised it. Your nephew was not too pleased, dropping heavy hints that the throne was the Crown's prerequisite, business reserved for him alone. But,' Thibault smiled slyly, 'that matter came to nothing and now it is gone. The same is true, when we went to pray in the abbey for a safe and successful visit to the Scottish March.' Again the smile. 'We demanded that the abbey be emptied in order to protect you. We prayed, we left costly gifts, precious linen and pounds of pure beeswax.

Again, royal eyebrows were raised, but that business is finished, a matter for the past.'

'And of course there is our journey to Scotland. My beloved nephew blames me for that. My attempts to treat with King Robert . . .'

'Oh, I am sure he does. I know only too well how that hymn goes! How you deserted your young nephew the King. How you fled from the troubles in the south to lurk and take shelter in the north. That is a nonsense. You went, you returned. The Great Revolt lies crushed and the situation in the north is at least stable.'

'Now the Scots come to us.'

'A mere courtesy visit, nothing more. The envoys bring felicitations and greetings from one royal cousin to another. They will perhaps once again raise the question of the Stone of Destiny and, once again, your royal nephew will declare he does not wish to discuss the matter. Please remember, your Grace, the Scottish envoys are led by Prior Sinclair, a Benedictine eager to make his name as a chronicler. He wishes to write about the events of last June and has expressed a desire to talk to those involved. He'll talk to me and others. I suspect he would love to discuss matters with the Earthworms, which is why he will be directed to St Erconwald's where he can talk to his heart's content. Athelstan's parishioners were deeply involved in matters they should have avoided. As you know, your Grace, during the revolt, the parishioners of St Erconwald's were taken into protective custody, so in truth they were not rebels, but they were certainly steeped in the villainy of the Upright Men and their Earthworms.' Thibault waved his hand. 'Sinclair is harmless enough! Every great abbey, be it in Scotland, England or France, wants to boast of possessing a full chronicle of the times. Sinclair's mission is part of that and the other items on his mission are just as mundane, even banal.'

'But these murders at Westminster? God knows, Thibault, who is behind them. However, as I have said, what truly worries me is that these murders could draw Cranston and Athelstan deeper into the affairs of the abbey.'

'Your Grace, remember. First I have spies who watch both our Lord Coroner and his little friar.'

'You have?'

'Yes, both in the abbey and St Erconwald's parish. These will keep me fully apprised of all developments. Secondly, a savage killer, the Flayer, has emerged in the city. He murders and skins his victims. Now, I have expressed our concern, your Grace, to the lords of the Guildhall. I have insisted that such a ghastly assassin be hunted down. The Guildhall lords will certainly add their voices, demanding that the Flayer be trapped, caught and hanged. The Guildhall has every confidence in our coroner: they will commission him to catch the killer, so he and Athelstan will be busy enough.' Thibault drew a deep breath. 'And finally, your Grace, only you and I know the truth. We know everything.'

'No, no,' Gaunt countered. 'Thibault, my friend, Robert of Scotland and his council also know the truth of the matter.'

'Your Grace, I must disagree. All the Scots know is what you told them. They also realize that any attempt to twist your words or proclaim them to Christendom will ruin forever whatever they truly hope for.'

'But perhaps that threat has brought them south.'

'Your Grace, they are here as a courtesy to discuss the usual agenda. Please,' Thibault leaned across the table and lightly touched his master's arm. 'Remember,' he whispered, 'we have what we have. We know what we know. Nobody can take from us what we hold. All we have to do is stay silent and watch.'

The killer, the assassin, the murderer known as the Flayer had struck again. He had wandered the needle-thin alleyways of Billingsgate. He'd prowled there, snouting like a wolf at the sheepfold. He had crawled, slinking like a rat through the shadows, staying well away from God's light and that of man. The Flayer had glimpsed his victim, a poor slattern sheltering in a doorway, leaning against the cracked, broken wood. To others, she was a miserable creature, almost invisible, but for the Flayer she was his natural victim. He had closed with his prey, enticing her for a penny into the stinking cellar of a rotting tenement, a place of deep darkness and wretched filth. He had coaxed her gently. Once she was down the crumbling steps he had killed her with a hammer blow to the poor woman's forehead. She had died immediately and now he was ready for further enjoyment. Humming softly to himself, the Flayer crouched beside the blood-soaked corpse. He grasped his razor-thin dagger and, as skilful as any skinner in the guilds, began to peel his victim's flesh.

Once finished the Flayer squatted with his back to the wall, taking deep breaths as he reflected on what was happening. He felt sated, relaxed, even ready for a sleep. He took another gulp from his wineskin and let his mind wander back to his former life as a mercenary, fighting . . . no, he wasn't really fighting, more plundering whatever he and others came across in France. As a hired mercenary, a member of a free company, the Flayer could do what he wanted when he wanted and be commended for it. Some village in Normandy turned into a sea of flame was just part of a day's work, as was his cruel torture and abuse of any prisoner, be they man, woman or child.

The Flayer had returned home with other veterans and he soon realized that what he had done in France could not be done here. Sheriffs, bailiffs and beadles imposed order. Above all, the likes of fat Jack Cranston, the Lord High Coroner and his faithful friend Friar Athelstan posed a real danger. These men hunted the likes of the Flayer and, he understood, they had done so with outstanding success. Cranston loved to spread a net, to provoke those he hunted to break cover. The Flayer ground his teeth. He had heard about the proclamations coming out of the Guildhall, the rewards being offered for information leading to his arrest and a slow hanging from one of London's gibbets. The Flayer quietly cursed. He turned and looked at the corpse of his most recent victim. 'How dare they?' he demanded. 'How dare Cranston and Athelstan interfere in my world, my life! How dare they boast that one day I will be caught and despatched to dance in the air for the delight of the London mob.' The Flayer wiped his lips on the back of his hand. Earlier in the day he had risen to the challenge and sent Cranston a small present, a token of the Flayer's sheer contempt for the coroner. Indeed, that was the problem, Cranston personified it. Order and good government! What a contrast to those years of the plague when he and Adele had done whatever pleased them so they could prowl the City and beyond without let or hindrance.

The Flayer closed his eyes. He recalled God's Acre, that vast lonely cemetery around St Erconwald's, when it was a truly desolate place. Now it was all changed, transformed by that Dominican friar. The Flayer snorted with fury. He opened his eyes and, leaning forward, breathed out noisily, as if this very gasp could inflict a wound on his opponents.

The Flayer crossed his arms, wetting his lips as he recalled the dramatic events in that cemetery some twenty years ago. The dark night, the flaring torches and the cowled, visored figures. Now it was different, yet it shouldn't be. The cemetery of St Erconwald's was his fief and he should really wage war against those who had persecuted Adele to a most cruel death. Nevertheless, he knew no names. The parishioners who tried Adele were strangers, hooded and visored, though he had his suspicion! Ursula the pig woman! He believed she, or those of her family, had been involved in the capture and destruction of Adele.

The Flayer leaned forward, cracking his finger knuckles. Ursula was a fat bitch who smelt like the creature she fussed, that great lumbering sow with its flapping flanks and ears. 'Two great mounds of fat,' the Flayer whispered. 'I'd love to skin, to peel both of them, but that would be difficult.' The Flayer's mouth watered at the prospect of such a killing! He hated Ursula for what she was and her endless chatter to anyone who bothered to reply to her. She warbled like a bird about angels shedding their wings as they flew through God's Acre. What a nonsense, what a nuisance! The Flayer was also intrigued. He'd recently learnt that Ursula was the widow of the hangman of the parish, so he may well have been one of those who tried Adele. One day he must bring Ursula and her sow to a place like this. The Flayer scrambled to his feet. 'So much to do,' he murmured, 'and so little time to do it. Busy, busy, all the day long.'

Cranston and Athelstan were grateful to reach the main Cheapside thoroughfare with its Standard, Cross and Tun. A frenetically busy market place, row upon row of stalls sold everything under the sun, from leather saddles made in Cordoba to the finest gold-chased goblets from Cologne. Despite the freezing cold, the crowds pressed backwards and forwards, a mass of moving colour and different scenes, be it a funeral party carrying a coffin to a nearby church or a cohort of market beadles leading a line of peace-breakers down to the stocks. Chanteurs, standing on plinths or barrels, proclaimed the most fantastical stories about kingdoms of glass far to the East, or a castle in the dark forests along the Rhine, where demons gathered to plot man's downfall. Whores in their gaudy wigs, their sly-eyed pimps not far behind, solicited for custom, keeping a wary eye on their herders as well as the bailiffs.

At last they reached their haven, The Lamb of God. Cranston paused in the porchway to greet Leif the one-legged beggar and Rawbum, Leif's loyal henchman. These two beggars plagued Sir John and haunted the entrance to his favourite tavern. Cranston knew that if they were not paid, they would visit the Lady Maude to inform her that, 'The illustrious coroner, her most loving husband, was cheery and well, that he was enthroned in The Lamb of God at a time when he could be visiting her and their two sons the poppets, Stephen and Francis.' Cranston spun each of them a penny and both beggars disappeared into the crowd, shouting Cranston's praises and promising that they would pray for him in every church in Cheapside.

Cranston and Athelstan entered the tavern. Minehostess, pink-cheeked, blue eyes dancing, her buxom figure almost hidden by a snow-white apron, greeted Cranston enthusiastically. Once kisses had been exchanged, she ushered them both, her 'special guests', into the solar reserved for 'visitors of quality', Sir John Cranston in particular. It was well-known as the coroner's favourite spot in Cheapside, if not in all of London. The solar was truly luxurious, with a deep-cushioned window seat providing a full view of the tavern garden, yet close enough to a roaring fire, its flames leaping merrily in a hearth shaped like a dragon's mouth. Minehostess served stoups of home-brewed ale and platters of tender slices of capon and pheasant, all delicately cooked and spiced. Cranston and Athelstan ate in silence; they had both risen early and the harsh, cold weather had sharpened their appetites. Once they had finished, they waited for the table to be cleared, then Athelstan opened his chancery satchel and laid out his writing materials.

'On reflection, not really necessary,' Cranston murmured,

sitting back against the cushion settle. 'Summarize, my little friend, the sea of troublesome problems confronting us.'

'Westminster, Sir John, the royal abbey, the home of the Benedictines, the Blackrobes. Peace and harmony reigned there until earlier this week when a most curious incident occurred. Brother Robert, the sub-sacristan, was to lock the entire abbey church. He was to make it secure except for the Devil's door, a narrow postern in the north transept. According to what we have learnt, this was supposed to be left off, both lock and bolt, so the abbey could be swiftly emptied if some mishap occurred after dark. On that particular night it did. Our poor anchorite heard sounds echo through the abbey. He glimpsed a darting figure dancing about, bells ringing.' Athelstan waved a hand. 'The anchorite was certain that someone had entered the abbey at the dead of night. So, agitated and fearful, the anchorite left his anker-hold. He discovered nothing amiss except the Devil's door was locked when it shouldn't have been so. He raised the alarm. A few days later, Brother Robert the sub-sacristan admitted that he might well have locked the Devil's door by mistake, yet this does not resolve our mystery. It's a well-known fact that the anchorite raised the alarm by ringing the tocsin. There was no other way because he found the Devil's door locked. Moreover, when Brother Robert, together with his superior, Sacristan Sylvester, reached the church, they and others also found the Devil's door locked though nothing amiss in the church. However, if the door was locked, who was responsible for those strange sights and sounds?'

'It might be the anchorite? Maybe he was fey-witted, seeing and hearing things which simply did not exist except in his own disturbed humours.'

'Sir John, there is no evidence for such a conclusion on that particular night or any previous one.'

'The intruders could have hidden away in the shadowy recesses; there are enough of them in the abbey church.'

'Very dangerous, Sir John. Remember, after the tocsin was sounded, the Devil's door was opened. No other. It would have been difficult for an intruder to leave at a time when that door was under the care of Sacristan Sylvester and Brother Robert, not to mention other monks streaming towards the church. In a word, any intruder would seriously risk being noticed and seized.'

'In which case my little monk . . .'

'Friar, Sir John.'

'The intruder had a key. He opened the Devil's door or some other postern, entered the church and left, locking the door behind him.'

'But, Sir John, nothing was found missing, disturbed or damaged, so why? And if the intruder was busy in the church and had a key, surely someone would have noticed? The intruder would have left their mark, some trace of them being there?'

Cranston simply sipped from his tankard, shaking his head.

'What happened that night is both unique and very strange,' Athelstan mused. 'And we must ask if it was connected to the next swirling mystery, the murder by poison of three Blackrobes as well as Ricard the anchorite? Why, how and who are the pressing questions. Was the anchorite poisoned because of what he saw or heard that night? One additional consideration. All four victims were Blackrobes, Scottish and, apart from the anchorite, self-proclaimed Guardians of the Stone, a coven bonded together to honour the Stone of Destiny, that sacred relic of Scottish kingship now held firmly by the English Crown.' Athelstan paused. 'Sir John, we do face a true mystery. These Blackrobes were poisoned, we don't even know how it was done. We are now in Advent, when the Benedictine rule imposes a great fast in preparation for Christmas. The good brothers could only eat one full meal a day, taken late in the evening. Everything except water is strictly forbidden.'

'And we have established that they all drank from the common supply, so how, and this must include the anchorite?'

'I agree, Sir John. So far we have found no trace of any tainted food or drink.'

'Or the source of the poison?'

'Well, the abbey has its own infirmary, herbarium and medicine chest. The murderer could have helped himself, but not without the very real risk of being discovered.' Athelstan bit the corner of his lip. 'So we have this to contend with, Sir John; then we must stop that great sinner, the Flayer.'

'Indeed, Brother, for there is nothing even remotely human about his filthy crimes.'

'It could be anyone, Sir John. An unrepentant sinner and, I suspect, one with a deep and lasting hatred for women or, indeed, anyone else.'

'Brother?'

'Our evil-minded Flayer selects what he regards as the lowest of the low, the raddled, diseased, blighted whores who wander our streets, poor women forsaken by everyone.' Athelstan sipped from his blackjack and stared around the comfortable, even luxurious solar, with its turkey cloth carpets, gleaming oak furniture and well-carved candelabra. The chamber's walls were pink-plastered and decorated with delicately painted cloths, a sharp contrast to the cold dark horrors confronting them.

'Brother, you said anyone else?'

'Oh, I think the Flayer, a sick-souled killer, has a deep and lasting hatred for humankind, women in particular. He is a demon, a slayer, his soul echoes the words of Christ: "Satan was an assassin from the start." The Flayer loathes fellow humans, yet this hatred, curdled by his own upbringing and experiences, has to be cunningly managed. He wants to vomit his loathing but not against anyone who enjoys some status in our community, an individual whose murder would provoke justice into action. Oh no, our assassin wants to kill and kill again with impunity, and he does so with his specially chosen victims. No one really cares for the raddled whores he's tortured and killed. So believe me, Sir John, what you do now is God's work.'

'In which case I wish God would give us both a little help.'

'Oh, he will, Sir John. What you said earlier to Paltoc was very shrewd. You have interfered with the Flayer's murderous enjoyment. You have challenged him, but let's leave that for the moment. You have sown the seed of a possible trap, you've prepared the lure. So let us now move to those two worthies, Halpen and Mildew. You received my brief message about their murders?' Athelstan then described in detail what had happened at The Piebald. Cranston heard him out and softly whistled.

'You mean to say, Athelstan, that two killers, professional assassins and Judas men, for that's what they were, caroused, ate and drank in the taproom? Afterwards, they adjourned to

bed in a locked, sealed chamber, all from within, yet both were
found hanging by their necks?' Cranston shook his head. 'With
no sign of forced entry or attack? Satan's tits!'

'What do you know about that precious pair, Sir John?'

'Oh, I've been to the chancery office and searched the secret
memoranda rolls. I also had urgent words with Thibault, our
Master of Secrets. So listen,' Cranston lowered his voice,
'Halpen and Mildew were Upright Men. They sat high on the
councils of the rebel leaders, Wat Tyler, Jack Straw, Grindcobbe
and others of their ilk. Halpen and Mildew were also leading
captains in the ranks of the Earthworms.' Cranston took a gulp
from his wineskin. 'In truth, this was all a nonsense. From the
very beginning, Halpen and Mildew were Thibault's creatures,
his spies, his henchmen, body and soul in this life and the life
to come. That treacherous pair didn't just turn King's evidence,
they were King's evidence from the very start.'

'Sir John!'

'Don't look so shocked, Brother. Halpen and Mildew were
steeped in villainy. In a sense, they truly deserved their deaths
and yet,' Cranston pushed the stopper back into the wineskin,
'two men were murdered.'

'And I was threatened.' The friar then described his meeting
with his midnight visitors, the Reapers. Once again, Cranston
whistled in surprise.

'I am astonished,' he murmured. 'I always thought the great
cause was finished, the revolt crushed. Most of the leaders, if
not all, either dead or fled beyond the Narrow Seas. However,'
Cranston tapped the tabletop, 'Halpen and Mildew took a leading
part in the Great Revolt. They were both deeply involved in the
rebel's attack and plundering of John of Gaunt's luxurious palace
of the Savoy. Of course, they later asserted that they acted as
secret servants of Gaunt and did their level best to save the
palace and protect its many treasures.' Cranston gave a short
bark of laugher. 'Now that was a tissue of lies if there ever was
one, a folio of fables concocted to protect and enhance themselves. So, what did happen there? Well, as you know, Brother,
the Savoy was sacked and burnt to the ground, along with most
of its furnishings. However, a certain treasure chest containing
sacred and precious items . . .' Cranston paused and scratched

his face. 'I am not too sure if what Thibault told me is the truth. Anyway, this chest, according to Halpen and Mildew, was taken from its arca in the palace's chancery room, transported down to Queenhithe quayside and taken over to Southwark side.'

'What! How do you know this?'

'Because Halpen and Mildew maintained they were forced to do this by the masked leader of a gang of rifflers. Remember Halpen and Midlew were born liars: their story is probably a mixture of truth and what they spun to enhance themselves. Anyway, on that afternoon they were told to carry the chest down to a waiting barge and row the same across the Thames. They were to berth at a small deserted quayside close to the church of St Mary's Overy, not far from the Southwark stews, that hunting ground for a horde of whores. Once there, the masked stranger took care of the chest. He ordered Halpen and Mildew to row wherever they wished across the river. They could go anywhere except follow him and his coven who would take care of the chest. Halpen and Mildew had no choice but to agree. Now,' Cranston clicked his tongue, 'speculation abounds about what that chest contains.'

'But Master Thibault has told you?'

'Under oath, yes, little friar, but there again, I am not breaking my word but sharing what might be important in resolving the murderous mysteries which now confront us.' Cranston took a generous mouthful from the miraculous wineskin. 'So, Brother, let me give you a short, sharp lecture. In 1296 Edward I, the self-styled Hammer of the Scots, invaded Scotland, defeated its army and seized all the royal regalia enjoyed by a succession of Scottish kings.'

'This included the Stone of Destiny.'

'Oh yes, and much more. The Scottish royal orb, sceptre and crown, not to forget a most precious sacred relic commonly called "The Black Rood", a fragment of the True Cross kept in the most exquisitely fashioned gold reliquary. Once possessed by the illustrious St Margaret.'

'Scotland's most famous saint and Queen.'

'Very good, little friar. Edward I seized all this and took the precious items south. He deposited them in his treasury, the cavernous crypt of Westminster Abbey. In 1303 this treasury was violated, robbed by an audacious criminal, Richard Puddlicot. The Scottish treasures, along with others, were seized and taken. The gang was hunted down and broken, Puddlicot was captured, tried and hanged on a special gallows outside the gates of Westminster. Oh my goodness,' Cranston's fingers fluttered to his lips, 'oh my goodness, what a coincidence,' the coroner murmured, 'Richard Puddlicot was hanged but then, on the express order of the King, his corpse was flayed and the skin nailed to a door leading down to the crypt. Strange, yes? We now have a prowling assassin who also skins his victims . . .'

Athelstan stared into the fire. He repressed a sharp shiver, as if something cold and malevolent had swept across his soul. Was there, he wondered, some connection between the desecration of a thief's corpse so many years ago and the present horrors?

Athelstan drained his blackjack then absentmindedly refilled it.

'A great deal of the treasure was found,' Cranston continued. 'The crypt was never used again. The King moved his store of precious items to the Tower. John of Gaunt, after he proclaimed himself regent, took some of that treasure and hoarded it in his palace of the Savoy.'

'Why those particular items?'

'Brother, when the Great Revolt swept London, Gaunt was in the north negotiating with King Robert. According to Master Thibault, one of the items to be raised in those negotiations were the terms of the Treaty of Northampton of 1328, agreed some fifty-three years ago.'

'That the Scottish royal regalia be handed back?'

'Precisely, little friar. According to Master Thibault, Gaunt had prepared for this. The treasure chest stolen from the Savoy and taken across the Thames held the Scottish royal regalia: the crown, the sword, the sceptre and the Black Rood. The only item missing was the Stone of Destiny, but that was also included in the negotiations which, in the end, came to nothing.'

'Could Halpen and Mildew have stolen the chest?'

'Possibly, Brother. They might have known where it lay hidden and were waiting for the right moment.'

'Which is?'

'Well, the treasure would be difficult to sell. However, for those who allegedly found it, a most lavish reward.'

'Do you think Halpen and Mildew were plotting this?'

'Possibly.'

'Had there been other attacks on those two worthies?'

'Halpen and Mildew received pardons, amnesties. They became King's approvers. In other words, they were traitors, Judas men, and had been from the very start. They betrayed many of their comrades, and for this they were lavishly rewarded. I also believe they held out the prospect of discovering the missing treasure so that Master Thibault would favour them. No one dared accost them which, little friar, makes what happened all the more puzzling. The re-emergence of the Reapers, the mysterious executions and, of course, the Reapers visiting you.'

'And Paltoc?'

'Oh, I have scrutinized the records. Paltoc was a member of Gaunt's retinue. He was despatched north of the border to inform Gaunt about the destruction of the Savoy and the disappearance of his treasure.'

'And Gaunt?'

'As angry as a rampant stag, and apparently he still is. He dismissed Paltoc and others and swore they were proscribed, excluded from any office in the service of the Crown.'

'Could Paltoc be secretly searching for the treasure, a peace offering to his former master?'

'Believe me, Brother, Paltoc could find the Holy Grail and get no thanks for it. No, Paltoc was dismissed from Gaunt's household. From what I've learnt, he tarried a while in the north then wandered south as a mercenary, a man-hunter intent on catching or killing any wolfshead. Oh yes . . .'

Cranston broke off as Minehostess came into the solar, gripping a street-swallow tightly by the ragged scruff of his dirty neck. The urchin, dressed in a long, drab jerkin, battered sandals on his feet, was holding a thin roll of linen clenched tightly in his fist. At Minehostess's insistence, he thrust this at Cranston, who took it.

'A present,' the urchin squealed. 'A man hooded and visored

in a nearby alleyway. He gave me a penny. Told me to give this to you, Fat Jack. I have.' The street-swallow twisted free from his captor's firm grasp, turned and sped like a whippet through the solar door, across the crowded taproom and back into the crowded street.

'Let him go,' Cranston ordered, placing the linen package on the table. He carefully unrolled it to reveal what looked like thin, wispy strips of gauze, stained here and there by flecks of blood. Athelstan edged closer, using a chicken bone from the platter to lift the folds. He leaned over and sniffed a rancid odour.

'Satin's tits,' Cranston whispered. 'Brother Athelstan, I believe . . .' The coroner broke off and smiled at Minehostess. 'Madam, it's best if you were gone.' The lady promptly fled the solar.

'I know what you are going to say and I agree,' Athelstan whispered, staring in horror at the linen parcel. 'I know what it is, Sir John, human skin. It's a mocking gift from the Flayer. Little shavings from his most recent victim, some poor wretch whose bloodied corpse now lies in a filthy cellar, her soul gone to God. Sir John, this is truly wicked and you are correct: the Flayer has responded to your challenge and will do so again.'

'And what should we do with this?'

Athelstan neatly folded the thin linen cloth in which the pieces of skin had been wrapped. It started a memory but he could not place it. 'I will give honourable housing to these pathetic remains. I will bury both cloth and skin in the Poor Man's Lot in God's Acre.' Athelstan paused at a knock on the door and Tiptoft the courier slipped into the solar.

'Sir John, my apologies. I come with urgent messages from Westminster. The monk Donal has been found poisoned in sanctuary.'

Athelstan stared at the wall painting which decorated the sanctuary enclave in the apse behind the high altar of Westminster Abbey. He desperately tried to hide his deepening exasperation at what he heard, saw and felt. The painting he was studying, with its gold-headed demons prancing around the bed of some hapless dying sinner, seemed to reflect his own turbulent mood.

This was no longer some splendid abbey with its ornate nave and splendid sanctuary, but a place of dark deceit and murderous mayhem. He closed his eyes and whispered a prayer, then crouched down beside the twisted corpse of Brother Donal. The dead Benedictine must have died in agony, his body now lay sprawled, head to one side and, when Cranston turned him over, the friar tried not to flinch at the dead man's face contorted, full of horror. The eyes were rolled back, cheeks sunken, the skin a hideous pallor, streaked with patches of light-purple, his swollen lips parted and stained with a dirty-white mucus. Athelstan felt for the life beat in Donal's throat but the flesh was cold and hard.

He glanced up at Norbert and Sinclair, who stood in the shadow of Sylvester the sacristan. Cranston had now moved to sit on a sanctuary stool. He'd doffed his beaver hat and was staring down at the exquisitely tiled floor. The brilliantly hued mosaics celebrated the Eucharist with golden chalices crammed with purple grapes, full to bursting, around a huge silver, bejewelled ciborium containing a snow-white host. The friar took a deep breath and turned back to the corpse, pulling up the sleeves of the black gown, examining both wrist and ankle for any ligature, but there was none.

'How?' Athelstan glanced up at the three Benedictines. 'How was Donal poisoned here, in almost full view of this community, at the very heart of this abbey?'

'Brother, we don't know,' Sylvester retorted. 'Donal was left here. A lay brother brought him a stoup of water. Donal insisted that the lay brother taste this, which he did. The water was pure. Other brothers came through the church on this business or that. No stranger was seen, nothing out of the ordinary occurred. Prior Sinclair and I went into Westminster, we only learnt about the death on our return. Brother Donal's corpse was discovered by a lay brother bringing fresh cloths down to the sacristy.'

Athelstan thanked him and got to his feet. Cranston followed suit. They talked to the three Benedictines for a while then took their leave. Athelstan walked down into the shadow-filled north transept to examine the Devil's door, the one Robert the sub-sacristan should have left unlocked on that fateful night. He opened the door, flinched at the cold and stared out across the bleak expanse of heathland. The stonemasons laying the slabs further down the side of the abbey, close to one of the other doors, now seemed to be finished, loading their mattocks, hammers and spades up onto a cart. A noisy group of burly men, shoving and pushing each other, sharing out a wineskin in celebration of their finished work. Athelstan watched them for a while, his mind a medley of conflicting thoughts about what was happening in this great abbey.

'Brother,' Cranston whispered, hurrying up, 'it's getting cold, let us go, yes? There is nothing for us here.'

'Oh, but there is.' Athelstan closed the door, turned and smiled at the coroner. 'Sir John, there's something for me here, a warm comfortable bed in the guest house for a start. I am tired and cold. I do not want to face a journey back across the Thames.'

Cranston nodded understandingly. 'I will send Tiptoft,' he declared, 'to advise Benedicta. Brother Athelstan, is there anything else I can do?'

'Yes, Sir John. Pick at the thread at what we saw and heard today. Think! Reflect! Remember!'

'And tomorrow?'

'I will go back, Sir John, and truly rest in my little house. Once I am refreshed, I will enter the meadows of murder. I will hunt assassins and dissipate the heavy mist of murder which hangs over this holy place. Now listen, Sir John, please, if you can. Get your clerks to go through the Exchequer and chancery memoranda, not to mention the schedules at the Guildhall.'

'What am I looking for, little friar?'

'The name Puddlicot, my Lord Coroner. Anyone called Puddlicot; anything he or she may have done. Murder, as we know, Sir John, passes like blood from one generation to another. My good friend, I bid you adieu. God bless your sleep. I will see Prior Norbert, say my prayers then retire.'

The coroner and friar exchanged the kiss of peace. Cranston strode off, shouting over his shoulder that Athelstan should get a good night's rest. In the end, the friar certainly did, awaking just after dawn. He hastily washed and dressed, then celebrated his Mass in a small chantry chapel, Sacristan Sylvester assisting. After he had broken his fast in a nearby buttery, Athelstan collected his possessions and made his way across the abbey grounds towards King's Steps, where he hoped to hire a barge. He was almost there when he heard his name being called and turned to greet Prior Sinclair. The Blackrobe, hooded and mantled against the cold, informed Athelstan that he too was crossing to Southwark and that Moleskin and his crew had agreed to meet him at King's Steps shortly after the bells tolled for the first solemn High Mass of the day. When they reached the mist-hung quayside, Moleskin and his six oarsmen were waiting. The bargemen ushered his special guests into the stern, protected by a thick leather canopy. Sinclair and Athelstan made themselves comfortable against the bolstered backrest. Moleskin deftly lit the lanternhorns in the prow and along each side and gave the order to cast off.

The barge turned and made its way across the swell, lanterns glowing, oars rising and falling in unison, Moleskin blowing repeatedly on his horn to warn off other craft. They passed the Fisher of Men's massive, freshly painted war barge, which cut through the current in a sweep of long oars. Icthus, the Fisher's henchman, stood as usual in the prow. A voice bellowed across the water, greeting Athelstan and Moleskin, then adding how the harvest that previous night had been rich, no less than six corpses being plucked from the Thames. The majestic sombre barge ploughed on, Moleskin shouted at his oarsmen for greater speed, and the boat lurched forward through a bank of rolling mist and into daylight so clear Athelstan could glimpse the Southwark shore. The barge turned, heading like an arrow towards the quayside of St Mary's Overy; this was dominated by the massive Scottish war cog, *The Bannockburn*. The Scottish ship occupied almost the full length of the quayside. As Moleskin's barge carefully made its way in, Athelstan stood up and stared at *The Bannockburn*.

'Truly majestic,' he murmured, 'I wonder what it's like on board.' He glanced down at Sinclair. 'Could you take me up? I mean, I have never seen such a majestic cog?'

Sinclair looked uncertain then smiled. 'Very well, Brother, as soon as we berth. I will take you up to meet its master, Nicholas Gromond.'

Moleskin brought his barge in, Sinclair paid the coin, and

he and Athelstan stepped gingerly ashore. *The Bannockburn* was only a short walk away, its broad gangplank well-guarded by heavily armoured men-at-arms. There were six of them on the quayside and the same number covering the entrance on to the deck. They came to attention as Sinclair swept by them leading Athelstan up on to the broad, slightly swaying deck. Master Gromond, thickset, balding, with a jovial, rubicund face, greeted them, showing every deference to Prior Sinclair. He offered wine and sweetmeats but Athelstan shook his head, staring around the great cog. A massive, fat-bellied ship of war, *The Bannockburn* boasted two masts and a high, fortified stern and jutting poop. The ship lay quiet, rocking gently against the quayside. Athelstan sensed that the ship was ready to sail at a moment's notice. The crew were all on board, scampering like squirrels across the deck. Athelstan also noticed how the ship was well prepared for either attack or defence, it was even armed with new-fangled bombards and culverins, as well as sealed buckets of lime to be used if a favourable wind could blow the deadly dust into the enemy's eyes. The crew seemed to be well-seasoned veterans whilst the rest of the ship's company were soldiers, hobelars, archers and men-at-arms.

'Master Gromond, you are berthed on Southwark side, you are well armed for war and seem ready to leave, it's . . .'

'Strange?' Prior Sinclair smiled.

'Not strange at all.' Gromond took a step closer, his light-blue eyes watery from the salt-tinged breeze. 'Not strange at all, Brother Athelstan. England and Scotland enjoy an uneasy peace. A truce to last, or so they say. But . . .' The master turned, hawked and spat into the water swilling across the deck. 'Life is very short, Brother. Times change.'

'In other words, if matters took a turn for the worse . . .?'

'You have it, Brother. We are well provisioned, heavily armed and ready to sail. Here at Southwark, we cannot get entangled with other ships. We can soon be out in midstream and heading like an arrow for the estuary. Of course,' Gromond bowed mockingly, 'we are also very close to our noble envoy, Prior Sinclair, should he need assistance of any kind.'

'Quite, quite,' Athelstan murmured, staring around. He was sure he'd glimpsed something curious, out of place, but for the life of him he could not now see anything amiss or articulate his concern.

'Brother Athelstan?'

The friar bowed towards the captain. 'Master Gromond, many thanks. Prior Sinclair, it is time I returned, we returned, to the bosom of our parish.'

Athelstan, in fact, found his parish very quiet. He and Prior Sinclair parted company at The Piebald, Athelstan continuing on up to the church. He found this securely locked and thanked God for Benedicta. The church enclosure was also desolate, and God's Acre a silent sea of moving gorse. He reached his house, all locked and shuttered, and searched out the key hidden in a place known only to him and Benedicta. He opened the door, went in and heaved a sigh of relief. He again thanked God for Benedicta; everything was in order. The house looked and smelt clean. The bedloft was tidy. The great kitchen table scrubbed. The small buttery and kitchen immaculate. A small, banked fire glowed in the hearth, its warmth enhanced by wheeled braziers full of sparkling charcoal. Athelstan made himself comfortable, as he did the following day. He rose early, celebrated his Jesus Mass, then took care of parish business, be it visiting the sick or listening to the Hangman of Rochester's ideas for a range of fresh paintings, brilliantly hued frescoes to decorate the walls of the south transept. Athelstan studiously ignored his parishioners' plea to hold a council meeting. The likes of Watkin and Pike were insistent on discovering what actually happened at The Piebald. If they were not pleading for this then they would return to their usual concerns about staging the festival for Advent with masques, plays or other such mummery. Athelstan relaxed and, two days after his return from Westminster, he decided to concentrate on the mysteries confronting him for, despite his best efforts, they nagged at his peace of mind.

Athelstan decided to study in detail what had happened at The Piebald. He took a square of parchment and used this to recreate the murder chamber. He carefully noted how the window was far too small to force any entry, whilst the door was held fast from within by a heavy lock and two sturdy bolts. No secret entrances existed. The victims' food and drink were untainted. Finally, no disturbance was seen or heard, not a single shred of evidence existed to indicate defence or attack. Athelstan had also learnt that the gallery was deserted except for the chamber next to the murder room, this had been occupied by Prior Sinclair, who had reported nothing amiss. Nevertheless, both Halpen and Mildew, killers to the core, had certainly been murdered. One of the parishioners had mentioned suicide as a possibility.

'Nonsense,' Athelstan murmured to himself. 'We don't even have the stool or table they would've stepped off.' Athelstan stared down at his rough drawing. 'Very well, very well,' he whispered, staring at Bonaventure, the cat now sitting on the table, tense and watchful as if he fully shared Athelstan's concerns. 'My friend,' Athelstan rubbed his hands together, 'let's look at all the possibilities, yet, in truth, there is surely only one, and that's the door!' Athelstan sat chewing the corner of his lip as he recalled the chamber being forced. He had been there. He had seen it for himself, the bolts were drawn across, the lock fully turned. Nevertheless, there was something he'd glimpsed, as he had when he boarded *The Bannockburn*. Something not quite right, but what? The friar closed his eyes. He fully conceded that he had no idea of why his mind could turn and twist as it did. Was it a gift or a curse? He'd see something, remember it, then wait and see if was important or insignificant. That was the situation here. He'd seen something outside that chamber which concerned him, a fleeting thought. He was about to return to the question of the so-called Reapers when he heard a knock on the door. He rose, turned the lock, opened the door and forced a smile.

Ursula the pig woman, along with Remart the relic seller, stood shivering, their cloaks pulled fast about them. Athelstan, hiding his exasperation, invited both of them in, including Ursula's sow. The grossly overweight pig, ears flapping, flanks billowing out like bellows, trotted in and immediately sank down in front of the fire. Bonaventure, who regarded such a place as his birthright, rose, stretched disdainfully, and walked away with as much dignity as a cat could muster. Hubert the hedgehog, however, nestling in the inglenook, simply rolled himself into a threatening ball. Athelstan took some comfort in the fact that the sow was probably better off in his kitchen than rooting up the friar's precious vegetable plot.

For a while there was confusion as Athelstan offered
and served bowls of steaming oatmeal laced with nutmeg,
together with fairly fresh bread, butter, honey and jugs of The
Piebald's morning ale. Both guests made themselves very
comfortable. Athelstan delivered a blessing and his guests ate
hungrily. Athelstan watched them curiously. Like so many in
his parish, Athelstan knew very little about their past, upbringing
or work. Ursula had a wizened, doughy, plump face, her deep-
set eyes like small black holes in the snow, her nose more of
a snout, whilst her lips, as usual, were clumsily carmined. Ursula
lived in a tenement along an alleyway off the main thoroughfare
to the bridge. She did not work, being too old and frail, but
depended on the alms and generosity of the likes of Benedicta
and others in the parish. Ursula was eccentric, the source of a
great deal of laughter. Parishioners still talked of her clash with
Joscelyn at The Piebald over the price of certain kitchenware
she had sold the taverner late that summer. Ursula, so Athelstan
understood, had lived in the parish for decades; she was regarded
as one of its ancients, having a wealth of knowledge about the
past. Athelstan was determined to talk to her about the parish,
its history, and some of the strange characters it housed.

Remart, on the other hand, was different. He was a newcomer
who created a great deal of amusement over his claims about
the relics he kept locked away in his long wheelbarrow. Remart
had a pale, pock-scarred face, and lank grey hair bound in a
queue behind his head. From the little Athelstan could recall,
the relic seller originally hailed from the mid-shires. He had
been a novice in the Dominican order until he found he had no
vocation. He had arrived in St Erconwald's and settled down
as a relic seller, being given every support and lodged in the
death house. Athelstan had agreed to this at the behest of Prior
Anselm at Blackfriars. In the end, Remart had proved to be a
good parishioner. Athelstan had employed him as keeper and
surveyor of God's Acre. Lodged in the old death house, Remart
had been given his task, to keep a sharp and wary eye on God's
Acre, a place beloved by the legion of wandering witches and
warlocks of Southwark. Athelstan stared at the slightly hunched-
back relic seller and idly wondered what the future might hold
for him.

'Father?' Ursula tapped the table with her horn spoon. 'I have been waiting, we have been wanting to speak to you.'

'I am sorry, I am sorry.' Athelstan held up his hands. 'I know you were looking for me but other business presses hard.'

'It's that other business,' Ursula intervened sharply. 'We all know what happened at The Piebald. We have also learnt about how Sir John is pursuing that dreadful demon, the Flayer. How Sir John has even hired the mercenary Paltoc in his hunt.' Ursula paused, fingers fluttering to her lips, her fat face abruptly falling slack.

'What, Mother?'

'Nothing, Father, just something I saw in God's Acre, but I have forgotten it now. My humours are not as sharp as they used to be.'

'Don't worry.' Athelstan patted the old woman on the hand. 'Ursula, my friend, I often lose my thoughts.'

'Thank you, Father, which brings me back to what I came to see you about.' She turned to Remart. 'Shall I tell him?'

'Please do.' The relic seller's voice was almost a whisper; he blinked watery eyes and stared beseechingly at Athelstan. 'Ursula and I have become good friends. We wander God's Acre to ensure all is well, but so does Paltoc. He searches amongst the dead. He seeks out ancient graves.'

'You know he's trying to discover where his parents and brother lie buried?'

'Yes, yes, he told us the same,' Remart replied. 'But you know he's disturbing the ground. He claims his family were not buried in shrouds but proper coffin caskets, so the sharp rod he uses can pierce the soil to tell him what lies beneath.'

'But he has also been hired to hunt the Flayer,' Ursula added crossly. She then rose abruptly as the great sow stirred. Ursula knelt and stroked the pig along its ridged back, soothing it as she would a child. Athelstan caught Remart's glance, smiled and raised his eyes heavenwards. Ursula retook her seat, tapping her fingers against the tabletop. 'There is also something else, Father.' She rubbed the side of her head. 'I remembered this. My past can be sealed, its iron-bound doors firmly locked. Anyway, that's what I tell Hilda.' She pointed at the sleeping sow. 'But, since Remart and I became friends, this Flayer business, memories have come floating back.'

'Tell him,' the relic seller insisted, wiping a dripping nose on the sleeve of his jerkin. 'Tell him now.'

'This talk of the Flayer stirred the past,' Ursula declared. 'Well, at least my past. Things I'd thought I had forgotten, I find I have not. Father, many years ago St Erconwald's was not the parish it is today. It was a dark, sinister place, the church and its benefice were gripped by a pastor who was more wolf than shepherd. Oh yes. Little wonder, Father, the warlocks and wizards still come back. There was a time when you could see their fires blazing at night and they would bring the remains of hanged men to lonely parts of God's Acre, if you could call it that, so they could indulge in their filthy practices. If the priest was malignant, the same could be said of some of his parishioners. Anyway, there was a corpse-dresser, Adele Puddlicot if I remember correctly.'

'Puddlicot, you are sure?'

'Yes, Father, I am, and yes, Father, I have heard rumours about that name. A gang leader, a chieftain amongst the rifflers, a roaring boy, but that's all. Adele dressed corpses here at St Erconwald's.'

'What year was that?'

'The season of the wolf,' Ursula retorted. 'The time of perpetual winter.'

'Ursula, that means nothing to me.'

'During the time of the Great Plague, when buboes appeared on the neck and groin. A deadly pestilence raged. People sweated to death. Corpses were piled to a man's height. Funeral pyres roared at the dead of night.'

'Ursula?'

'The Black Death,' she whispered, 'as the chroniclers described it. A time of swift, savage infection.' Ursula chomped on her toothless gums and wiped away a drip of saliva. 'A time of terror,' she continued, 'we thought it was the day of anger, the end of the world and the rise of the Anti-Christ. Corpses were left unburied. Anyway, this Adele Puddlicot, she was a witch. She loved to skin corpses, the pathetic mortal remains of someone who was never cared for in life, let alone death.

She would collect cadavers in her barrow and take them to the cellar of a tenement in Weasel Lane. Do you know it, Father?'

'As a reeking, evil-looking runnel.'

'Oh yes, Father, that's the place. The Great Pestilence raged on.' She sniffed. 'Corpses lay piled high. No one really cared. However, stories, rumours began to swill through the parish, but you must remember, Father, law and order had collapsed. There was no Jack Cranston, no Brother Athelstan, souls like Adele were common enough, wolves incarnate. Of course, time passed. Hell had its day and the plague began to peter out. Life grew better. People began to look around to try and repair what was damaged and replace what was lost. Now you may not know this, Father, but St Erconwald's is a very ancient church. It lies outside and beyond the authority of the city. The parish enjoys certain rites, privileges and liberties. One of these is to empanel a jury to listen to a bill of indictment and reach a judgement. The jury elects its own leader, a judge who would sit in the church porch where people come to present a petition.'

'I have heard of this,' Athelstan intervened.

'Father, it was a liberty few people invoked because it lay in the hands of the priest and, believe me, Father, most of those should have been indicted.' She smiled, her fat face creasing. 'Of course, since you arrived, Father, what's the use? Moreover, if things go wrong, we have always got Fat Jack to protect us.' Her face grew solemn. 'It wasn't always like that, oh no.' Again, she sucked on her gums. 'In those hurling days when the Great Pestilence was dying out and law and order were being imposed, such a jury was convoked. Bills of indictment were drawn up and, from what I recall, a number of these levelled the most horrendous accusations against Adele Puddlicot.'

'And?'

'I am not too sure. You see, Father, Adele just disappeared.'

'How?'

'Rumour has it that the grand jury sat in the dead of night after darkness had fallen. Adele was seized and dragged for trial before it.'

'Then what happened?'

'According to rumour, Adele was buried alive in St Erconwald's graveyard. She was wrapped in a filthy sheepskin and interred beneath the cemetery's oldest yew tree – planted, or so they say, more than a hundred years ago.' Athelstan repressed a shiver. St Erconwald's, before he was despatched to this parish, had gained a fearsome, even sinister reputation. A house of malignant ghosts and malevolent spirits, they claimed, the haunt of sorcerers and spell-binders, the home of night people and dark-dwellers. Athelstan lifted his head and stared at his two visitors, pathetic souls who floated aimlessly along the river of life. They were rejected and despised by those who should know better, dismissed as petty, of no real importance or value whatsoever. He briefly closed his eyes and crossed himself. He was guilty of the same. He opened his eyes and smiled at his guests.

'Are these just parish tales?'

'I used to think so, Father, until I heard those stories about the Flayer now prowling the city. Frightening stories, so I went out to the ancient yew tree. Father, someone has been there. They have sacrificed God knows what. A black cockerel at the midnight hour?'

Athelstan flinched at the cold dread which seemed to caress him, ghostly hands plucking at his peace of mind. He got slowly to his feet. 'I must,' he stammered, 'I must see this, even though I detest even the signs of such sacrifice. Ursula, how did you discover this?'

'I wander the cemetery,' Ursula eased herself up, 'I've seen Paltoc poking the ground and, of course, Remart . . .'

'I said she must tell you . . .' the relic seller intervened.

'I only discovered it by accident.' Ursula gestured at the great sow. 'As you know, Father, Hilda loves to forage. So, on this occasion she went under the branches and began to snout and tear at the ground.'

'I must see this.'

Athelstan put on his heavy sandals, throwing his cloak about him. He grabbed the lighted lanternhorn, then ushered his visitors, including Hilda, out of the priest's house and across the darkening God's Acre. Ursula led the way, swinging the gnarled staff she always carried. Athelstan swiftly gazed around this memorial to the dead, truly desolate on this winter afternoon. A forbidding place! Stark plinths, battered crosses and crumbling memorial stones broke the sea of gorse, grass and bramble, which swayed backwards and forwards under a harsh bitter breeze. Athelstan realized they were going to the northern part of God's Acre, beyond Poor Man's Lot, reserved for the burial of strangers and others. They pushed through the gorse and into a stretch of land dominated by ancient yew trees, their trunks almost hidden by their own branches, which curved down to form a thick curtain around them. Ursula went into one of these, its branches pulled apart. Athelstan, carrying his lantern-horn, followed into what was a circular chamber created by the branches which, over the years, had stretched out, curved down then entwined. Athelstan sniffed and pinched his nostrils. The place had the reek of the slaughterhouse, that iron-like tang of dried blood. Some gathering had taken place here. The ground in the centre had been cleared for a fire, was still littered with charred embers; the soil beneath these was loose and damp. Athelstan murmured a prayer and crossed himself. Angry by what he'd seen, the remains of some macabre, midnight cere-mony, the friar walked back to his house. Here he thanked Ursula and Remart, wished them a pleasant evening, then washed his hands and face. Benedicta arrived to see if all was well and he asked her to summon Watkin and Pike and others to meet him, adding that they were to bring their spades, mattocks and lanterns with them. A short while later, Athelstan met his leading male parishioners by the church steps. He ignored their questions and led them out across the cemetery to the ancient yew tree.

'Please,' he asked, 'go in there. You will find the remains of a fire. Ignore that and anything else. Just dig.'

'For what?' Pike demanded crossly.

'You will know when you find it. Once you do, send for me.'

Within the hour, Watkin returned, shaking his head as he met Athelstan at the priest's house.

'No, Father, I won't speak. It's best if you see for yourself. It's a skeleton, a woman's, we think. Come, Father.'

Athelstan, holding his lantern, followed the dung collector back across God's Acre to the ancient yew tree, where the others stood clustered around what they had discovered. Athelstan crouched down, wrinkling his nose at the foul smell from the rotten sheet which covered the skeleton.

'It's sheepskin,' Benedicta murmured. 'A rotting sheepskin,
Father. I think the skeleton is a woman. Notice the long, white
wispy hair. She was buried alive, I am sure.'

Athelstan nodded. The skeleton was twisted grotesquely, a
truly gruesome sight. The skull was still attached, with long
tendrils of dirt-encrusted hair. The arms and legs were contorted.
What caught Athelstan's attention, and proved the manner of
death, was the rotting leather gag pushed between the jaws and
tied with hempen cord at the back of the skull.

'There's no trace of any clothing,' Benedicta added. 'No
jewellery or ornament.'

Athelstan whispered his agreement and continued his study.
The skeleton was grey and brittle, its twisted limbs indicative
of a hideous death, slowly suffocating in that sheepskin buried
deep in the soil. The heavy gag was used to mute all protests
and cries whilst the soiled sheepskin was a well-known method
for abusing or mocking a corpse. Athelstan could only guess
what had happened here so many years ago. The grand jury of
St Erconwald's, and Athelstan was determined to remember
that privilege, had tried Adele Puddlicot, probably in secret at
the dead of night. They had judged her guilty of heinous cruelty
and condemned her to a living death: that should have been the
gruesome end to a very grisly story.

'But it wasn't,' Athelstan exclaimed to himself.

'Father?'

Athelstan startled from his reverie, smiled at Benedicta.
'One question,' Athelstan declared, 'who knew about this?
Ursula certainly did. Anyone else? Well?'

Watkin and Pike shuffled forward. 'We heard rumours,' the
ditcher confessed, 'parish gossip, tittle-tattle but . . .' Pike fell
silent.

'I heard the same,' a voice declared and Paltoc, pushing at
the branches, came into the clearing. 'Rumours,' he murmured
staring down at the skeleton, 'stories, tales.' The mercenary
pulled back his hood. Athelstan stared at the pale, unshaven
face. Paltoc certainly looked agitated.

'You have not discovered your family grave?'

'Oh, Father, I know the area but not the precise plot. I asked
Ursula to help. Although she could remember the funerals,

she could not recall where the graves lay.' Paltoc seemed distracted.

'You buried what I gave you?'

'Yes, yes, Father, where you told me, in the hummock of earth over Godbless's grave.'

'God rest him too,' Athelstan murmured. 'And have you discovered anything about the Flayer?'

'No, no, not really.' Paltoc was now openly evasive. The mercenary turned and walked back into the cemetery. Athelstan let him go now, busying himself. Watkin, Pike and the rest were to carry their grim findings to the death house whilst Benedicta and Crim agreed to take messages to Cranston. Athelstan returned to his house and the problems which now truly taxed him.

The next morning Athelstan celebrated his Mass, recited the Divine Office and tended to parish business when he had to, including the burial in the Poor Man's Lot of that hideous find beneath the yew tree. Athelstan scrutinized the parish records for any trace or mention of Adele Puddlicot, but this proved to be a fruitless task. The Great Plague years had brought an end to all parish business, a situation not helped by the devil-may-care attitude of the priest at the time. Cranston received his message and sent a reply that he too could find no reference to Adele Puddlicot. The coroner offered to visit Athelstan but the friar declined, saying it was best to wait for further developments.

Prior Sinclair asked to see him, a fleeting meeting in which the prior thanked Athelstan for his help and support. He reassured the friar that despite the mysterious murders of Halpen and Mildew, he'd amassed a great deal of information for his chronicle. He also informed Athelstan that Sylvester the sacristan would be accompanying him back to Melrose to attend a very important chapter meeting. Athelstan heard him out and then expressed his own deep regret about not resolving the murders at Westminster. Sinclair reassured him that the Blackrobes knew Sir John was doing everything in his power, adding that the deaths of the four Scottish Benedictines weighed heavily on the community. However, they still hoped Sir John and Athelstan would make some progress before the delegation departed for Edinburgh.

Athelstan watched the prior leave, going down through God's Acre, and the friar repressed a slight thrill of excitement. He closed the door and went back to his broad kitchen table where Bonaventure was waiting, all solemn and attentive.

'My dear, dear friend,' Athelstan whispered, 'if I have one fault amongst many, it is that I fail to see the obvious, in this case the very obvious! Prior Sinclair made me realize that. He is correct. The mysteries of Westminster are tightly woven together but not, as I first thought, by mere chance. All the murder victims are Scottish. Secondly, they define themselves as Guardians of the Stone. Thirdly, at the same time these dreadful murders are being perpetrated, we have a Scottish delegation visiting Westminster. Its leader, Sinclair, has a deep interest in the doings of my parish. Fourthly, the massive Scottish war cog *The Bannockburn* is not berthed at Queenhithe or Dowgate but here in Southwark. No, no,' Athelstan breathed, 'there's more to all this. I am dealing with the strands, separate strands. However, in truth, a very clever web of intrigue has been woven. So, what is the purpose of all this, eh Bonaventure? We shall see.'

The cat blinked his one good eye and continued his vigil, staring fixedly at Athelstan until the little friar realized that a bowl of milk was Bonaventure's reason for being so attentive, that and the fire, as well as the affection of his constant friend. Absentmindedly Athelstan rose, went into the buttery and brought back Bonaventure's bowl, which he placed before the hearth. Whilst the great tomcat feasted, Athelstan sat, face cupped in his hands. He recalled going aboard *The Bannockburn*, watching the crew members, and he realized what had intrigued him. He was sure of this. He'd seen one of those crew members before and it certainly wasn't here in the parish. A knock on the door startled him and Benedicta burst in, all agitated.

'Father you must come, you must see this.' The widow woman's fingers flew to her face. 'In God's name you must see this, it's hideous, terrible!'

'What is?' Athelstan asked, clutching her by the arms. 'Benedicta, in God's name what is it?'

'Ursula the pig woman. She, and her sow Hilda. They lie, they lie, both slaughtered. Come, come!'

Athelstan followed Benedicta out, hurrying through God's Acre along the lane past The Piebald. Athelstan shouted to those who wanted to accompany him to stand back. He and Benedicta entered the narrow, reeking runnels which coursed through Southwark like the strands of some giant cobweb. Here, the dark-dwellers and shadows met and plotted their mischief. Athelstan's name was proclaimed, voices shouted eerily and the shadows in the doorways and at the mouth of alleyways crept back. They reached the crossroads, nothing more than a roundel of cobbles. Watkin and another dung collector were waiting for him. Both men were subdued, whispering their fear as they led the friar down the needle-thin alleyway lined either side by shabby, decayed tenements leaning drunkenly across the street to block out both light and air. A truly filthy place, with its decaying doors, crumbling walls and ill-fitting window frames. The dung collectors pushed one of these doors open. Both picked up the lanternhorns glowing in the darkened hallway and led Athelstan along the mildewed passageway, down crumbling wooden steps to a cellar. Two cresset torches flared brightly and cast a strong pool of light around the abomination awaiting them. Athelstan caught his breath. He fought back the tears as he stared at poor Ursula's pathetic remains. He had no trouble recognising her immediately. The pig woman's head and face had deliberately not been touched so it would be easy to identify her, but the rest was a blood-soaked mess. All clothing had been removed, the woman's flesh cruelly flayed, reduced to a squalid, gore-soaked tangle. Ursula's beloved sow lay on its side at her feet. The pig's throat had been slashed, the blood gushing out to form a great puddle which winked in the dancing light.

'She was killed by a blow to the back of her head,' Watkin whispered. 'A hammer blow, she must have died immediately.'

Athelstan, overcome by the sheer horror of the tragedy, fell to his knees on the hard-paved floor. He put his face in his hands and sobbed uncontrollably at the sheer wicked waste of what lay before him, a human being with all her loving eccentricities reduced to nothing more than a bloody mangle. The only consolation was Watkin's comment. Ursula must have died immediately, not even aware of the horror about to engulf her.

Eventually, with Benedicta gently stroking his shoulder, Athelstan regained his composure and stood up now, fighting a surge of his fiery temper. He glanced quickly at Benedicta standing pale-faced and thin-lipped.

'You are stronger than I am,' he whispered.

'No, Brother,' she stretched out and took his hand between hers, 'I just draw strength from you. I know you will see justice done.'

Athelstan asserted himself. He walked to the foot of the steps where Watkin was waiting and asked how the corpse had been discovered. Watkin bellowed for his fellow dung collector to step forward. The man gave his name as Dicken and, still trying to control his own fear, explained how he had been clearing the runnel outside. He had glimpsed a great blotch of blood on a slab of stone, placed to cover a pothole close to the battered front door. Intrigued, Dicken pushed the door open and discovered another splash of blood. He realized this was freshly spilt so he checked the ground floor, adding that the stairs to the upper storeys were too dangerous. Apparently, the house was rat infested, and Dicken noticed how many of the vermin were scampering down to the cellar where a grisly feast awaited them. Dicken followed the rats down. He lit torches and these revealed Ursula's corpse and that of her sow in all their horror. Now and again Dicken would pause as he fought to control his urge to retch and vomit. Athelstan calmed him, reassuring Dicken that he had done well. He thanked him, blessed both dung collectors, and gave them each a coin for a tankard of ale. Despite his own agitation, and the ice-cold sweat which seemed to grip him from head to toe, Athelstan was sharp enough to realize that news of this outrage would soon spread. He had words with Benedicta to persuade Watkin to organize the swift removal of Ursula's corpse to the new death house at St Erconwald's. He also asked Benedicta to visit Ursula's chamber and bring all her goods to his house as soon as possible. Athelstan then left, striding through the gathering murk, eager to reach the comfort and solace of his own warm house.

PART FIVE

'Many devils are busy carrying him off.'

T he following morning, the second Sunday in Advent, Athelstan finished reading the Gospel and went straight into the pulpit to deliver a homily which truly startled his parishioners. Watkin, Pike and the rest were accustomed to Athelstan pleading with them to be gentle to each other and how, at Christmas especially, they should prepare for the birth of Christ in their hearts as well as the manger in Bethlehem. Instead, his voice full of fury and scorn, the friar delivered a truly angry denunciation of the Flayer who, in his view, was excommunicated and fit for hell as any Herod. He attacked the Flayer for his repulsive murder of innocents and the ghastly desecration of their corpses. He then spoke warmly about his 'dear sister Ursula' and his genuine affection for Ursula's constant companion, the great sow Hilda. Athelstan then returned to the attack, damning the Flayer as worse than a demon incarnate, a soul bound for hell where the demons would welcome him like a brother. Athelstan's parishioners sat chilled by the ferocity of their parish priest's invective. It ended with a heartfelt prayer that God send an angel to intervene and bring this malicious malignant to a well-deserved end on the gallows outside Newgate.

Once he had finished, Athelstan swept into the sacristy, where he hastily took off his Mass robes.

'You weren't just condemning the Flayer, were you?'

Athelstan turned to confront Paltoc, who had slipped like a shadow through the sacristy door. 'What do you mean?' Athelstan asked, slightly cross at this stranger creeping up so silently behind him.

'You are trying to provoke him, yes?'

'Perhaps. My sermon is not really meant for my parishioners. I hope it will be repeated and proclaimed throughout Southwark, across the bridge and into the city. It may well provoke the Flayer to show himself. Anyway,' Athelstan continued briskly, 'to what do I owe this honour?'

'First, when I have found the family grave, I would like your permission to dig. I understand,' Paltoc's words came in a rush, 'and you may well know this, my family were buried in caskets not just shrouds, and their names and titles were carved on the coffin lids. I assure you, Father, there will be no disruption . . .'

'To the others during their final sleep before the resurrection.' Athelstan finished his sentence, taking the words from the rite of exhumation. 'Go ahead, my friend, but be respectful and prudent.'

'And secondly, Father.'

'Of course there is always a secondly.' Athelstan bit his lips. He did not mean to be so tart and blunt.

'Secondly, Father, this . . .' Paltoc dug into his pocket and took out a strip of grubby linen. 'You asked me to bury the linen parcel containing human skin. I did so, but I first took a strip of the linen so I could examine it. Father, it's quite coarse, not fashioned in this kingdom but from Hainault or Brabant. Their looms produce a tougher and indeed a cheaper linen. Not the sort of material you would carry around with you. What I am saying is this. The Flayer used that linen for his own gruesome purposes, but it could be evidence that the assassin is a linen merchant in this kingdom or beyond.'

'It could be anyone, as linen is on sale all over the city.' Sir John came striding into the sacristy. 'The Flayer could be anyone. You know what reward beckons you, so continue your hunt, Master Paltoc. Brother, I walked through your blessed parish, I heard all about your sermon. Dangerous, very dangerous. I also received your message about other doings here. Master Paltoc, I wish you well. Be on your way. I need urgent words with my fiery friar.'

Paltoc made his farewells and left. Athelstan led Cranston out of the sacristy and across the sanctuary to St Erconwald's chantry chapel, where the reliquary of the great saint hung on a silver chain next to that holding the sacred host in its gold, bejewelled ciborium.

'It's a wonder,' Cranston pointed at them, 'that they have

never been stolen.' The coroner lowered his bulk on to the cushioned wall bench, whilst Athelstan moved the chancery stool to sit opposite the coroner.

'Oh no, Sir John, don't worry about that. I doubt if such a thief would leave this church or parish alive. Now, you received my messages?'

'I did and I have brought help. Master Catchpole. You will learn all about him soon enough. He is busy supping with all those other rogues in the taproom at The Piebald. You have ideas about what truly happened at that tavern?'

'I certainly do but, for the moment, that will have to wait. Now Westminster?'

'All quiet. Of course, the Blackrobes are shocked and trembling at the murders. The abbot intends to close the church for the rite of purification. I also understand that our Scottish brethren are preparing to leave, though there seems to be some delay or the other. God knows what's happening there.'

'Well, Sir John, I have been reflecting. We have,' Athelstan emphasized the points on his fingers, 'first, the four monkish victims were all Scottish, they were also self-appointed Guardians of the Stone of Destiny, the ancient Stone of Scone used for the coronations of Scottish kings, seized by the English some eighty-five years ago. The anchorite, although Scottish and a former Benedictine, cannot be included in this group. Accordingly, his death is truly shrouded in mystery. Secondly, we have Prior Sinclair's visitation, which includes a stay here at St Erconwald's parish. Sinclair is allegedly compiling a chronicle and wishes to discover more about the Great Revolt. In truth, he couldn't have chosen a better place: what my parishioners don't know about the Great Revolt is not worth knowing. Thirdly, we have the Scottish war cog *The Bannockburn* moored nearby. Finally, we have what began this chain of murder mystery, the night the anchorite was disturbed by strange sights and sounds and the poisonings which have taken place since.'

'And your conclusion?'

'Sir John, I have strange suspicions and deep doubts about everything we have been told. I believe we could be caught up in a veritable web of a very clever and subtle conspiracy. I have noticed something amiss, but, let me hasten to add, not enough to formulate an indictment. Nevertheless, we must make preparations and I would like your influence in arranging this.'

'Which is?'

'Well, what I call "sealing the trap" can wait. First, we must bait the lure.'

'What is that?'

'When you return to Westminster, seek out the archivist, the librarian. We need to study any manuscript the abbey may possess which describes the Stone of Destiny. Sir John, I need you to make great play of this. Make sure that what you want is trumpeted the length and breadth of that blessed abbey.'

'And for sealing the trap?'

'As I have said. Let us wait. Let us deal with the lure. Mysteries untangle, Sir John. We pick a loose thread, nothing happens. You pick at another and suddenly everything begins to unravel. This business at Westminster is such a tangle. I believe we are being used, Sir John, and certain people are being silenced but, be that as it may, it will have to wait.'

'Are you in danger, little friar?'

'Yes, Sir John, I think I could be. But that's part of the trap. Now, Master Catchpole?'

'As I said, drinking with the other sinners in The Piebald.'

'Then, Sir John, let us join them.'

The arrival of their parish priest, accompanied by the Lord High Coroner, created an immediate silence across the bustling, noisy taproom. Certain individuals fled like snow before the sun, be it through a window or the nearest door. Cranston bellowed his greetings, adding that he was not here to finger the nape of anyone's neck, though if any individual wished to confess to any felony, he, as Lord High Coroner, would be more than happy to listen. Even more of the customers now fled, much to the quiet amusement of Athelstan's parishioners Watkin, Pike, and the rest of their coven. Cranston, however, had espied his true quarry, Catchpole, a thin-faced, mousy-haired individual dressed like a Franciscan in an earth-coloured jerkin and hose, at first sight a truly placid individual with his soft, beseeching eyes and quiet speech. Cranston, however, now sitting next to his 'guest', with Athelstan on a stool close by, introduced Catchpole as a man who could sneak in and out of a chamber without anyone noticing. A highly skilled felon with a unique talent for turning any lock, weakening any bolt, lifting any latch, be it on a window, even a shutter behind iron bars. Indeed, Cranston declared, gripping his innocent-looking 'guest' by the shoulder, Catchpole could ease himself into any chamber where he had no right to be, having removed any obstacle set up to keep out people such as himself.

'Very good, Sir John, but excuse me.' Athelstan rose and walked over to have words with Minehost Josceyln, who looked surprised but nodded in agreement. He handed a key over and Athelstan returned to Sir John. 'I have told Josceyln,' Athelstan declared, 'that I wanted the murder chamber emptied, and it is. The door has been repaired and Josceyln has set a guard so we won't be disturbed. So come, let us discover the truth if we can.'

They climbed the stairs, now guarded by Ranulf and his two ferrets. He assured them that the chambers along the gallery were now empty, including the one occupied by Prior Sinclair before his return to Westminster. They reached the murder chamber. Athelstan opened the door, ushering Cranston and Catchpole inside, and then locked and bolted the door. Two lanternhorns had been lit and placed to provide more light, the chamber had also been thoroughly cleaned. Athelstan showed Catchpole around, who quickly agreed that there was no secret entrance, whilst the window was far too narrow for anyone to get through. Catchpole then inspected the heavy bolts and clasps attached to the top and bottom as well as the sturdy lock. Finally, he scrutinized the hinges, very thick pieces of the toughest leather held fast between door and lintel.

'So, Master Catchpole,' Athelstan asked. 'Two men, former soldiers, hale and hearty, were brought here and hanged without protest or resistance. No disturbance was seen or heard.'

'Yes, yes, I have heard of this.' Catchpole pointed up at the ceiling beams. 'They were hanged from there?'

'Yes, as I have said, with no sign whatsoever of any resistance but,' Athelstan continued, 'that could be solved easily enough. Both men were mawmsy, deep in their cups, made even more so with some opiate. The real mystery is how those responsible left this chamber locked, barred and very secure from within. The window provides no solution, whilst we know the heavy lock and bolts were not tampered with.' Catchpole nodded, his eyes bright with excitement.

'And so, Brother?'

'Well, there is only one logical explanation, one possibility, and that's why Sir John and I need your expert advice . . .'

Later that day Athelstan, accompanied by Cranston, met twelve of his parishioners in the hosting place close to the baptismal font in St Erconwald's. Athelstan sat in the great sanctuary chair, Cranston on a stool beside him, the parishioners on benches facing them. The church had been cleared and doors locked. Athelstan drew grim satisfaction about how many of his parishioners stepped forward when he demanded that he only wanted to meet those who had entertained Halpen and Mildew on that fateful night – twelve in all.

'The same number as a jury,' Athelstan whispered to Cranston, 'and, as I have recently discovered, this parish enjoys the ancient right and liberty of presentment and conviction. In other words, a jury can sit to decide on a bill of indictment.'

'Yes, yes, quite possible,' Cranston retorted. 'In my great magnum opus on the history of London, I've come across such a right being given to certain parishes, guilds and wards. Indeed, when Richard Puddlicot stole the Crown Jewels from the crypt at Westminster, the royal justices investigated the crime by moving across London, compelling each ward and parish to make a presentment.'

'Oh, and did you discover much about Puddlicot?'

'Plenty about Richard himself,' Cranston lowered his voice, 'but about his family very little. Perhaps they moved across river. I have learnt about poor Ursula's death and what she told you.'

'Father, why are we here?' Watkin interrupted.

'Oh yes, why are you here?' Athelstan retorted. 'Let us go back to that evening when Halpen the Hare and Mildew retired to their chamber never to leave it. They may have drunk. They may have met Cecily and her sister, but they were definitely marked down for death.' Athelstan paused. 'They were true Judas men betraying their kith and kin for a few pieces of silver and some patronage from the likes of Gaunt and Thibault. Yes?'

A stony silence greeted his question.

'They were tainted. Innocent blood stained their hands yet they were well protected.' Athelstan smiled thinly. 'I am sure the Reapers were very happy when Prior Sinclair declared that he would love to speak to people who played an important role in the Great Revolt.'

'Whatever the Reapers did, we did no wrong,' Watkin protested.

'And I am not accusing you,' Athelstan retorted. 'I am just describing the way things were. Indeed, I will talk about the Reapers; yes, that's the most tactful and truthful way of presenting this bill of indictment. The Reapers were delighted to lure Halpen and Mildew out of the murk into the light of the taproom in The Piebald tavern! Oh yes, a place where, not so long ago, the Upright Men plotted their great enterprise, a time and place when Halpen and Mildew acted as their most fervent supporters, even as they plotted to betray everything and everyone for Judas's silver.' Athelstan stared down at the floor letting the silence deepen.

'Halpen and Mildew thought they were safe,' he continued. 'After all, the parishioners of St Erconwald's hadn't really been hurt by the violence of the revolt or, indeed, its sudden collapse. Anyway, like good hosts you made them most welcome, and your two visitors would flatter themselves, all secure and smug. Neither of those two realized the Reapers were simply waiting for them. On that fateful night, twelve of these Reapers entered Halpen and Mildew's chamber.'

'Why twelve?' Pike shouted, though he could not disguise the tremor in his voice.

'Well, I am not too sure,' Athelstan retorted. 'However, Ursula the pig woman, before her brutal murder, informed me about St Erconwald's ancient Right of Presentment, the power to invoke a jury, to discern a matter and reach a verdict on a bill of indictment.'

'And, with the appropriate law officer being present,' Cranston intervened, 'sentence could be carried out. But continue, Brother.'

'As I said, on that night twelve Reapers entered Halpen and Mildew's chamber. Both were caught in the deepest sleep, the result of ale, wine, the ministrations of Cecily and her sister and, of course, a sleeping potion slipped into their cups . . .'

'And who did that?'

'Why Watkin, the Reapers of course, who cleverly concealed their true nature and desire. They would, to the likes of Halpen and Mildew, be nothing more than other customers flocking into The Piebald to glimpse our two heroes and listen spellbound and wide-eyed to all the tales they spun about the Great Revolt. Anyway, overcome by sleep, Halpen and Mildew prepare to retire. God knows who, but again there would be people who would help them up the stairs and along the gallery. The two heroes are then visited by our two sisters – I doubt if it was for long. The ladies would leave. Halpen and Mildew do not bother with keys and bolts – why should they? Both men were honoured guests, but not for long. The chamber is open and the jury gathers outside. Once inside, the Reapers, who probably slipped in quietly one by one, delivered sentence. Halpen and Mildew were condemned and the Reapers hanged them by the neck from the roof beams in that chamber. They were powerless to resist. Perhaps the Reapers helped them on their journey into the dark by grabbing their legs and pulling them down.' Athelstan stared directly at the Hangman of Rochester. 'A common enough practice on execution day when relatives want to ease the agony of a prolonged strangulation.'

'Very clever,' Cranston intervened. 'Two swift executions without any sign of resistance.'

'You believe these Reapers simply merged with the rest of us in that taproom?' Crispin demanded. 'Yet they were seen, Benedicta saw them.'

'No, no.' Athelstan shook his head. 'All Benedicta saw were dark shapes down a dimly lit runnel. I myself was confronted by those dark shapes, who simply appeared out of the night as I made my way home across God's Acre. Whoever they really were, they claimed to be the Reapers. Perhaps it was the only way of emphasising that they and no one else were responsible for the deaths of Halpen and Mildew, and I am certainly not going to contradict them, whoever they may be. Yes?' Athelstan's question simply provoked a deep and uneasy silence.

'And so,' Athelstan continued, 'let us return to the execution of Halpen and Mildew. They died as they lived, dreadfully. The Reapers left their mark, an insignia to demonstrate the executions were their doing. They also wanted to hide behind a great mystery. They wanted to puzzle everyone as well as demonstrate that the Great Community of the Realm and its servants, be they the Upright Men, the Earthworms, the Reapers or all of these, still exercised power and influence. By executing Halpen and Mildew, the Reapers proclaimed their cause to the world.'

'The executions and the way they were carried out are not easy to resolve,' Cranston declared. 'Like a problem in the schools it taxes the brain. The Reapers were very cunning. They created a true mystery, an ingenious way of proclaiming what they'd done. The executions of Halpen and Mildew would be highly popular. The news of their deaths, as it has, would sweep the city and the surrounding shires. How could this happen? How could Halpen and Mildew be found swinging from their necks in a secure chamber locked and bolted from within? I listen to the chatter of Cheapside, the gossip of the alleyways and the scurrilous rumours along the runnels, I have eyes and ears in all the taverns and alehouses from Colchester in Essex to the very heart of Dover. The news is all the same.' Cranston paused to sip from his wineskin. 'Do you know what they say?' he continued. 'They are talking about an angel sent from heaven, one of the Lord High God's messengers, who carried out justice on the behalf of the great cause. This angel meted out deserved punishment against those who had harmed Heaven's innocents. Wonderful, isn't it?' Cranston added sarcastically. 'A marvel to behold. I know it won't give you any comfort, but my Lord of Gaunt and Master Thibault are truly perturbed.' He paused as Pike sniggered into his hand.

'I am sorry,' the ditcher lifted his head, 'I am truly sorry. I was clearing my throat. I am, like the rest, stricken to the heart that my Lord of Gaunt and Master Thibault are perturbed.'

'Oh, I am sure you are,' Cranston retorted. 'I am sure you will weep into your hands tonight but, Brother Athelstan, let us continue.'

'The chamber was well prepared,' Athelstan declared. 'The remains of food and drink lay untainted, the bedclothes orderly, no overturned furniture, nothing disturbed, damaged or filched, just those two corpses dangling by their necks. Indeed, the room was found sealed and locked from within. So what really happened there? I have reflected, prayed and fasted. I have eagerly sought the advice of Sir John and Master Catchpole and I have reached the only logical conclusion: that room had only one way out and that was through the doorway.'

'But the chamber was locked and bolted from the inside,' Watkin shouted. 'Father, you saw that yourself.'

'Of course I did: that's what everyone looks at, the lock, the bolts. We forget about the hinges, those thick pieces of leather glued between the lintel and the door. Hinges which were destroyed shortly after I arrived when that door was forced.' Athelstan shook his head. 'Very clever.' He murmured. 'Hinges are items constantly used but very rarely studied. True? They are fashioned out of the toughest and most hardened leather, which is then folded, the two ends or tongues being coated with the most powerful glue to be had, a substance formed by boiling seasoned horse hooves. Anyway, one tongue of the hinge is fixed to the lintel, the other to the door. Usually there are two such hinges, one at the top and another at the bottom. Occasionally there are three, the third being inserted in the middle.' Athelstan pointed at Josceyln. 'That chamber door had two, yes?'

'Father.' Josceyln, who regarded himself as a born storyteller, lumbered to his feet, shaking his head and muttering under his breath at Crispin who also rose, face all sad.

'Don't tell me,' Athelstan snapped, 'let me guess. You know nothing about those hinges. You had a journeyman, an itinerant joiner working in The Piebald shortly before Halpen and Mildew were found hanged.'

'Precisely,' Josceyln snapped back. 'A travelling journeyman who has now left the parish, going south into Kent, or so he said.'

'And why didn't you use Crispin, our parish carpenter?'

'Too busy, Father,' Crispin declared. 'And Josceyln is very slow to pay.' His words were greeted with murmurs of approval. 'Father, what are you hinting at? The journeyman did some work on that door. Are you saying he might have been a Reaper?'

'Oh, anyone could have been a Reaper; indeed, anyone in

this parish could be a Reaper. Let us move on, who repaired the chamber door after we broke it down?'

'I did, Father.'

'Really, Crispin, I thought you were too busy and Josceyln was a late payer?'

'I did it as a favour and for free. I mean, Josceyln did lavishly entertain us.'

'And when you repaired the door, did you notice anything untoward?'

'Nothing at all, Father. The hinges, like the lock and bolt, were totally beyond repair. I didn't give the hinges a second thought. I mean, as you said, Father, very few people, if any, examine hinges.'

Athelstan hid his smile behind his hand.

'Father?'

'Oh nothing, Watkin. I just recall something I thought strange at the time when we forced the door. We used the battering ram, the yule log against the hinges rather than the lock and bolt. Crispin, you advised that.'

'Father, for the life of me I cannot recall saying . . .'

'No, no, I am sure you can't. However, to return to the matter in hand, those hinges certainly played a major part in the mystery surrounding Halpen and Mildew's execution. You see, once judgement had been carried out, the Reapers left the chamber, except for someone thin and wiry, someone like you, Pike.'

'Thank you, Father, and what did this person do?'

'Oh, let me explain. Sometime before that evening, the old hinges on that door had been quietly and quickly replaced by new ones. The leather would be soft and subtle, the glue not so thick or rich. Once the executions are carried out, the door is locked and bolted on one side, but not before the hinges are removed from the other side. An easy enough task. The door is held upright by the lock and bolts but the other side, now free of the hinges, can be moved to create a narrow gap through which the last Reaper, who has ensured all is as it should be within that room, leaves the murder chamber, squeezing and crawling through, given every help by his comrades waiting outside. The door is now pulled square to fit. The hinges, wedges of soft, supple leather, acquire a generous coating of strong glue then are pushed back into the gaps. As long as they are positioned correctly it doesn't really matter. Within a few hours, the door, its locks and, above all, its hinges are going to be skewered and shattered beyond repair.' Athelstan cleared this throat. 'The Reapers,' he continued, 'would scrupulously clear up any stains and remains of their handiwork. Of course there was little danger of anything untoward being noticed. After all, that gallery is dark at the best of times, and I was summoned long before daylight.'

'But how could the Reapers work so hard in that gallery? After all, Prior Sinclair was in an adjoining chamber?'

'Nonsense, Watkin! The rooms along that gallery were empty.' Athelstan smiled thinly as he stared at Joscelyn. 'God knows how the Reapers arranged that.'

'But Prior Sinclair?'

'Oh, Watkin, you know the answer to that. Didn't the good prior say he slept well and deep, because he had drunk well and deep, helped, I am sure, by a little sleeping powder that a Reaper poured into his goblet during the festivities in the taproom. On that night the tavern was crammed to overflowing. Didn't you, Joscelyn, have to use every cup and goblet, including those poor Ursula sold you earlier in the year?' Athelstan's reply provoked guffaws of laughter. Ursula's sale of kitchenware to the taverner and the hard bargain she pushed was well known in the community and a constant source of amusement. Athelstan let the laughter fade away.

'And so we have it,' he murmured.

'But, Father . . .?'

'Yes, Watkin?'

'Nothing,' the dung collector murmured. 'Nothing at all, Father.'

'Well.' Athelstan rose. 'As I said, that's what happened. Heaven knows who the Reapers truly were. Parishioners? Or others invited to St Erconwald's? Dark mysterious shapes to be glimpsed by Benedicta or myself, walking through God's Acre. Anyway, gentlemen, I have said enough and I bid you goodnight.'

Athelstan and Cranston left the church and walked silently back through God's Acre to the priest's house. Only when they were safely inside and the door locked did Athelstan sit at the table, laughing softly to himself.

'You think that's what happened, Brother?' Cranston asked, sitting down opposite. The coroner took a generous swig from his wineskin and offered it to Athelstan who did likewise. The friar, staring down at the floor, continued to laugh to himself. Then he glanced up, wiping his eyes.

'To answer your question, Sir John, I don't think that's what happened, I know it did. Young Catchpole's observations about doors and hinges convinced me. Of course,' Athelstan spread his hands, 'perhaps I am wrong in a few details, but I think we almost have the truth of all this nonsense!'

'Almost?' Cranston demanded.

'In brief, Sir John, in brief. Prior Sinclair, for God knows what reason, chose St Erconwald's. A strange decision. After all, there are other parishes, other taverns in Southwark, which were hotbeds of conspiracy and revolt. I certainly have my suspicions about our good prior, Sir John, but for the moment they are based on pure speculation. Secondly, I was also deeply intrigued by the reaction of my beloved parishioners. You see, Sinclair asked to meet individuals who were swept up in the Great Revolt.'

'Your parishioners were truly delighted to be chosen.'

'True, Sir John, and that also mystified me.'

'Why?' Cranston pulled a tray of sweetmeats, a gift from Merrylegs to his parish priest, closer to him: he popped two of the honeyed comfits into his mouth.

'Well, my learned coroner, thanks to your good offices, the Upright Men of St Erconwald's were, in the main, taken out of the parish. True, they were ardent supporters of the Great Community of the Realm but, for those few fateful days of the revolt, they were in protective custody organized by you. However . . .' Athelstan sipped at the tankard of ale he poured himself and absentmindedly helped himself to some of the sweetmeats. 'However,' he repeated, 'when Prior Sinclair announced the reason for his visit, my parishioners, and in truth they are the Reapers, seized it as a marvellous opportunity.'

'For what, justice?'

'More than that, Sir John. First, they could redeem themselves.

Many of their comrades were killed during the revolt. Others were hanged afterwards, yet Watkin and his comrades emerged totally unscathed.'

'Prior Sinclair gave them the opportunity to balance the scales?'

'Precisely, Sir John. Halpen and Mildew were two dyed-in-the-wool Judas men, traitors and betrayers. They were enticed out of the shadows, away from any protection, and ever so gently led into a deadly trap. Halpen and Mildew happily obliged. They accepted the invitation. They were arrogant. They would regard my parishioners as dull and stupid. What they didn't know – what they failed to realize – was how clever Watkin and his crew were. My parishioners hastily prepared to deal out justice: that gallery would be left empty. Prior Sinclair would be flattered and cosseted with wine, a good deep bowl of Bordeaux laced with a sleeping potion. The door to Halpen and Mildew's chamber was tampered with long before the victims arrived; the old stiff hinges were removed and new supple ones lightly fixed. There was no real danger, after all those hinges would only be used for a very short period of time. Halpen and Mildew were silenced with jugs of wine. They fell asleep. Execution was carried out. The door to the murder chamber locked and bolted on one side by a Reaper who stole through the gap on the other. The hinges are then put back and the mystery posed. Oh, my parishioners were certainly involved, though perhaps they brought in others, including those gentlemen who confronted me in God's Acre. So to another issue.' Athelstan took a deep breath. 'What does Master Thibault truly think? Never mind about being perturbed. How will he view Halpen and Mildew's deaths?'

'In truth, good riddance!'

'For a short while he will.'

'What do you mean, Brother?'

'Well, I come to a further reason for this murderous masque. Sir John, the Great Revolt is over. The Lords of the Soil ride high and mighty, the rebels are utterly crushed yet the seed remains. The battle was lost but the war continues, and will do so as long as injustice reigns.' Athelstan sipped from his tankard. 'The execution of Halpen and Mildew, two hideous traitors, is a shouted protest, a cry that the cause is not yet finished. The Upright Men may be gone, the great Council of the Realm a dream, the Earthworms dispersed but the Reapers, the Guardians of the Flame, remain.' Athelstan tapped the table. 'Believe me, Sir John, the revolt is not really over and that's the message the Reapers, whoever they are, whomever they include, have proclaimed for all to see and hear, including Master Thibault. Now,' Athelstan rubbed his face, 'what do we do, Sir John?'

'We have no real proof. Halpen and Mildew were villains, treacherous to their very marrow. They certainly reaped what they sowed. We will leave it. We have little evidence for any bill of indictment. More importantly, Brother, I have neither the time, the energy or the inclination to prosecute.' He paused. 'Bearing in mind that Halpen and Mildew were once attainted traitors who died the death they deserved, I may well ask for a royal pardon for any and all involved in their deaths.'

'Is that possible, Sir John? Even though you have no actual names, no real proof about what really happened?'

'It's been done, little friar, up and down this kingdom. It would be protection should anyone,' Cranston grinned, 'produce proof positive about what really did happen in that chamber at The Piebald on that most fateful evening.' Cranston gave a deep sigh. 'Much more serious, Brother, much more perilous is your public condemnation of the Flayer. What you did was very dangerous.'

'It was necessary, Sir John. We must provoke the Flayer even further. We must make him break cover from the forest of lies and deception he lurks behind. We have baited him. We have taunted him. Like all such assassins, he is lost deep in his own twisted arrogance. Let us be patient. He will emerge. Until then, Sir John, let us wait.'

Cranston left a short while later, striding down the lane, cloak thrust back, beaver hat firmly on. No one could mistake it was Sir John Cranston, heading like a well-aimed slingshot for London Bridge and, once across, the warm embrace of his beloved wife and equally beloved poppets. Athelstan also prepared to end the day and make ready for the morrow. He was about to retire to bed when he heard a rapping on the door. Athelstan grasped the small arbalest Cranston had given him some months earlier. He winched back the cord, placed a bolt in the groove, then held it down as he hurried to answer the insistent knocking. When he did so, he was surprised to see the Hangman of Rochester, lantern in one hand, ave beads wrapped round the fingers of the other. The hangman looked ghastly: tears wetted his cheeks, his eyes red-rimmed as if he had been crying for hours.

'Come in, come in,' Athelstan urged. He ushered his visitor to a stool, then pressed a goblet of the best Bordeaux that Cranston could buy into the hangman's gauntleted hand.

'I have been to the death house, Father. No, not where the relic seller lives but the new one. I saw Ursula's corpse. I took a Christmas rose to place on her corpse and that of her poor sow. Father I saw, I saw . . .' The hangman gulped from the wine cup. 'Dreadful, dire, disgusting! Who could do that to poor Ursula?'

'You knew her well?'

'Father, she was a great wanderer, especially around God's Acre. She loved that place. You know that. She liked nothing more than to walk there and chat to anyone she met, be it in the cemetery or outside. You know she was the widow of a hangman.'

'No!'

'Oh yes, Father. Ursula's husband was chief hangman at Newgate. According to Ursula, he hanged the traitor Mortimer at Tyburn in November 1330. Mortimer was the first man to be executed there. Anyway, we often met.' The hangman stretched across to the tray of sweetmeats, plucked one up, then smiled apologetically through his tears.

'No, no,' Athelstan urged. 'Eat.'

'A gift from Merrylegs,' the hangman retorted. 'Well, really a gift from the parish. I mean, after what happened, what you told us in church . . .' The hangman's voice trailed away.

'Gone now,' Athelstan replied quietly. 'Giles, look at me.'

The hangman lifted his tear-stained face.

'It's finished, it's over. All my beloveds on the parish council will be a little subdued for a while but that will pass. One thing, Giles.' Athelstan himself took a sweetmeat and popped it into his mouth, inviting the hangman to a further helping. 'One thing,' Athelstan repeated. 'Did Prior Sinclair specifically ask to meet Halpen and Mildew?' The hangman shook his head.

'No, that was . . .' He paused and grinned. 'I forget now but someone suggested them.'

'But there must be others like Halpen and Mildew who turned traitor and betrayed the cause.'

'Halpen and Mildew were different. You saw them: they had no care for God or Man. They swilled ale with people who only seven months earlier they'd plotted to betray, to be handed over to torture and a very cruel death.'

'True, true.' Athelstan helped himself to another sweetmeat. For some reason the gesture startled him and he realized he had hardly been aware of picking up the little honeyed cakes and popping them into his mouth. The hangman was no different, nor were other people. Memories crowded in, things Athelstan had seen and heard, but he couldn't reflect, he was tired and distracted.

'Father, we were talking about Ursula.' The hangman dug into his purse. 'Can I pay for a requiem, a stipend?'

'No, no, my friend.' Athelstan stretched across and gripped his visitor's wrist. 'In your next painting. Well, whenever you depict Heaven, place Ursula and her sow there, all golden and glorified.'

'Will there be sows in Heaven?'

'If you want them to be.'

The hangman smiled. 'Strange woman, Father. A great talker. She and I would wander God's Acre. More recently with Paltoc.' He added darkly, 'That man seems to haunt the place. Ursula thought the same. Anyway, Ursula loved nothing better than to sit in the precinct before the church, on that bench close to the steps. She would lean on her stick, now and again poking the sow. Anyway, she would chat to the traders, tinkers, chapmen, pilgrims, and above all the moon people who wander the face of God's earth. You know, Father, all those going in and out of Kent and the ports and harbours along the East Coast. Ursula learned a great deal.'

'What precisely?'

'Ursula informed me that this killer, the Flayer, is not just in London. In fact, he's been at work here and there in different towns and shires. But more than that she couldn't or wouldn't say. I'm not too sure. Ursula could be fey. Recently she started to claim that feathers from an angel's wing were drifting through God's Acre, fragments floating on the breeze. But that was Ursula. Ah well, Father, it's time I was gone.'

Athelstan retired soon after the hangman left and woke just before dawn. As he washed and dressed, the friar felt uneasy. Some sort of disturbance of the humours. He grabbed his staff to steady himself on the ice-covered path, picked up a lantern-horn and left the house. He closed the door behind him and stared around. *'Tenebrae Facta Est* – and darkness fell,' Athelstan whispered. He walked down to the church, climbed the steps to the main door, lifted the lantern and stifled a scream at the abomination fastened by a sharpened pole through what Athelstan realized was a skinned cat. 'Bonaventure! No!' Athelstan groaned, but then closed his eyes in relief at a meow behind him. Athelstan turned and stared down at the great one-eyed tomcat. 'Thank God, thank God.' Athelstan crouched, putting the lanternhorn down. He stroked Bonaventure then got to his feet, struggling to control his stomach. He stepped closer to study the gruesome mess of a fairly young cat, its tail removed and completely skinned. 'You wicked, wicked soul!' Athelstan breathed. 'You perpetrated this abomination to warn me. Will it be Bonaventure next time or indeed some other soul I love?'

'Father.' Athelstan whirled round as Benedicta and Crim emerged out of the darkness. They both glimpsed the grisly corpse and abruptly turned away. Benedicta retching, Crim yelling and shouting. Others alerted by Crim's screams and shouts came hurrying through the faded dawn-light. Athelstan, who had managed to compose himself, gratefully accepted Watkin and Pike's offer to remove the gruesome sight. They would then scrub the door and the steps beneath so that no trace of the abomination remained.

The news of the shocking sacrilege pinned to their church door soon swept the parish. Athelstan refused to become involved in the speculation. He recognized the outrage as a clear warning to himself from the Flayer so he had quiet words with Watkin and Pike about setting a close guard, day and night, over Benedicta. After celebrating his morning Mass, Athelstan withdrew to his own house. To divert himself, he became immersed in a litany of ordinary things. Scrubbing the buttery, tidying the kitchen table before going out to purchase ale, wine, dried meat and fresh bread, honey and butter, from Merrylegs' pastry shop. Late in the afternoon, Paltoc visited him, asking permission to go through certain documents kept in the parish arca, the great chest lodged beneath the sacristy floor.

'I trust you, Paltoc,' Athelstan smiled. 'Though there is nothing of great value there.' Athelstan handed him a key to the corpse door. 'Use that,' he declared, 'but lock yourself in, we do have wanderers who like to take up residence in our church.' Paltoc agreed, thanked him and left. Athelstan then took a square of freshly scrubbed parchment and swiftly wrote the title, 'The Mysteries of Westminster'.

'Item,' Athelstan whispered as he wrote, 'on the Wednesday before the beginning of Advent, the abbey was locked and bolted for the night. Silence and harmony should have reigned. On that particular night, however, chaos broke out. Apparently the anchorite, who resided there, was terrified out of his wits by ghostly phenomena; a scraping sound, as if something was being dragged across the ancient paving stones of the nave. Then the anchorite glimpsed a shadow flitting between the great drum-like pillars. A ghostly shape with cap and cloak who moved to a mysterious tinkling of bells. The anchorite became so terrified he decided to leave his cell and flee the abbey church. He tried the Devil's door, which, according to custom, should have been left on the latch, unbolted and unlocked. However, on that particular evening, it was not. The anchorite, now beside himself with fear, panicked and sounded the tocsin.

'Item. The brothers were roused, a thorough search was made but nothing untoward was discovered, either then or during the subsequent investigation ordered by the abbot. Robert, the sub-sacristan, simply admitted he had made a mistake. He'd forgotten to leave the Devil's door unlocked, and that was that.

'Item. However, that was not the end of the matter. The sacristan's monkey escaped and, more seriously, five murders took place soon afterwards. All perpetrated in a short space of time.

'Item. Were these murders connected to the events of that

Wednesday evening?' Athelstan continued to speak as he wrote using abbreviations only known to himself. 'In my view there must be a connection. Brother Robert was most probably murdered because of that evening. I believe the sub-sacristan saw, heard or suspected something was very wrong and he had to be silenced.

'Item. As for the other victims, monks in Westminster and so-called Guardians of the Stone of Destiny. Why were they murdered? Ruthlessly removed? And the anchorite?' Athelstan sat back in his chair, recalling what he had said to Cranston. 'It is,' he murmured 'all part of some great conspiracy.

'Item. What is Prior Sinclair really involved in? True the Great Revolt was an extraordinary rebellion which provoked great interest across Europe, or so Cranston had informed him, but what was Sinclair truly searching for?'

There was certainly a connection between Sinclair and Paltoc. They could try and disguise it behind that search for the graves of Paltoc's family, nevertheless his suspicions had been aroused. He recalled Prior Sinclair knowing Paltoc's full name, whilst the Blackrobe could distinctly recall not only the names of Paltoc's parents but the dates of their death. 'You are allies!' Athelstan exclaimed. 'Sinclair even offered to help you search God's Acre, but you are not looking for tombs, you are looking for treasure.'

Athelstan, all tiredness forgotten, got up and excitedly paced up and down. He recalled what Thibault had informed Cranston about the treasure looted from the Savoy: a chest which apparently containing the sacred regalia of Scotland. Was Paltoc hunting for that? Was Sinclair involved? Were they both searching for the treasure under the pretext of seeking out a family grave?

Athelstan paused in his pacing and stared down at Bonaventure, who had been watching the little friar intently. Athelstan knelt and stroked one tattered ear. 'Do you know, my dear friend?' Athelstan made himself more comfortable before the hearth. 'Years ago, when I was young and handsome, I studied in Rome. A dear friend of mine had discovered a most exquisitely fashioned floor mosaic, a relic of ancient Rome, more beautiful than anything created in our present age. Anyway.' Athelstan tweaked the cat's ear. 'Many of the small pieces had become loose, mixed together and scattered. We had to put them back together to form the picture. And that's what I am trying to do now. So, my friend, why is *The Bannockburn* moored on Southwark side? I now recall what intrigued me! Did I really see a red-haired labourer working on the paving outside Westminster Abbey on board that great cog?' Athelstan rose to his feet and stared at the crucifix on the wall. 'Now the Blackrobes I cannot question. They'll hide behind their privileges. Paltoc, on the other hand, is a different matter.' Athelstan checked the hour candle in its corner recess. 'Indeed.' Athelstan went and plucked keys from a peg driven into the wall. 'Master Paltoc has been away far too long. Let us see what he is doing.'

Followed by the ever inquisitive Bonaventure, Athelstan, wrapped in his cloak, sandals on his feet, left the house. The light was dying, the day drawing on. Athelstan went round to the Devil's door. He unlocked it and walked in, calling for Paltoc. His voice rang through the dimly lit church, echoing ghostlily back. Athelstan went up into the sacristy. He took a tinder, lit some candles and carried one out, walking back under the rood screen into the nave. 'Master Paltoc,' he shouted, 'Master Paltoc,' but only the echo answered him. Athelstan returned to the sacristy. The arca lay open, its lid thrown back, the occasional scroll or sheet lying next to it. Athelstan swiftly glanced around. 'Nothing,' he murmured. 'Nothing amiss.'

Athelstan left the sacristy now, carrying a candelabra, and walked into the north transept. He reached the chantry chapel of St Erconwald's. The door in the lattice screen was slightly ajar. He pushed this open, went in, and almost stumbled over the body lying on the floor. He crouched down and a dead-eyed Paltoc glared back. The mercenary's face was twisted by the shock of death caused by the barbed crossbow bolt loosed deep into the right side of his chest. Blood had burst out of both the horrid wound as well as through Paltoc's nose and mouth. Athelstan hastily blessed the corpse, whispering a plea for God's absolution for this dead man's soul. He knelt, trying to control his breathing, ears straining for any sound. There was none. Just that ominous silence, as if the world of the spirits was intensely watching that corpse sprawled in its own blood.

The friar moved the candelabra closer to inspect the dead man. He heard a sound and whipped round but it was only Bonaventure, who had come in to stand by the half-open door. Athelstan returned to his scrutiny of the corpse. 'Your knife is still sheathed,' he whispered. 'Your purse,' Athelstan tapped the bulging pouch, 'has not been touched, so the attack was not robbery, it was certainly swift. You were a daggerman, Paltoc, a street fighter, God rest you. Yet on this occasion you never even armed yourself. And why are you lying like this?' Athelstan rose to his feet and stared down. Paltoc lay stretched out, slightly twisted to one side, one arm out as if pointing to the chantry chapel altar covered in its precious cloth.

Athelstan blessed the corpse again then walked around the church. Every door was securely locked. He found the key to the corpse door in Paltoc's wallet and, when Athelstan checked, he also found that door locked and bolted from within. Athelstan walked the full length of the transept, watching the faint mist which had seeped into this ancient church. The friar knew St Erconwald's, every stone, every carving, its different marks and signs. There was no secret entrance. 'Strange,' he mused.

He unlocked the corpse door, drawing back the bolt, and went back into the chantry chapel. 'So.' Athelstan narrowed his eyes as he stared at the candles on their spigot. 'You came here, Paltoc, ostensibly to search amongst the records. But you were wary – of what? Why did you not only lock but bolt yourself in? What were you fearful of? And if so, how was a man of war like you so easily and so quietly slaughtered?' Athelstan then searched the corpse, opening both wallets, but he found nothing except scraps of linen. Athelstan returned to the sacristy. He looked at the disturbed arca and the documents strewn around the floor. 'You were here, weren't you?' the friar whispered. 'And then something disturbed you, but what? How does a daggerman like yourself get killed in a church with every door locked? How did the assassin get in and how did he get out . . .?' Athelstan broke off as the corpse door crashed open followed by Benedicta calling his name. Athelstan hastened to meet her. The widow woman had glimpsed the door to the chantry chapel was open and stood on the threshold, hand to her mouth, as she gazed at Paltoc's corpse. She turned as

Athelstan hurried up. 'God knows what happened here,' he declared. 'Benedicta, what you see is what I saw when I first came in. Yet every door was locked.'

'Could the assassin still be here?'

'No, I have searched.' Athelstan paused as Remart, the relic seller, lumbered through the corpse door, pushing his long rattling barrow. The relic seller had looped a battered wineskin over one of its handles. It looked empty and, by the way Remart was staggering, Athelstan suspected the relic seller had been imbibing generously in the death house. He waited patiently. The relic seller stared at Paltoc's corpse before turning fearfully away, eyes all bleary, face slack, fingers to his mouth like some frightened child. Benedicta went over and stroked Remart's arm. The relic seller muttered something before slumping down at the base of a pillar. 'Leave him for a while,' Athelstan murmured. 'Benedicta, fetch the funeral barrow, we must move poor Paltoc to the death house.'

'Shall I send for help?'

'No, no, Benedicta, that would take time and only spread confusion. Let us deal with it ourselves.' Athelstan hastily blessed the corpse and then, helped by Benedicta, loaded Paltoc's mortal remains into the funeral barrow. Remart continued moaning as he sat propped up against the pillar. A short while later, after asking Benedicta to arrange the corpse in the mortuary, Athelstan returned to the church to find Remart fast asleep, snoring his head off. Athelstan shook him awake and helped him stand. He took him outside and gently pushed the relic seller in the direction of the old death house. 'Go home, my friend, sleep the sleep of the just.' Athelstan returned to the church and wheeled out Remart's barrow. 'You'll wake up and come looking for this soon enough,' Athelstan whispered, setting it down. 'God have mercy on you.'

The friar stood for a while, staring up at the sky, wondering why the stars seemed so distant on a night like this. He remembered the books he had studied at Blackfriars. Search as he could, he never truly discovered a satisfying explanation of why on one night stars would seem so distant and on others hang so very low. The cold breeze startled him from his star-gazing. He went back into the church, lifted the lanternhorn and, as he did so, glimpsed one of the hangman's miniature paintings. The lantern light brought it to life. The picture was a satire on court life, where the nobles were depicted as beasts clothed in fine raiment. One figure in particular caught his attention, and he smiled as he recalled Barak's corpse, as well as what he'd seen in different fairs and mummers shows. The monkey the hangman had painted was clothed in coat and cap with bells around his wrists and ankles. Athelstan stood for a while then started as Bonaventure slipped through the door and padded softly towards him. Athelstan raised the lantern and watched the cat's shadow, greatly enhanced, dance against the wall. The friar stood transfixed. He moved the pool of lantern light closer. Bonaventure thought this was a game and darted backwards and forwards. 'I wonder,' Athelstan murmured, 'I truly do.' He went out on to the path, picked up some pebbles and returned, watching Bonaventure. The cat, now bored, sloped off into the darkness on his silent hunt for vermin. Athelstan waited for him to go then, lifting the lanternhorn, threw the pebbles hard across the transept to bounce against the wall. Bonaventure immediately returned, swift and sure, twisting and turning as he tried to search out the cause of the disturbance. Athelstan threw more pebbles and watched Bonaventure's elongated shadow dart and dance against the flickering, shifting light.

'And so it is, God be thanked,' Athelstan prayed, 'and so it was. Thank you, Bonaventure, for making me a wiser fool.'

After finishing his Mass early next morning, Athelstan studiously ignored his parishioners who had flocked into church all agog with the news about Paltoc's murder. Instead of meeting Watkin and the council, the friar returned to his house, locked himself in, broke his fast and began his studies. He followed the same method he had when analysing the deaths of Halpen and Mildew at The Piebald. He took a square of parchment and drew a crude map of his church, marking all the entrances. 'Now,' Athelstan murmured to himself, 'all the entrances were locked from within. Paltoc must have made sure of that, so how was he murdered and why?' He returned to the church and went through the corpse door, which he kept opened as he studied its ancient woodwork and the ground around it. Going down on his hands and knees, as if creeping to the cross, Athelstan slowly crawled, searching for any bloodstains, on the paving stones, or the wood of the door. He could detect none. Shaking his head in disbelief, Athelstan got to his feet and returned to his house. Benedicta arrived, carrying a coffer or chest containing what she called 'poor Ursula's earthly possessions'. Athelstan studied the coffer closely, wiping away the dust. 'Look, Benedicta,' he declared, 'this coffer is of the finest wood. I am sure it is walnut, a treasure in itself, fashioned by a master craftsman then polished by his apprentices. In its time it must have looked magnificent. And study these!' Athelstan tapped the clasps and locks along the rim. 'Again the work of a guildsman, a true expert, a master locksmith. Somebody broke these, shattered them so as to force open the coffer. I do wonder how Ursula came to own something like this.' Moving the chest into the centre of the table, Athelstan peered along the side where the finely carved medallions had been roughly gouged out, destroying the insignia displayed there. He opened the coffer and glimpsed a piece of cloth piled up to cover whatever lay beneath.

'Father, that's all I could find.'

'And no one went there?' Athelstan asked, returning to his chair.

'Oh no, Father, once the news about Ursula's murder was known, the parish council set up a strict guard over the place.

'Good, good,' Athelstan replied absentmindedly, and returned to his studies.

Benedicta could see the friar was totally distracted, so she prepared a platter of bread and meat in the buttery, patted the friar gently on the head and left. Athelstan became more and more immersed in his studies, staring down at his drawing. He became cramped so he rose, stretched and walked across to where he had placed the battered coffer close to the stairs leading to the bedloft. He opened the lid, removed the cloth and stared down at the contents; small, white objects. Athelstan's stomach lurched. He picked one of these up and carefully unwrapped the thick white linen covering. He put down the scrap of linen, staring at it as he leaned against the bedloft ladder. Athelstan closed his eyes as he imagined what could be the truth. He thought of Paltoc opening the corpse door to greet his killer.

Athelstan was certain that the Flayer had murdered the mercenary. Paltoc must have been seen as an upstart, a challenge, a taunt, an insult which had to be met and countered. Curbing his excitement, Athelstan grabbed his cloak, swung it around him and hurried down to the church. He now recognized what had baffled him. Athelstan unlocked the corpse door, went in, closed it behind him and leaned against it. 'You opened this door,' he whispered, 'you were distracted. You may have had your suspicions but that's the mistake you made. You didn't check before you opened this.' Athelstan turned, pulled back the corpse door then slammed it shut. 'You were wounded here,' Athelstan murmured. 'You staggered away. You went to the chantry chapel where you collapsed but, in your dying moments, you point to the altar. What is there? A cross, the ciborium containing the sacred hosts and St Erconwald's reliquary. Oh yes!' Athelstan curbed his surge of excitement. 'You must have bled, you must have done, yet I can find little trace if any of your blood.' Athelstan stared up at the painted glass window celebrating scenes from the life of St Erconwald. 'Lord of light help me,' he whispered. 'I need to trap this fiend and send his soul to hell.'

Athelstan continued to sit in the chapel as his mind turned and twisted. He stared down at the spot where Paltoc's corpse had sprawled. Benedicta had worked wonders in removing the stains left by the murder. 'And there's other types of stains,' Athelstan declared, 'more difficult to remove but, if it's to be done it's best done quickly.' Athelstan continued to sit and plot. He could not directly confront the Flayer. No, Athelstan reasoned, like the killer at Westminster, the Flayer had to be teased out, enticed into an ambush. Athelstan plotted. The trap would be simple, preparing the lure was the most difficult task, but he would try then to see what happened. Athelstan left the church and, despite the cold darkness, he walked across God's Acre. He reached the old death house and paused, his sandalled feet causing a noisy crackling. Athelstan stared down. Remart had strewn the ground with a host of dried twigs and small branches. Athelstan glanced at the light peeping through the shuttered window and walked slowly towards the door, which opened and Remart, wrapped in a cloak, slouched out.

'Your path of bracken,' Athelstan declared. 'It creates a great deal of noise.'

'Aye, Father, it alerts me to visitors and provides good protection against the mud. Are you well, Father?'

'Very much so, thank God. I am looking forward to tomorrow. I intend to return to my indictment against that great fool and stupid sinner, the Flayer.'

'How is that, Father?'

'Oh, Sir John believes it will be easy to trap that hell-born creature. I have been sitting in the church reflecting on how I can help Sir John trap that fool and I'll continue my studies throughout the evening. Anyway, I assure you, Remart, God's Acre is desolate and empty, except for Watkin. He's emptying the cesspits and jakes pots.' Athelstan raised his hand in blessing and passed on. He did not immediately return to the priest's house but hurried to The Piebald, where he had urgent words with Watkin and Pike about what he needed. Both of them were surprised but agreed, Crim being immediately despatched with an urgent message for Sir John. Once he was satisfied with his arrangements, Athelstan made his way back to the priest house where he finished his preparations and waited. He smiled thinly at the expected knock at the door. He shouted at his visitor to come in, then turned to greet Remart, who slipped through the door like the snake he was. Athelstan studied him from head to toe. This was a different Remart. The relic seller was no longer slack-faced or wet-eyed: the hunched shoulders had disappeared, the nervous mannerisms had changed. He was not drunk or dim-witted. The relic seller looked what he was, a hard-eyed, cunning killer who clutched the arbalest he carried like a man highly skilled in its use. Remart kicked the door shut and lifted the crossbow, the jagged barb only inches from Athelstan's face.

'Good evening, Father, Brother, or whatever else I am supposed to call you.'

'Good evening, Remart. I have been expecting you.'

'Really, priest?'

'Oh yes, have you decided to leave, Remart?'

Athelstan pointed at the arbalest. 'You sent me a warning through that poor cat you nailed to the church door. I suspect

you would have loved to have snared Bonaventure, but even he
is too cunning for you.'

'Shut up, priest.'

'I think I'll sit down.' Athelstan, steeling himself, returned
to sit at the table, pushing away the heap of clothes placed there
and pulling the tankard of fiery hot mulled wine closer to him.
'Remart, tell me your real name, or the one that you took for
yourself, Pudlicott! Yes, your mother or the woman who raised
you was Adele Pudlicott, who created such tumult in the parish
some years ago during the Great Pestilence. Well, well.'
Athelstan joined his hands together as if in prayer. 'Remart,
you certainly are a cunning man. Much more so than Sir John
and I ever imagined.'

'Good, good,' Remart purred. Still holding the arbalest, the
relic seller made himself comfortable in Athelstan's chancery
chair. He smiled as if he and the friar were old friends, only to
rise and hurriedly lock and bolt the door. He retook his seat,
still beaming, and Athelstan realized his adversary was not just
a killer to the very marrow but a consummate mummer. Remart
could, in the blink of an eye, change his mood and appearance.
No longer the shabby beggar, the travelling tinker with his
tawdry items, but a man of deep menace, highly dangerous in
his madness and cunning. Remart's face seemed longer, harder,
like that of many a veteran Athelstan had met. Even the relic
seller's speech had changed, betraying a northern burr Athelstan
hadn't noticed before. The friar sat quietly watching. Remart's
deep weakness would be his arrogance, a devilish belief that
he was superior to all and sundry, especially Athelstan. The
friar was determined to exploit this. He knew from experience
that Remart would not only love to boast but fence words with
his opponent.

'You killed Ursula, you murdered her! You abused her
corpse!'

'Of course.' Remart wagged a finger reprovingly. 'The cowl
doesn't make the monk. Ursula was a cunning old bitch; she
noticed things, you know.'

'What things?'

'Oh, I brought back skins – well, you know that. They would

corrupt. Some of the fragments, little white wisps, would be blown across the cemetery. I mean, it couldn't be helped. Anyway, that silly old bitch thought they were fragments from the wings of an angel. Well at first she did.' Remart shook his head. 'I do wonder if she changed her mind, she was certainly dangerous. You see the old troll loved to wander the cemetery watching this, watching that. She was too nosey, too inquisitive for her own good.'

'And you kept your parcels, relics of your murders, of your killings,' Athelstan hastily corrected himself, 'in the death house, yes? That's why you had the approach strewn with bracken so you'd be warned of any visitor.'

'Yes, yes, that's what I did. Something I learned when I served in the royal array in Normandy. We used to do the same outside our bothies and tents.'

'So you have been a soldier?' Athelstan stared in genuine surprise at Remart. Then, 'Of course,' Athelstan murmured. 'Les Écorcheurs.' He continued. 'The Flayers, English mercenaries. The dregs of humanity, pardoned, armed and sent to France to fight for the old King. I heard stories about how they flayed their victims.'

'All true, Friar. Did you know that Paltoc served in the same for a while?'

'A prime reason for killing him.'

'Yes, yes, one amongst many. There were times I did wonder if he recognized me or he might do so. I was furious when that fat bastard Cranston, that moving mountain of flesh, which I would love to skin, hired Paltoc to hunt me.' Remart wiped the spit frothing from between his lips. 'Of course, that wasn't the truth, was it? Paltoc wasn't really hunting me, nor was he searching for any family grave. No, no, I was there when the Savoy was burnt. Fascinating how the fire and heat make the human skin buckle, bubble and peel.' Remart smacked his lips, as if savouring a tasty meal. 'Yes, yes, I believe Paltoc was looking for a treasure chest, which, I suspect, he spirited away from the smoking ruins of the Savoy and brought here. He chose his family burial plot as a memorable place to hide his ill-gotten gains. But, as he soon discovered, it is so easy to forget where something is buried, especially when that godforsaken cemetery was occupied by hordes of rebels during the great revolt. Anyway . . .' Remart placed the arbalest on the table. 'Not such a good idea, Paltoc roaming the cemetery like an unquiet ghost. He became curious about the slivers of skin blown by the breeze to be caught tangled in the brambles and gorse.' Remart shook his head like a magister in the schools dealing with a recalcitrant scholar. 'Oh yes, Paltoc was becoming dangerous, even more so when he began to gossip with Ursula.'

'About what?'

'Oh, how the Flayer, as I am well known, lurked in Southwark. Then of course Ursula found the burial pit of my dear mother Adele, a place where I performed the sacrifice.'

'You are Adele Pudlicott's son?'

'Yes, priest, I like to call myself that, Richard Pudlicott's grandson.'

'And how did you get to know all this?'

Remart's face abruptly fell slack, then it sharpened; the killer glanced slyly at Athelstan and pulled the arbalest a little bit closer.

'Tell me.' Athelstan's voice took on a pleading tone. He just hoped he could exploit the killer's great weakness, his desire to talk, to lecture, to boast.

'Adele told me all about Richard Puddlicot's execution. How his corpse was peeled on the scaffold and the skin nailed to a door in Westminster Abbey. How it was allowed to hang there until it rotted. Anyway, the Great Plague came. Adele was a corpse-dresser. She collected cadavers and sewed them in their shrouds. She seemed fascinated by the dead. Then she would have nightmares about her father and she'd have terrible thoughts. Here, here.' Remart tapped the side of his head. He then paused, muttering under his breath. 'Terrible times, priest! Terrible times! No one could help, especially people like you. We lived with the dead, corpses stacked high. Anyway, Adele started to peel this cadaver, that cadaver. She just loved human skin, called it her silk. As she skinned, so she would perform a dance, sinuously, calling herself Salome. I would watch her. Adele prepared the corpses in the same cellar I met that silly bitch Ursula. She was so knowing.'

'What do you mean?'

'It's just. It's just,' Remart repeated himself, 'that the past releases humours here in my head. They are like devils, priest, demons, constantly chattering to me. Anyway, I know what happened to Adele. She was seized, taken in the dead of night: judged, found guilty and buried alive beneath that yew tree.'

'How do you know all this?'

'I was there, priest, though I hid my past from Ursula. Nevertheless, she was quicker than I thought. Sooner or later she might begin to wonder about me, the hapless relic seller trying to trick people with the corpse of a mummified monkey.'

'And, of course,' Athelstan replied, 'you encouraged her to inform me about Adele Puddlicot, or at least some of the story, otherwise I would have become suspicious if you hadn't.'

'Oh yes, priest. I tried to keep everything hidden but, on reflection, I can see that I made mistakes so I had to act. Paltoc was supposed to hunt me down and I learnt about your sermon.' Remart's voice turned ugly. 'There were other things. The wisps of skin blown around the cemetery. The linen I used to wrap my relics in. I overlooked such issues. Suspicions might be raised so I reached the conclusion that it was time to go. Wouldn't you agree?'

Athelstan nodded. Even as he heard a sound from outside, the clink of metal, he tried to distract Remart from hearing this by coughing noisily.

'True, true,' Athelstan declared, clearing his throat. 'You certainly made a mistake with that linen you wrapped your pathetic relics in, as well as the skin of your victims. Paltoc himself made the very shrewd observation, which I did not reflect on until too late, that not many people carry such linen around with them. But you did.'

'How do you know that?'

'Remember the hideous gift you sent Sir John at The Lamb of God in Cheapside? I suspect you did that immediately after you'd slaughtered and skinned your wretched victim. So you must have had the linen with you.'

Remart just grinned, though Athelstan glimpsed the anger in his opponent's eyes. Soon, Athelstan quietly reasoned, he must bring these matters to a close.

'You had marked Paltoc down for death, hadn't you?'

Remart just grinned wolfishly.

'You did, didn't you?' Athelstan repeated.

'He brought it on himself,' Remart protested. 'He kept wandering God's Acre, talking to Ursula. He was a most vexatious man.' Remart laughed abruptly. 'I mean, he was always here, constantly watching me. In the end, Ursula had to go and so did Paltoc.'

'And how did you do it?'

'Oh, Ursula was very easy. I asked her to help me with something I discovered in that cellar. The stupid bitch believed me. I delivered a good clean blow to the back of her head. Of course her sow, as stupid and as fat as its mistress, immediately began squealing. I took care of that with one swift slash of my knife.'

Athelstan fought to hide his revulsion at the cruel callousness of this hardened killer. 'And Paltoc?' Athelstan murmured. 'So clever, so subtle?'

'Don't indulge in false flattery,' Remart retorted. 'I admit I made a mistake, Paltoc closing that door in my face. I will be honest, that's the reason I'm here. Well, one reason amongst many.'

'And the others?'

'Well, for a start your attack on me and those of Fat Jack . . .'

'You mean . . .' Athelstan decided to gamble. 'You mean . . .' he repeated softly, then his voice rose to a shout. 'You mean no less a person than Sir John Cranston, Lord High . . .' Athelstan wasn't allowed to finish speaking. The door rattled, cracked and creaked under the hammer blows from outside. Remart, startled, lifted the arbalest, but Athelstan flung the tankard of hot posset, scalding the relic seller's face. Remart screamed. Athelstan jumped up, knocking the arbalest away. He then punched his enemy's face, shouting with joy as he felt the man's nose crumble under his hard, muscular fist. Again he struck. Remart, his face drenched in fast-flowing blood, lurched to his feet even as the lock snapped. The door was flung open and Cranston charged into the chamber, smashing into Remart, pinning the assassin between himself and the table. Pike and Watkin followed, all agog at what was happening. At first there

was confusion but eventually Remart was held and bound
securely. No one did anything to wipe the blood which dried
like a mask over his face. Athelstan made the prisoner sit on a
stool whilst he pulled his great chancery chair closer, with
Cranston standing behind him and Watkin and Pike guarding
the door.

'So, Sir John,' Athelstan declared. 'Here we have a prisoner
who has confessed to his hideous crimes as well as one cleverly
caught by me.' Athelstan smiled coldly at the fury blazing in
Remart's eyes. 'Oh yes.' Athelstan let his voice drop to a whisper.
'Like all your kind, Remart, you are arrogant and overweening.
You,' he pointed at the prisoner, 'stalked your last victim Paltoc,
the mercenary, the graveyard wanderer, the hunter allegedly
searching to trap the Flayer. In truth, however, Paltoc's real
business was to find buried treasure, which I am sure you would
also covet and hope to find. You were prepared to wait. I gave
you the old death house to live in. I am sure that once Paltoc
was removed and all the hubbub had died down, you would
conduct your own hunt. However, that was for the future. In
the meantime, you watched Paltoc closely and, on that lonely,
misty afternoon, you followed him. He entered our church. You
watched and waited, armed with your arbalest. You approached
the corpse door and knocked. Knock, knock again. Paltoc,
distracted by his search, would answer it. Perhaps he asked who
it was, perhaps he did not? What I do know is that he opened
that door and you loosed the bolt, striking him here.' Athelstan
patted himself high in the left breast. 'A mortal wound.'
Athelstan paused for effect. 'What happened next was sheer
chance or perhaps the will of God.' Again Athelstan struck the
left side of his chest. 'As I said, the barb struck here. Now Sir
John – and indeed any veteran – would testify that a man, even
one struck with a mortal wound can, for a short while, act as
if nothing had happened.'

'Very true,' Cranston murmured, mystified by the proceedings
in this most singular of parishes.

'I have,' the coroner added, 'seen men fight for a while even
if they have lost a hand, or even an arm.'

'Quite so, Sir John, and remember Paltoc was a veteran, a
mercenary, a true daggerman.'

'A fool,' Remart spat back. 'As you all are.'

'Not so foolish,' Athelstan retorted. 'You are our prisoner. But to return to my indictment. You loosed the killing bolt but Paltoc instantly pushed the door shut. He locked and bolted it. A matter of a few heartbeats. He is wounded, mortally so. He staggers into the chantry chapel and collapses. Even in death he continues his struggle. I found Paltoc, his body strangely twisted, arm out, finger pointing towards the altar. At first I thought he might have been praying to the cross or the pyx. One last desperate plea before death. In truth, Paltoc was pointing at our reliquary, the most accurate allusion he could make to you; his last desperate attempt to name his assassin before the darkness descended.'

Athelstan blessed Watkin and Pike, standing on guard, silent and still as statues. 'God bless you, Watkin.' Athelstan turned back to Remart. 'Fancy that, eh sir?' He mocked. 'Being trapped by a dung collector. And so you were. You were elated after killing Paltoc, as well as being provided with a means of deepening the mystery. Paltoc had sealed that door, locking himself in. So how could his murder be explained? How could someone enter a locked church, carry out such a dreadful deed, and then leave that church still locked against any intruder? And again, no one would even think of you, Remart, the beggarly relic seller, all stooped and twisted, shambling and shuffling across God's Acre. However, God be thanked, you made the most dreadful mistake, didn't you?' Athelstan leaned over and pushed his face closer. 'Are you listening?' he taunted. 'You made the most dreadful mistake, didn't you?' Athelstan, to provoke the prisoner further, wagged a finger in front of his face. Remart coughed, cleared his throat, then lunged forward on the stool and spat a mouthful of sputum at the friar. The spit narrowly missed. Athelstan drew back and the relic seller screamed as Cranston pressed forward and twisted Remart's battered, bloody nose. The friar waited until Remart's sobs faded away.

'You wanted to deepen the mystery as well as remove any evidence about what actually happened. You see, when you loosed your bolt and Paltoc lunged forward, his blood spurted out, and it must have done, to stain both door and floor. Of course, it is very dark in that transept and the corpse door is only one possible entrance amongst quite a number. You had to be careful, cunningly so. You determined to remove anything which could indicate how Paltoc's murder occurred. Now remember, Remart, after I discovered Paltoc's corpse and was viewing it with Benedicta, you pushed your barrow into the church and waited for us to leave with the corpse. You acted the drunk, a man deep in his cups, ale-sodden and bleary, but that was all pretence. Once Benedicta and I had left, you locked the door behind us. You then took some of the linen out of your barrow and used that as a cloth to remove any blood streaks or spots. If anyone had come and wondered what was happening in the church, you'd reply you were frightened and locked the church to protect yourself.' Athelstan paused as Remart moaned, rocking backwards and forwards on the stool. 'Once you had finished removing as many bloodstains as you could find, you put the linen cloth into your barrow and left; by removing all bloodstains, you'd deepened the mystery. You wanted to hide the very obvious fact that Paltoc had been killed at the door, how he had closed it and staggered back to the chantry chapel. I strongly suspected you would do this, your last fatal mistake. You were determined not to keep a blood-stained linen in your barrow. You decided to get rid of it down one of the jakes holes or cesspits around the church; in particular, one close to the corpse door, which is used by parishioners if they are taken by a sudden urge during a ceremony. I asked Watkin to clean that jakes hole and, more importantly, I also informed you of what I intended. You quickly realized what might happen if Watkin drew out that blood-soaked piece of linen. Blood is very distinctive, it catches the eye even under a smear of dirt.'

'Anyone,' Remart snarled, 'anyone could have thrown a piece of bloodstained linen into that jakes pot.'

'Ah, so it was the jakes pot. How did you know?'

Remart just glared back.

'It was at the top,' Watkin declared. 'And freshly done, so who else could it be? The church and God's Acre were deserted except for you, Father and Paltoc.'

Athelstan crossed himself. 'God rest him,' he declared. 'But I am sure Paltoc was becoming suspicious. Like Ursula he must have seen those strange white wisps, in truth fragments of human skin blown across God's Acre. At my insistence, he buried some human skin in its linen parcel. He'd seen the same fabric around the pathetic relics you gave to poor Ursula. You took care of Paltoc but then there was me. Once I mentioned to you what Watkin would be doing in God's Acre, you decided to act. Time to punish me and Sir John for daring to hunt you, to condemn you and to interfere in your hateful practices. Remart, you will certainly hang, and for what you did to poor Ursula, I shall watch you die slowly!'

'I know things,' the relic seller blurted out. 'I've seen things.'

'Oh, for heaven's sake,' Athelstan snapped. 'Be silent, there is nothing further you can say.'

'You'll be lodged in Newgate,' Cranston declared. 'Now let us search your house. Watkin, Pike, Tower archers will arrive within the hour. Until they do, guard this wretch. Strike and strike hard if he even tries to move to the left or the right.' Cranston and Athelstan left the priest's house, tramping through the cold dark of that bitter winter afternoon. The cemetery looked especially bleak, made even more so by what had happened that afternoon.

'The child is certainly the father of the man,' Athelstan murmured. 'I suspect that as a boy, Remart had to witness Adele peeling corpses. Early in his life he must have tried to fight such demons. For a short while he joined the Dominican order, but of course, our black and white robes do not take away sin, they only hide it more cleverly. Ah, here we are.' They stopped outside the old death house. 'As I said,' Athelstan continued, 'Adele would make Remart watch. She would sing and dance. He became tortured and twisted inside. Spiritually he would not survive such an ordeal, not then, not now. A seed was sown, and when Remart reached manhood, the harvest came to a full and bloody fruit.' Athelstan tapped the bracken with the toe of his sandal. 'This was laid so Remart could hear anyone who approached the door.'

'Which I will do now,' Cranston declared. He then strode forward and gave the door such a powerful kick it flung back with a crash. Athelstan following Cranston in. A lantern still glowed. The air smelt fragrant.

The friar stared around. 'Everything,' he explained, 'so neat, so tidy, more like a lady's chamber than the hovel of a relic seller.'

'Or a killer.'

'Yes, but just look, Sir John, turkey carpets and the bed with its flower-festooned coverlet. So many cushions, so many bolsters,' Athelstan added. He walked over and climbed up to the bedloft. He reached the top and stared down at the coverlet, the pillow, and he repressed a shiver. Sometimes in his ministry Athelstan came across pure evil, so deep, so malignant, it assumed a form and exuded itself like water being wrung from a filthy cloth. This was such an occasion. The walls could be freshly lime-washed, the floor well swept, the hearth cleared, the air all fragrant, but there was something else here. A real malevolence hovered, brooding over what to do next. Athelstan touched a bolster and squeezed.

'Brother?' Athelstan looked over his shoulder. Cranston had opened a battered coffer. He was sifting through scraps of parchment. He was clutching another piece, scrutinising it carefully in the poor light.

'What is it, Sir John?'

'Nothing much, just a collection of dates, recent ones. There's the day and the month, most of them in the last week or so. Beside each date there are the initials, P and S.'

'Paltoc and Sinclair,' Athelstan replied. 'I am certain Remart kept both individuals under careful scrutiny. Sir John, please open these.' Athelstan threw down a cushion, followed by the bolster and the quilted coverlet. 'Use your dagger, Sir John. Slash them open.'

Cranston drew his dagger and ripped the bolster. Athelstan came down the ladder and stared in horror at the flimsy pieces of human skin scattered all about. 'God have mercy,' Athelstan whispered. 'He murdered his victims, flayed their corpses, took the skins and brought them here. I suggest he cured them to make them last longer, but eventually they would dry out and crack. Little wonder fragments and wisps floated across God's Acre.'

Cranston continued, cutting and ripping until Athelstan asked him to stop. 'Every cushion, every bolster,' Athelstan exclaimed.

'They are all stuffed with human skin. Remart sat on these and leaned his head against them. This was his life, revelling in the same macabre practices his mother followed during his childhood.' Athelstan paused as he heard the bracken outside crackle and snap. Watkin and Pike appeared in the doorway to announce the Tower archers had arrived and were now guarding the prisoner.

'Good, good. Now look Watkin and Pike.' Athelstan dug into his purse and handed each a penny. 'Search this place. If you find anything of value, have Benedicta take it to my house. Promise?' Both solemnly nodded. 'I need to see everything.'

'And for the rest, Father?'

'Oh yes, once you have done that, collect the kindling from outside. Heap it around here, drench it in oil, then set fire to it. You are to burn this house to the ground.'

'Brother Athelstan!' Cranston exclaimed.

'Father.' Watkin demanded. 'Is that necessary?'

'Yes, it certainly is.' Athelstan stared around and shivered. 'This is a truly evil place; I want it razed to the ground. Another house can be built but this and all it contains must be destroyed. Watkin, Pike I don't want one stone left upon another. Level it! Now, Sir John . . .' Athelstan paused as Benedicta appeared. He murmured a prayer of thanks, took her aside with Cranston and told her what had happened. He politely stilled her questions and wouldn't satisfy her curiosity. Instead he insisted that if he was missing for a short while, to take good care of the parish and see especially to the total destruction of the old death house. He smiled at her spate of questions, then pressed a finger against her lips. He said he could say no more, adding that he needed to have the most urgent words with Sir John about what was planned for the morrow . . .

PART SIX

'Let us drag him from the water.'

Early the next morning, before he left, Athelstan strove to curb his excitement as well as his deepening apprehension about what might happen. He had given Cranston his final instructions the night before and the coroner had solemnly assured him that he had acted on the friar's earlier request, going into secret council with the lords of the Guildhall. Cranston had desperately tried to make Athelstan swear that he would not endanger himself but the friar had been obdurate. 'Sir John, my friend, as I have told you, I truly think this is the only way I can trap, confront, gain a confession and provide justice and judgement. You must accept my word on that.'

Cranston reluctantly agreed. They'd exchanged the kiss of peace and the coroner left Athelstan to his preparations for the morrow. Athelstan slept well, despite the excitement of the day, which continued long after dark with the old death house being turned into a raging inferno, the flames only dying shortly before Athelstan left his house to celebrate the dawn Mass. Once finished, Athelstan had a further meeting with Benedicta, asking her to keep a careful eye on the parish and ensure the church was kept safe. Once again the widow woman tried to question Athelstan, but he merely kissed his fingertips and pressed them gently against her lovely lips. 'Pray for me,' he murmured, 'and all will be well.' Satisfied that he'd done all that he could, Athelstan, wrapped in his cloak, hurried through the cold murky dawn light, down to the quayside where Moleskin had his barge prepared for a choppy passage across the Thames to King's Steps. Once he reached the abbey, Athelstan had to wait in the visitors' vestibule until he was met by Prior Norbert, who was accompanied by Sylvester and Sinclair. The Blackrobes were friendly enough but questioned Athelstan closely on the request the Lord High Coroner had passed on to their abbot, demanding that Athelstan be given any and all documents describing the Stone of Destiny. Athelstan cleverly fenced back. He pointed to the hour candle, murmured that time was passing and the matter was urgent.

Prior Norbert grudgingly led him up to a specially prepared carrel in the scriptorium furnished with chair, lanterns and candelabra. A sheaf of documents had already been prepared. Athelstan thanked the prior and, without further ado, settled down to his studies. The number of manuscripts he had been given was fairly slight, extracts of chronicles and annals which mentioned the Stone of Destiny. Athelstan, although left to his own devices, was very wary. He knew he was being watched and again prayed that the path he was following would lead to a true and just conclusion. Nevertheless, Athelstan realized he was fully committed. He swiftly read the extracts as if deeply interested, but concentrated on the different physical descriptions of the stone. One in particular was most specific in its analysis. Athelstan repeatedly read this, committing it to memory. By the time the noonday angelus sounded, the bells booming across the abbey, Athelstan declared he was finished in the scriptorium but he urgently needed to speak to Prior Norbert and the others. The Blackrobes arrived and became all flustered at the friar's request, whilst his two companions Sylvester and Sinclair stood hard-faced, lips compressed as they shook their heads. 'We cannot,' Prior Norbert stuttered, 'we cannot remove the stone from beneath the coronation chair.'

'Brothers, brothers,' Athelstan sat down wearily 'If I have to, I will summon Sir John Cranston. The Lord High Coroner will arrive here very angry but armed with licences and letters signed by the King himself. I cannot see what is wrong with my request. I need to examine that precious stone – nothing less, nothing more.'

'Why?' Sacristan Sylvester demanded.

'If I find out, then I will tell you.'

'You talk in riddles, Brother Athelstan.'

'Ah yes, but I am still searching for the truth. Now, is it yes or no?'

The Blackrobes reluctantly agreed. They left the scriptorium.

Athelstan tried to act calm and composed even though he was distracted by the surge of events. The trap was about to close. It might prove highly dangerous to him yet '*alea iacta*; the die was thrown.' Athelstan and the three Blackrobes hurried down the hollow stone passageways, their sandalled feet echoing loudly to mingle with the other noises of the abbey: catches of plainchant, the closing of doors, the clatter from kitchens, butteries and refectories.

As usual the air was perfumed with the scent of incense, candle smoke and cooking odours. Other Blackrobes slipped by them, moving shadows in the dappled light pouring through the windows. They entered the great abbey church, bitterly cold despite the rows of braziers cracking merrily, the heated coals glowing a fiery red. They reached the sanctuary. Athelstan waited until the three Blackrobes had moved the great throne-like chair so the stone could be slid on to a cushion the sacristan fetched from his stores. At Athelstan's request he also brought two lighted lanterns and placed these either side of the stone. Satisfied, Athelstan knelt down and examined the rectangle of reddish sandstone most carefully. He noted the different symbols, cuts and marks. He betrayed no emotion but finished his scrutiny and got to his feet, brushing his hands on his robe. 'Brothers,' he declared. 'Many thanks, but now I must return to my parish.' Sinclair's reply was almost word for word what Athelstan had imagined it would be.

'Brother,' Sinclair urged, 'come with us. I also need to visit your parishioners again.' Prior Sinclair picked up Athelstan's chancery satchel.

'Be our guest,' he declared. 'We have a barge waiting at King's Steps.' They left the abbey and hurried down to the quayside. Athelstan remained impassive. Again, it was what he'd expected. The waiting barge was manned by Scotsmen, crew members from *The Bannockburn*. Norbert, who had accompanied them down, lifted his hand in farewell and the barge cast off. Athelstan, seated between Sinclair and Sylvester in the canopied stern, recited a line from the psalms. Prior Sinclair swiftly murmured a prayer for safe passage then leaned closer, touching Athelstan on the knee. 'My good friar, before we return to St Erconwald's, you must be our guest on board *The*

Bannockburn. Your previous visit was too short. I understand you were deeply impressed by the cog.'

The friar smiled his thanks and nodded in agreement. The trap was opening. They disembarked at St Mary Overy's quayside before walking over to the heavily guarded gangplank leading up onto *The Bannockburn.* Athelstan followed the Blackrobes up on to the deck, now moving quite sharply up and down on the strengthening tide. They were met by the master, Nicholas Gromond, who seemed dressed ready to depart, wrapped in his war cloak and issuing orders to a very busy crew. Athelstan stared round, watching the sailors scamper and slide across the slippery, water-soaked deck. A few of the crew were already grouped around the main mast, helping two of the ship's boys clamber up to where the great sail was reefed. Athelstan heard the snap and crack of canvas and rope as sails were loosened. He listened carefully to the shouted orders and Athelstan deduced that *The Bannockburn* would soon slip its moorings and allow the current to push it forward.

Now daylight was here, the sails would be fully loosened so the ship could take full advantage of the winds. The crew also realized that once they reached the estuary, they would have little time for anything except to man the sails and make sure the ship kept on course. Consequently, they would feast and dine before they reached the open sea. Charcoal fires in moveable stoves and ovens now flamed merrily beneath pots and platters laden with strips of meat, whilst the cooks were slicing vegetables and herbs using overturned barrels as tables. The air was thick with drifting odours, pitch, tar, cordage, salt and brine, as well as the flavour of roasting meat which could not quite mask the filthy odours from the bilges beneath. Athelstan stared around. He knew enough about shipping to realize *The Bannockburn* was ready for sea and he would not be disembarking.

He glanced over the side and glimpsed the Fisher of Men's massive funeral barge go swiftly by, its oars rising and falling in unison. Athelstan lifted a hand in salute at the tall hooded figure high on the stern, but the Fisher of Men did not respond. Gromond broke the uneasy silence of his visitors by inviting

Athelstan, Sinclair and Sylvester into his cabin, no more than a very large cupboard wedged beneath the stern, and furnished with a narrow cotbed, chests and small barrels positioned around a low-legged table. Goblets of mulled wine and platters of hot, fresh fish stew were served. Athelstan, committing himself quietly to God's mercy, ate and drank as he listened to the desultory conversation. He felt a surge of tiredness and glanced at Sinclair, who gazed sad-eyed back. Athelstan's eyes grew heavy. He leaned back against the bulwark and drifted into a deep, drugged sleep . . .

Prior Norbert crossed himself, as he always did whenever he entered the Tower. As soon as he disembarked from the royal barge, which had brought him from Westminster, Norbert became nervous. He went through under the Lion Gate, guarded by household knights and squires garbed in their half-armour. Above these, along the parapet walk, stood Cheshire archers, the most skilled of master bowmen. Inside the fortress, more soldiers patrolled the narrow lanes and thoroughfares which wound up and around the different towers. The late afternoon was cold, a river mist was rising, and Norbert, as he always did, felt as if the Tower was pressing closer about him. Little wonder people called this place the House of War. Plagued by the sooty stench of Satan, the Tower was a true haunt of ghosts: the wounded souls of those whose decapitated heads, soaked in brine and heavily tarred, now decorated the poles erected high above each gateway. The Tower people whispered how at night the ghosts of all those who had died violently in this House of the Red Slayer gathered on the execution green before the soaring, great white donjon. They would assemble there, then process silently and solemnly into the Chapel of St Peter in Chains, where they dolefully chanted the matins of midnight.

On that freezing late winter afternoon, Prior Norbert could well believe such stories. He had come to the fortress, as he did every month, to render an account of matters involving the abbey, the King's own chapel as well as one of the most impor-tant Benedictine abbeys in both England and beyond. The prior was the abbot's principal officer, but he was also John of Gaunt's informant amongst the Blackrobes. Usually Norbert's reports were mundane, even banal, yet Gaunt always listened carefully, as did his henchman, that most cunning of creatures, Master Thibault.

Norbert, trying to hide his unease, made his weary way up the narrow lanes, past the different small markets. Each of these contained a range of stalls selling local merchandise, as well as more exotic items such as oranges and dates, bought fresh from the cogs moored along the nearby quayside. The air was thick with the stench of blood billowing from the slaughter pens, as well as the odour of the cheap soap the washerwomen used as they scrubbed and cleaned around the Tower wells. Dogs barked and yelped, as strident as the screams of the Tower children who played on the great war machines, positioned for readiness close to gates and postern doors. The machines were massive contraptions which rejoiced in names such as 'Bone-Crusher', 'Head-Swiper' and 'Flesh-Gouger'.

The Tower, grim as it appeared, was a small town in itself, and the great white keep stood at its heart. The steps and doors leading up to the main entrance were closely guarded by knight bannerets in full armour emblazoned with the royal colours of blue, gold and scarlet. Norbert heaved a sigh of relief and murmured a prayer. He paused to catch his breath and stared up at the first ring of guards: Sherwood archers, in their Lincoln green jackets and earth-coloured hose, deadly war bows slung across their backs with quivers of goose-feathered arrows hanging by their side. Norbert searched through the warrants and letters in his chancery satchel then started as two glossy, black-feathered war ravens which, by tradition, guarded the Tower, came floating by; their screeching echoed, chilling and menacing. Norbert found his pass and the captain of archers escorted him up through the guards thronging at the top of the steps. They stood aside and Norbert entered the darkness of the White Tower. Accompanied by a man-at-arms, the prior climbed the steps past the entrance to the luxuriously decorated chapel of St John and into the council chamber.

John of Gaunt, still garbed in his hunting leathers, lounged at the end of a long polished oval table with Master Thibault sitting to his right. Norbert stopped, bowed, then sketched the usual benediction towards both men. Gaunt and Thibault swiftly crossed themselves. The regent's henchman gestured to the chair to the left of his master. Norbert sat down. The Spanish mercenary who had showed him in poured a goblet of white wine and placed it before him, along with a platter of toasted honey slices, small mouthfuls to delight the taste. Norbert tried to remain composed. He was accustomed to these meetings where he acted as the abbot's spokesman. He tried to maintain his own integrity, yet he knew some of his brethren at Westminster regarded him as the regent's spy.

Norbert sipped at his wine and nibbled one of the sweetmeats as he stared at these two powerful men. Gaunt was truly beautiful; he had the golden hair, olive skin and eerie light blue eyes of the Plantagenet. His face was a mask of serenity, though Norbert knew that could easily slip into one of insufferable rage. Thibault, Gaunt's sole confidant, was garbed in black from head to toe. In truth, he was no different to his master, a man of many moods. Unlike Gaunt, who sported a neatly clipped moustache and beard, Thibault was smooth shaven. He had a smiling, soft round face under a mop of closely crimped blond hair. The henchman had the eyes and look of a choir boy, or one of those angels painted on the wall leading into St John's chapel. Norbert knew different. Thibault was a viper in human flesh. A swift, deadly killer. He was his master's man, body and soul, in peace and war. If Gaunt fell from power, Thibault would certainly follow.

'You are well, Prior Norbert?'

'Yes, your Grace.' Gaunt smilingly nodded and fingered the Lancastrian SS collar around his throat.

'Lord Prior.' Thibault leaned across the table, his voice all silky. 'We have asked this before and we do so again. Early last summer, before my Lord journeyed to Scotland, before the hideous troubles broke out in the city, we visited our abbey. You do remember?'

'Of course, of course, Master Thibault. You asked for the abbey to be emptied so you and my Lord could pray privately before leaving for Scotland. London was restless, Westminster even more so. You did not wish to endanger yourself. You lit candles before the Lady Altar as well as in the chantry chapel of the Confessor. You . . .'

'A peaceful, serene visit,' Thibault broke in. 'Yes? Of course.' Thibault answered his own question. 'But tell us, has anyone questioned you about our visit?'

'Nobody, I assure you, your Grace, and why should they? That was Crown business carried out in its own chapel.'

'Very good, very good,' Thibault purred. 'And the present matters. These murders? Prior Norbert, tell us what's happening. Everything you know.'

'Sir John Cranston would . . .'

'My Lord Coroner is another matter,' Thibault snapped. 'You tell me, in particular, about any visit Sir John and Brother Athelstan have made to the abbey and any interest they have shown in the Stone of Destiny.'

'They have visited the abbey but more to investigate the murders and question those they want to. However, earlier today, Brother Athelstan spent considerable time in our library studying manuscripts which describe the stone. He then demanded to examine the stone, which he did, and then left.'

'And did he say why? Did he say anything about the Stone of Destiny?'

'My Lord, the Dominican is always tight-lipped. He examined the stone and left immediately afterwards with Prior Sinclair and Sacristan Sylvester. My brothers have finished their business here and wish to make hasty departure to Scotland for an important chapter meeting at Melrose. Prior Sinclair informed me of this before he left, which is why Sylvester accompanied them. They were impatient to leave.'

'Oh, I am sure they were,' Gaunt replied dryly. 'Prior Norbert, is there anything else you can tell us?'

'Your Grace, I can say nothing except the abbey is now a place of mystery and murder.'

'And Sir John Cranston and Brother Athelstan have not resolved the killings?' Gaunt mused. 'I understand all the victims, apart from the anchorite, were self-styled Guardians of the Stone. The good brothers were of Scottish origin and like to honour the stone, which is quite understandable. The Scottish delegation also wanted to pay their respects to it, as well as finish minor matters left from previous negotiations. Oh yes, and one further matter.' Gaunt smiled. 'Sinclair was a chronicler, deeply interested in the events which occurred last summer in London and the surrounding shires. He wanted to make diligent search about that infamous event. I saw no problem with that.'

'All true, your Grace. However, I can assure you, no light has been cast on how or why my poor brothers were so foully poisoned.'

'But the stone they guarded safely resides there?'

'Oh yes.'

'Anything else, Prior Norbert?' The Blackrobe scraped back his chair then paused to reflect on Gaunt's question.

'One minor mystery, your Grace. You may have heard that Sacristan Sylvester's pet monkey escaped and was later found dead.'

'And?'

'Strangely, the corpse of another monkey has recently been discovered in the abbey cemetery. I cannot inform Sacristan Sylvester; he too has left for Scotland and the meeting at Melrose.'

Thibault glanced at his master who simply flicked his fingers, as if what Norbert had said was of very little interest to him.

The prior gripped the side of the table and made to rise. 'Your Grace, Master Thibault, I must—'

'Go,' Thibault smiled, 'and many thanks, Prior Norbert.'

Both men waited until the Blackrobe had left, then Gaunt leaned forward, putting his face in his hands as if listening to the different sounds drifting through the council chamber. Thibault sat, head to one side as he gently hummed a hymn from Compline. 'Arise, oh Lord, arise and judge my cause.'

Gaunt took his hands away and slouched back.

'In God's name, Thibault, Cranston and his friar should not be involved in this business. Our fat coroner is sharp as a razor whilst Athelstan is a veritable ferret in human form.'

'Your Grace, we had no choice. Their commission was a direct request, indeed an order, from your beloved nephew Richard the King. To have ignored such a request in any way would have provoked a whole sea of troubles.'

'True, true,' Gaunt sighed. 'But Athelstan has scrutinized the stone.'

'Let him do that.'

'And what else do we know?'

'My spy . . .' Thibault paused to pop a sweetmeat into his mouth.

'My spy in St Erconwald's . . .'

'Who is?'

'Why Mauger, the parish clerk. He has informed me by swift despatch that Athelstan has trapped the hideous monster, the Flayer. He was caught red-handed, confronted by Cranston, who has had him locked up in Newgate.'

'Yes I have heard of that monster, but he can go hang as he surely will. What about our business?'

'Paltoc the mercenary is dead, murdered by the Flayer who must have resented Paltoc haunting the cemetery at St Erconwald's. You remember him, your Grace, once a member of your household? He was one of those who failed you at the Savoy. He may also have been responsible for removing that chest.' Thibault winked at his master. 'But we have no real proof, no evidence.'

'Paltoc was a fool,' Gaunt retorted. 'A man who couldn't even remember where he buried a chest. Not that its discovery would have done him any good. What else?'

'I mentioned this before. Halpen and Mildew were found hanged in their chamber at The Piebald tavern. I strongly suspect that Athelstan knows the truth about their deaths. I am certain that some of his parishioners were involved but really I couldn't care. Halpen and Mildew maintained that they saw the chest being removed from the Savoy but, your Grace, both men took to lying as a bird to flying. They were treacherous to the core. They should have hanged with the rest. Good riddance to them.' Thibault sniffed and primly dabbed his nose. 'Halpen and Mildew were very useful, their story about the treasure chest protects us who know the truth. You, my Lord, can now present yourself as totally innocent: you were the guardian of the regalia, you stored it safely and securely until your palace was destroyed and your possessions, the chest included, were feloniously robbed. No one can point the finger of accusation against you. I have imparted all this to Cranston who has no reason to doubt or challenge such a story: the treasure chest and the regalia of Scotland have disappeared and, quite rightly, you have no knowledge of their whereabouts. So, your Grace, stay comforted. We not only own the mystery behind all this but the keys to unlock it. Remember, the official story is that we journeyed to Scotland to treat on certain matters. We stayed at the abbey of Melrose. During the negotiations, the Stone of Destiny was mentioned, but we maintained our public attitude on that. We left Scotland and returned to London. A few months later, the Scottish court responded by sending a delegation to finish certain matters. Prior Sinclair's arrival here was only a courtesy, a response to our visit last summer.'

He paused. 'Now we know that during our visit to Scotland the Great Revolt erupted. Your palace of the Savoy was burnt. Paltoc came to report this and you, very angry, quite rightly dismissed him. In other words, your Grace, nothing extra-ordinary occurred in Scotland and whatever is beginning to unfold now does not touch on the secrets we hold. Of course, something very interesting is happening. I know that Cranston has been having urgent talks with the lords of the Guildhall on certain issues. However, that should not concern us. We must simply maintain our public face and not become involved.' Thibault sipped from his goblet. 'Of course, people might ask what truly happened to the regalia of Scotland, to the treasure chest stolen from the Savoy? Our response is that we are still searching for it, which is why we allowed the likes of Halpen and Mildew to be pardoned so that they could be involved in the hunt. We have done what we can and we can do no other.'

'I agree, I agree, but tell me, Thibault my friend. What if Cranston and Athelstan stumble on to this mystery and find their own key? What if they discover the truth?'

'Then, your Grace, and I will be blunt: that would make Cranston and Athelstan the most dangerous men in the kingdom . . .'

When he woke, Athelstan panicked at the strange sounds and smells, the deep blackness all around him. He rolled over on the heaped sacking and stared up into the darkness. He realized what was happening, very much as he had expected. He had been lured on to *The Bannockburn*. The Scottish delegation were leaving in haste for Edinburgh and they had decided to take Athelstan with them. The friar sniffed and gagged at the rancid stench of sweat, cordage, tar, and the ever pervasive odour of rotting fish. He became aware of the roll of the ship, the creak and groan of timber and cordage. He felt cold: his robes were damp and, when he licked his lips, he could taste the heavy salt. He stared round the captain's cabin but it was empty.

Athelstan rose. He used the jakes pot, then splashed cold water over his face from a bucket just inside the door. He murmured a prayer, crossed himself and went up on to the deck. He staggered as the cog suddenly pitched to one side, only to rise just as roughly on the surging tide. The salt-laden, pinching-cold breeze stung his eyes and face. The light was now a dull grey. Trails of mist drifted across like disembodied spirits to dance around the mast. The crew were busy enough, pattering across the deck shouting at each other. Athelstan abruptly staggered as the cog, sails snapping, lurched up and then sideways. Athelstan stumbled across to the taffrail then groaned as a cloud of spray slapped his face. He reached the rail, leaned over and was promptly sick, vomiting and retching. A sailor came by. The man stopped and asked if Athelstan was well, advising him not to look at the sea but the horizon. In a broad Scottish burr, he informed the friar that *The Bannockburn* had slipped its moorings late the previous night. They were now midstream, making their way down river to the estuary. Athelstan thanked and blessed the man who scurried away.

The friar wiped his mouth on the back of his hand and stared across the fast-moving river; he could, despite the shifting mist, glimpse lights and the outline of buildings on the far bank. He took deep breaths and thanked God his stomach was settling. Athelstan had done service in the Narrow Seas and, along with his brother, had fought in a sea battle off Calais. Nevertheless, the sea frightened him, be it beyond the estuary or these surging, powerful and highly dangerous waters of the Thames. Athelstan had experienced the nightmare squalls and demon-ridden winds. He quickly murmured the mariner's prayer: 'From the horrors of the sea and its devouring monsters, Lord deliver me.'

Athelstan glanced over his shoulder. Gromond the master was now exerting himself. Dressed in leather jerkin, leggings and fur-trimmed boots, the captain studiously avoided Athelstan's accusing gaze to shout at the ship's boy high in the falcon's nest. Athelstan gripped the taffrail, struggling against the swaying and lurching of the ship. He let the noise sweep over him: the sharp crack of wood, the grim creak of ropes and the constant snapping of the thick canvas sails. Athelstan composed his thoughts and quietly recited a line from the psalms. 'Oh Lord give light to my eyes, lest I fall asleep in death. Lest my enemies say I have overcome him.'

'Brother.' Athelstan turned to face the two Blackrobes, Sylvester and Sinclair. The sacristan offered a cup of posset. Athelstan took it then turned it, letting the contents spill out across the deck.

'You must be angry,' Sinclair declared, pulling back his hood. 'Let me explain.'

'I am angry,' Athelstan retorted. 'But as the Book of Ecclesiastes says: "There is a season under heaven for every-thing. A time for planting and a time for plucking up. A time for peace and a time for war."'

'Meaning?'

'The time has not yet come. The candle awaits the flame, the bell for the sign. Oh,' Athelstan forced a smile, 'don't worry, they'll all come soon enough.' Sinclair, eyes narrowed, face tense, came closer, then hurriedly stepped back when Athelstan moved towards him.

'What do you mean, Friar?'

'Let us wait and see, monk.' Athelstan turned to continue his study of the far bank. He stood rigid and calm, even though he still felt a little nauseous. *The Bannockburn* was now battling the full powerful thrust of the Thames. The friar watched as the massive cog manoeuvred its way through the sandbanks; dangerous, gruesome places where river pirates were hanged and their corpses, black twisted shapes, stood impaled on great stakes for all to see. Now and again they would pass a solitary herring boat or fishing smack and, when the mist parted, a cog or merchantman making its way along to the quaysides.

Athelstan, aware that the Blackrobes had left, glanced around. He'd already noticed the strong guard on the chamber built beneath the lofty poop. Athelstan smiled to himself. *The Bannockburn*'s precious cargo would soon be revealed. He now regretted his sharp words with Sinclair. Both he and Sylvester were now in deep conversation with Gromond who, one hand covering his mouth, seem perturbed by what he was hearing. He muttered something to the two Blackrobes, then ordered one of his crew, a young lad, back up into the falcon's nest.

Athelstan returned to leaning against the taffrail. He ached from head to toe, he was thirsty, his lips and throat were salt soaked, his belly empty and cold. In truth he yearned for a bowl of hot potage in his little house . . .

'Sail!' The lookout in the falcon's nest sung out. 'I see sail to the east, nothing to the north, nothing to the south, nothing to the west. I see sail to the east.' The lookout's clear strong voice swept *The Bannockburn* like God's own trumpet. For a matter of a few heartbeats, the ship fell silent. No one moved or made a noise. Even the sail and rigging, the pitch of the river and the harsh clattering whistle of the wind seemed to fall quiet.

'Another sail,' the lookout proclaimed. 'I see another sail. A cog fully armed to the west.'

The Bannockburn's crew broke from its surprise. Gromond shouted orders one after the other. A drum began to beat. *The Bannockburn* became a hive of activity. Sailors hurried along the deck, taking up position, awaiting the next spate of orders. They all knew that the great cogs sailing directly towards them meant bloody confrontation.

Athelstan, still gripping the taffrail, stared to the left and right. He could now see the two massive warships, sails fully extended, bearing down on *The Bannockburn*, tacking and shifting, to take full advantage of the blustery winds. The second cog was moving faster, now breaking free of the concealing mist to stand off the stern. Athelstan gave a deep sigh of relief. Sir John had been true his word. Two formidable war cogs had been despatched. One to control entry to the estuary, the other had remained concealed along one of the banks, waiting for *The Bannockburn* to pass. Now the trap was sprung and God knows how many other English cogs waited further downriver. Athelstan heard his name called and turned once again to confront Sylvester. The sacristan's face was suffused with anger.

'This is your doing, Friar,' he snarled, his face only a few inches from Athelstan's. Sylvester was wild-eyed, his lips coated with spittle, one hand deep in the pocket of his mantle which, Athelstan suspected, housed a dagger.

'Not my doing,' Athelstan retorted, 'but God's. And a wonder to behold! As I said, Blackrobe, there is a season under heaven for everything. My season has now arrived.' Sylvester was about to withdraw his hand but Sinclair hurried across, slipping and slithering on the shifting deck.

'Leave him,' he shouted. 'Brother, I tell you, leave him for the while.'

Sinclair plucked at the sacristan's arm. Sylvester threw Athelstan a hateful glance before following Sinclair over to the main mast where Gromond had gathered his officers. *The Bannockburn* was now preparing for war. The crew hastily armed themselves, donning rusty armour and chainmail over which they pulled animal pelts, the heads of dogs, foxes and bears still attached to them. Culverin, cannon powder and shot were brought up. Some of the sailors urinated into pieces of cloth creating makeshift masks to protect the eyes and face should the enemy, if the wind was right, release lime as the cogs prepared for boarding.

'Two war cogs closing fast!' the lookout shrilled.

'What names can you see?'

'To the east, *The Sanglier*, to the west behind us, *The Firedrake*.'

Athelstan closed his eyes and murmured a prayer of thanks. Cranston had persuaded the lords of the Guildhall to despatch their two most powerful warships.

'And their banners?' Gromond shouted.

'The City of London.' The lookout fell silent.

Athelstan leaning over the taffrail, stared to his right. The mist abruptly shifted. Athelstan caught his breath. *The Firedrake* was closing fast.

'They have unfurled the black banner and loosened beaussons.' The lookout's warning created a sudden silence on *The Bannockburn*. The constant creaking of wood, the rasp of cordage and the angry flap of canvas abruptly faded.

Athelstan peered through the mist. *The Firedrake* had now shifted slightly. It was no longer behind *The Bannockburn* stern but battling to run alongside. Athelstan could now make out *The Firedrake*'s black banners and the beaussons, brilliant red ribbons streaming in the wind. Both the banner and the ribbons were a clear proclamation by the master of *The Firedrake*. They were about to close with fire and sword in what would be a fight to the death. No quarter would be given, no mercy shown, no prisoners taken. *The Firedrake* began to edge closer to the portside of *The Bannockburn*. The mist parted. *The Bannockburn* rose and shook on a sudden surge, *The Firedrake* likewise.

'Archers,' the lookout shrieked. 'Archers to loose!'

Athelstan crouched down. He heard a clatter like iron raindrops smacking the deck followed by shrieks and yells. Athelstan glanced around. The master bowmen on board *The Firedrake* had loosed a hail of yard-long shafts. Some had thudded into the deck but a few had caught their victim. Here and there sailors screamed in agony at the shafts piercing chest or neck. A few just lay silent, blood streaming from the mortal wounds to their throat or face.

'Beware *The Sanglier* . . .' The lookout's warning ended in a shriek of pain as, clutching an arrow to his chest, he toppled from the falcon's nest to bounce against the deck, where he thrashed around then lay still.

Gromond, sheltering beneath the stern with his henchmen and the Blackrobes, shouted an order. The master then fell silent as a sailor, high in the stern, came clambering down the steps shouting and pointing. Athelstan peered over the taffrail. *The Firedrake* was now taking down both the beaussons and the black banner of anarchy, whilst some of its crew had removed part of their taffrail and were now lowering the ship's heavy bum-boat. Waiting for it to reach the water stood a tall figure garbed completely in black. Athelstan immediately recognized the Fisher of Men whilst the dwarf-like figures around him must be his disciples: Hackum, Soulsham and the rest. The Fisher of Men stood stark, threatening, ominous, even though he carried a cross wrapped in a white cloth which he raised for all to see.

'The Cross of Truce,' Athelstan shouted across to Gromond. 'Do you accept?' The master made to rise from where he crouched. Sacristan Sylvester tried to clutch his arm but Gromond shrugged this off. He shouted at a henchman to lower the royal standard and bring him a crucifix wrapped in a white cloth. Once he was satisfied that the banner was lowered, Gromond, clutching the cross, half-hidden by the white cloth, walked to the side of the ship and held it up. The Fisher of Men and his acolytes were already in the bum-boat.

At Gromond's signal, the boat pulled away from *The Firedrake*, making its way across the choppy waters. *The Sanglier* now stood off *The Bannockburn*'s bows, its poop and stern packed with Tower archers in their brown and green livery, war bows at the ready. Master archers, these would loose a veritable arrow storm at any sign of treachery or double-dealing. Athelstan, however, knew this would not happen. *The Bannockburn* was trapped. It would not survive a battle along the Thames, it had wisely accepted the truce cross symbol. The ceremonies surrounding this peace offering were sacred. Violation of a truce cross would provoke immediate condemnation by the Crown and excommunication by Holy Mother Church.

Athelstan whispered a prayer as *The Firedrake*'s bum-boat, its oarsmen the most skilled along the Thames, brought their craft across, then turned it gently so it nudged the side of *The Bannockburn*. Gromond had already removed the gangplank gate, a rope ladder was sent snaking down. Athelstan waited. The light was strengthening yet the day was still a dull grey, with lowering clouds over a swift-running river. *The Bannockburn* fought to keep still its sails, now fully reefed, its tiller men desperately trying to keep the ship on an even keel. Silence reigned, broken by the occasional screech of marauding gulls and the constant creaking and groaning of the cog.

'Sweet Jesus, save our souls!' The Fisher of Men's powerful voice rang across the deck to where *The Bannockburn*'s captain and crew now stood fascinated by this eerie apparition, garbed in black from head to toe. The Fisher of Men's face was hidden by a visor, his cloak thrown carelessly back so they could clearly see his sword and dagger, not to mention the small primed arbalest in his right, gauntleted hand. The Fisher of Men moved slightly forward so all three of his equally eerie companions could stand beside him. They were dwarves, though well-armed and as confident as their master. The arrival of the Fisher of Men only deepened the fraught silence across *The Bannockburn*. The friar, still crouching beneath the taffrail, almost jumped as the Fisher of Men shouted his name.

'Brother Athelstan,' he demanded, 'are you safe?'

'My friend,' Athelstan called out, getting to his feet.

The Fisher of Men turned and beckoned the friar to join him. Athelstan hurried to obey. The Fisher of Men clapped him on the shoulder, drew him closer and whispered heatedly.

'Sir John sends you greetings, and if we have to flee down the rope ladder, go faster than a ferret down a rabbit hole.'

Athelstan nodded then smiled at the Fisher of Men's acolytes.

'Will you give us a special blessing for this?' Soulsham hissed, his little wounded face wreathed in a mischievous grin.

'Of course!' Athelstan promised. 'You will all have my most solemn blessing.' He fell silent as the Fisher of Men pushed the cross of truth into Athelstan's hand. He then undid his wallet and took out a scroll of parchment. The Fisher of Men held this up as he stepped forward. 'I have here,' he proclaimed, 'a document signed and sealed by the Lord High Coroner of London. He has two lawful demands.' The Fisher of Men paused at the murmur of the crew of *The Bannockburn* now assembled around the great mast. 'First this. His Worship the Lord High Coroner demands the peaceful removal from this cog of his good friend and colleague Brother Athelstan, Dominican Friar and Parish Priest of St Erconwald's in Southwark. You have no objections to that?'

'None,' Gromond bawled back, totally ignoring the objections of the two Blackrobes.

'Secondly . . .' The Fisher of Men's voice thrilled with vibrancy. '*The Bannockburn* is immediately ordered back to moor at Queenhithe. The cog is in English waters and subject to English law. Once there, certain individuals and specific items, including baggage, will be removed. Having thus satisfied the authorities, *The Bannockburn*, its master and crew will not be harmed but given free fresh supplies and permission to sail across the King's seas unharmed and without challenge or obstacle.'

'Or what?' Gromond hurled back.

'A fight to the death. No quarter will be given. No mercy shown. No prisoners taken. Utter annihilation! Nothing more, nothing less, nothing else . . .'

By late the following morning, Athelstan felt he had recovered from the rigour of his forced imprisonment aboard *The Bannockburn*. He now sat shaved and bathed, garbed in his best black and white Sunday robes of the Dominican order. He made himself comfortable on the cushioned, throne-like chair next to Cranston.

The coroner sat in the seat of judgement, leafing through manuscripts on the leather top of the King's Bench, modelled on that in the kingdom's greatest court in Westminster Hall. On the far side of the coroner, his clerk and scrivener, Oswald and Simon, were busy preparing a side table of food and drink. Flaxwith and his bailiffs guarded the entrance, whilst within the doorway sat Cranston's green-garbed, red-haired, white-faced courier Tiptoft, ever-ready to hasten off on his master's behalf. No other person had been allowed into what Cranston called his 'secret chamber'. They were now waiting for the two Blackrobes, Sinclair and Sylvester, to be brought in. Cranston had tried to begin proceedings, only to grudgingly concede that he would wait for Prior Norbert to arrive from Westminster.

Athelstan gazed around the starkly furnished chamber, its oaken woodwork shimmering in the light from a host of candles and well-placed lanterns. Capped braziers mounted on wheels provided warmth, as did the fire roaring in the hearth on the far left of the chamber. Athelstan stared at the room's only real adornment, apart from a stark black crucifix, a tapestry describing Prophet Daniel's vision of the Last Judgement.

Athelstan crossed himself and reflected on the judgement yet to come. The confrontation aboard *The Bannockburn* had ended very swiftly. Gromond had totally ignored the Blackrobes' protests. He had no choice; his crew, faced with certain destruction, would have mutinied. Gromond had agreed. *The Bannockburn* turned and, escorted by *The Firedrake* and *The Sanglier*, made its way back to Queenhithe.

Athelstan was safely escorted over to *The Firedrake* where Cranston was waiting. Athelstan thanked him for his help. Cranston declared how, following Athelstan's advice, *The Firedrake* and *The Sanglier* had been prepared for some time, one taking up position close to the estuary, the other to close the trap by allowing *The Bannockburn* to pass then follow it downriver. On shore, the coroner had asked Benedicta to send some of Athelstan's parishioners to closely watch *The Bannockburn*. If Athelstan boarded the Scottish cog and never came off, Sir John was to be immediately alerted. In fact, there was no need. The Fisher of Men's spies had also noticed Athelstan being taken aboard *The Bannockburn*. Once this enigmatic lord of the river had been informed that Athelstan might have been taken prisoner, he had immediately sought out Sir John and offered his assistance. The coroner had ruled that the Fisher of Men would join him aboard *The Firedrake*.

Once all three cogs had berthed at Queenhithe, Sinclair and Sylvester tried to return to Westminster, loudly protesting at what was happening. In truth the two Blackrobes were terrified. The ambush along the river had been totally unexpected, and whatever plans they had concocted were now in total disarray. They loudly protested their benefit of clergy. They argued that they were tonsured clerics and so not subject to secular law. They also claimed that their allegiance to the Scottish Crown nullified any authority the Lord High Coroner wished to exercise. Cranston dealt with these objections in his usual brisk manner. He smilingly assured the two Blackrobes that they were not being detained but treated as his most honoured guests. They would be lodged in comfortable chambers at the Guildhall until certain matters were resolved. Cranston then dealt the crushing blow. He bluntly informed both monks that he had the full support of the Lord High Abbot of Westminster. This had quelled all objections, though Sinclair demanded that Prior Norbert should come and assist them in whatever challenges they faced. Athelstan heartily agreed. Tiptoft had been despatched to the good prior who now seemed to be taking his time in coming.

Athelstan opened his eyes and stared at the table to his right and the two great slabs of reddish sandstone resting there. He nodded to himself as he recalled Cranston clattering down the steps of *The Bannockburn* to remove the large crate from the cog's special hold. No one had protested or objected, and the same was true of the stone Cranston had removed from the abbey. Once again he had the support of the Lord High Abbot. Athelstan stood up to stretch and ease the ache in his muscles. As he did he watched a lay brother put out the trays of sweetmeats for the clerk, the scrivener, Sir John and those guarding the door. These sweetmeats had been hastily prepared by the pastry cook at Westminster at Cranston's urgent request. The coroner, at Athelstan's insistence, had also questioned the abbey pastry cook to discover certain information Athelstan needed . . .

'They are ready.' Tiptoft approached the dais on which King's Bench stood.

'They are ready,' Tiptoft repeated. 'Prior Norbert has arrived from Westminster, he came on a cart, little wonder he was slow. Anyway, he and the other two Blackrobes have been offered refreshment, they have refused.'

'Good,' Cranston retorted. 'Then bring them in and let us begin.'

The Blackrobes swept into the chamber like God's own messengers. They did not acknowledge either Sir John or the symbols of justice on the table before them, whilst they studiously ignored Athelstan. They took their places on the chairs arranged in front of the dais. Each had a small chancery table set before them.

'Let us begin,' Cranston demanded.

'Let us protest.' Prior Norbert rose to his feet. 'You have no authority,' the prior declared.

'This is not a trial,' the coroner retorted. 'It is in fact an Inquisicio Coronae, a legal and justifiable enquiry on matters affecting the Crown. I carry the royal writ,' Cranston plucked up a document decorated with seals along the bottom, 'and this writ has been accepted, indeed it has to be, by your Lord High Abbot. So Prior Norbert, shut up and sit down.' Cranston pointed at the hour candle in its recess to the left. 'Time passes, the hour has come. Brother Athelstan, present your indictment.'

The friar rose to his feet and walked around to the table. He touched each of the sandstone slabs.

'The Stone of Destiny,' he began, 'sacred to the Scottish Crown. On this, princes sat to be hailed, proclaimed and anointed. Its true origins lie deep in the mists of history. Its hallowed status cannot be denied. This,' Athelstan patted one of the stones, 'is why Edward I seized it from Scone Abbey when he raged through Scotland with fire and sword almost one hundred years ago. He seized the stone and sent it to Westminster Abbey, placing it beneath the English throne; a symbol, I suppose, of English dominance over Scotland.'

'And much resented,' Sinclair interrupted.

'True, true.' Athelstan smiled thinly. 'You are now showing where your true allegiances lie, for that is where all this murderous mayhem began.' Athelstan paused. 'I concede the stone should have been given back to the Scots, that is its rightful place. The stone should never have been seized in the first place and its return was solemnly agreed by the English Crown under the terms of the Treaty of Northampton in the Year of Our Lord 1328. However, due to the opposition of the Londoners, the stone was never returned. The English completely failed to understand the deep bitterness such a move provoked.'

'It certainly did,' Sinclair almost shouted, pushing away Norbert's restraining hand. Athelstan, however, noticed that Norbert's attitude was subtly changing. Ever since the proceedings had begun, the prior had sat staring, mouth gaping, at the two sandstone slabs.

'Now,' Athelstan continued, 'early this year my Lord of Gaunt went north to the Scottish March to negotiate with King Robert on a number of matters. The Stone of Destiny was one of them. Gaunt, however, already wary of the deepening opposition to him across London, refused to even debate the issue of restoring the stone.' Athelstan pointed across at Cranston. 'My Lord

Coroner informed me of that, it can be found in the official record. Now,' Athelstan rubbed his hands together, 'whilst Gaunt was away, London erupted in the Great Revolt. The palace of the Savoy was sacked and razed to the ground. During the pillage a certain treasure chest was taken from the Savoy by the mercenary Paltoc. He carried it across the Thames and buried it somewhere in St Erconwald's cemetery, probably in Paltoc's family grave. True, all of this is conjecture, we have no firm evidence.' Athelstan held up a hand. 'I concede I have very few details. I am not too sure what really happened or who was truly responsible. Two Judas men, Halpen and Mildew, were also involved but, there again, I have few details. Whatever! I truly believe the treasure chest was buried in St Erconwald's. Paltoc was responsible and he immediately left London to inform his Master Gaunt about the devastation of the Savoy.' Athelstan laughed abruptly. 'He got little thanks for that. Gaunt dismissed him from his service, leaving Paltoc on the Scottish March without office or revenue. Paltoc became a highly discontented man. I understand from Sir John that during his sojourn in Scotland, Gaunt lodged in Melrose Abbey, a Benedictine house. The same place where you, Prior Sinclair, began to spin a web of the most subtle intrigue, a plot to return not only the Stone of Scone – the Stone of Destiny – to Scotland, but also the Scottish regalia including the precious Black Rood of St Margaret.'

'And how did I manage all this?'

'Because you befriended Paltoc, who had been turned out of his living. The mercenary was resentful and penniless as he hung around the precincts of Melrose Abbey. You became his hand-fast friend. Paltoc confessed to you what had happened to him and informed you about the treasure chest, plucked from the burning Savoy, and cunningly interred in a grave at St Erconwald's. You wove the first great strand of the web. You, Prior Sinclair, would lead a diplomatic delegation to treat ostensibly with the English royal council at Westminster. I suggest these were fairly mundane matters, your visit being depicted as a courteous response to that of my Lord Gaunt's visit earlier in the year. You gathered your household and sailed south on *The Bannockburn*, which berthed at Queenhithe.

You lodged at Westminster where you would begin your diplomatic work. However, once there, you began to weave the second strand of your web. Prior Sinclair, you are a chronicler, interested in recording the turbulent events of our time: the Great Revolt was certainly one of these. I do not doubt your real interest and curiosity in that most singular event. Nevertheless, your studies provided an excellent cover to retrieve that treasure chest. In this great enterprise, you were assisted by your confederate Paltoc; the only real fly in the honeypot was Paltoc discovering that, due to our cemetery being occupied by the peasant army, Paltoc's family grave could not be located. Crosses, plinths, tombstones, shrubs and bushes had been pulled up and cast aside. The burial ground had changed in appearance.

'We all know the danger of burying something precious. You must mark the spot most carefully or you could swiftly become involved in searching for moonbeams. Both you and Paltoc, however, pursued the matter. Paltoc had an excuse to wander God's Acre. No one would disturb him and, of course, you were close by to provide any assistance. However, your offer to help was not an act of charity but a real attempt to find the regalia. Paltoc's presence in the parish was greatly enhanced by his offer to assist Sir John in his hunt for the Flayer. Poor man; his murder, however, did lead directly to the Flayer being caught. He now lodges in Newgate awaiting sentence.' Athelstan paused. 'I do wonder, Prior Sinclair . . .'

'About what?'

'Well, you had planned the great robbery and you must have known how such matters are dealt with here in London. If you were involved in the parish, either chronicling events or helping Paltoc, you could keep a close eye on me and any dangers I might pose to the plot being concocted across the river at Westminster. What better place to observe any involvement by myself and Sir John than being lodged in my parish at The Piebald tavern.'

'You flatter yourself, Friar.'

'No, I speak the truth. Now, in the great scheme of things, such activity is common enough across the courts of Europe, people putting on masks to face others who have also donned masks. Intrigue, deception and downright lies are common currency between kingdoms. This one, however, was truly murderous.' Athelstan paused to drink from his goblet. 'You . . .' Athelstan pointed at the sacristan. 'You, Brother Sylvester, were, I am sure, the real architect of this plot: Sinclair wove the web but only according to the design you devised. You are a Scotsman good and true, and God bless you for that, but you are also a Blackrobe and, I suggest, a very ambitious one. You were about to return to Scotland to attend a very important chapter meeting. Yes, Prior Norbert?'

The prior, who slouched wide-eyed, just nodded agreement to Athelstan's question, then he exerted himself, sitting up, resting both hands on the chancery desk.

'Athelstan, you are correct,' he retorted. 'Brother Sylvester is very talented, with the ambition to match. He was about to return to Melrose for a very important chapter meeting. Whispers and rumours abound in our order that Sylvester was due to be elected Lord High Abbot of that important abbey.'

'Of course,' Athelstan intervened. 'And what better prize to bring back to Scotland than the Stone of Destiny and the sacred regalia? You, Brother Sylvester, would have been hailed as a hero, worthy of all rewards, and what could the English Crown do but protest? And what use would that be? King Robert would point to the Treaty of Northampton which declared that the stone should be returned to Scotland, its rightful place.' Athelstan rose. He went back round to the slabs of stone and scrutinized them both, particularly the one brought from *The Bannockburn*. Athelstan stood tense, hand to his mouth, as if he'd glimpsed something he'd not expected. He stood for a while, lost in deep reflection. Only when Cranston coughed did the friar walk back to his seat beside Sir John, who, like the others in the court, sat fascinated by what was being alleged.

'On the Wednesday before the first Sunday in Advent,' Athelstan paused, staring back at the stone, lost in his own thoughts until Cranston loudly cleared his throat.

'Oh yes, oh yes!' Athelstan smiled apologetically. 'On that fateful Wednesday, Sylvester, you began your deadly game. Daylight faded, darkness fell. The abbey church emptied and,

at the appropriate time, your sub-sacristan Robert locked all
doors except for the Devil's door – it was firmly shut but not
bound fast. It was the custom for that postern to be left on its
latch. All was quiet until someone stole into that church. That
was you, Brother Sylvester, and you became very busy.'

'Doing what?' the sacristan snapped.

'You know full well. Under the pretence of strengthening
the path outside the nave, you had assembled workmen to
take up old slabs and lay new ones.' Athelstan pointed at
Norbert. 'Father Prior, when I first noticed those workmen,
you spoke as if you had organized the labourers but, in truth,
it was Sylvester – yes? He is responsible for doors, gates,
indeed all entrances.'

'That is correct, at the time, it was a minor matter . . .'
Norbert shrugged. 'I never gave it a second thought.'

'Of course, that was all a sham, a pretence,' Athelstan
continued. 'The workmen who looked so nondescript were in
fact sailors from *The Bannockburn*, who'd hired a cart and
acted like so many workmen across this city. Now, these
labourers secretly brought a slab of coarse-grained, pinkish
sandstone, this had been fetched south on *The Bannockburn*.
The quality of stone is very good and can be found close to
the abbey of Scone in the province known as Perth and Angus.'
Athelstan waved a hand. 'Whatever legend says, I believe this
locality furnished the reddish Stone of Destiny. I found such
information in manuscripts kept by the abbey library. Now
the slab, I will call it "The Bannockburn Slab", was left
near the Devil's door. All you had to do, Sacristan Sylvester,
under the cover of darkness and with the assistance of your
labourers, was to replace the true Stone of Destiny with The
Bannockburn Slab. A simple enough task. You are sacristan
of the abbey and therefore in charge of security, you are the
master of the keys. The exchange was made. True, the anchorite
declared he'd heard a strange scraping; that of course would
be the noise created by the stones as they were pushed out or
in under the English throne. In the end, who would really care
about what the anchorite babbled about? He would have been
ignored, but of course a mistake occurred. An unforeseen
circumstance . . .'

'The monkey,' Prior Norbert exclaimed. 'Barak. Sacristan Sylvester's pet monkey.'

'My Lord Prior, you are correct,' Athelstan replied. 'On that same night, Sacristan Sylvester's monkey allegedly escaped.'

'I thought of that,' Norbert interrupted, scratching the side of his face.

'What?' Sylvester demanded.

'Your pet monkey,' Norbert retorted just as brusquely. Athelstan sensed the breach between Norbert and his two companions was widening.

'Prior Norbert?' Athelstan asked gently.

'Well, Sylvester loved that wretched animal.'

'He even brought it a cape and a hat with bells, didn't he?' Athelstan asked.

'Yes, yes he did. I hated the creature and yet,' Norbert blinked, 'there is something else I must say on this issue, but perhaps not now.' The prior fell silent, as if reluctant to commit himself to changing from being an ally of Sylvester to helping Athelstan in drawing up his indictment.

'Prior Norbert,' Cranston called out. 'We are here for one purpose and one purpose only: the truth!'

'I had no part in all of this,' Prior Sinclair abruptly burst out.

Athelstan steeled himself. Cranston lowered his head to hide his smile, the Blackrobes were definitely beginning to separate.

'No part in what?' Cranston insisted. 'Prior Sinclair, in what?'

'I don't know,' Sinclair mumbled. 'It's best if I keep silent.'

'For the time being, yes,' Cranston agreed. 'But in the meantime, Prior Norbert?'

'Sylvester.' Norbert's tone now turned accusatory. 'You were devoted to that creature, even though it was a real nuisance, eating and shitting all over the place, but we tolerated it because of you. Yet when the animal escaped, when news of its death was brought, you did not seem perturbed or greatly saddened by what had happened. I wondered then, as I wonder now, why this change of mood.'

'Oh, I can tell you,' Athelstan declared. 'I was also mystified. Sylvester, you never raised the matter with me. But, on
reflection, you wouldn't, would you? Any talk or speculation
about Barak's escape might attract more questions about what
actually happened to that creature, as well as about the mysterious events of that particular Wednesday night.' Athelstan gave
a deep sigh. 'Ah well, now we know.'

'Know what?' the sacristan shouted.

'How on that Wednesday night you exchanged an ordinary
slab for the Stone of Destiny, which you had transported to the
hold of *The Bannockburn*. The anchorite heard sounds, but what
truly frightened him was that long dark shadow fluttering about
to the sound of bells.'

'Barak?'

'Of course, Prior Norbert. Barak, garbed in his little cape, cap
and bells. Many pet monkeys are dressed like this. I have seen
the likes at fairs and markets. Indeed, whenever monkeys are
described in any painting or fresco, they tend to be depicted in
some form of costume, with little bells pinned to their clothes
or fastened around neck, wrist or ankle.' Athelstan paused. 'That
the dead do speak to the living is a favourite saying of mine. I
truly believe it. Those who now walk with Christ, also walk with
us. They assist us as they did me. I noticed in my own church,
with darkness falling and the lantern light flitting, how the
shadows of my cat, Bonaventure, became elongated, shifting
fitfully, a trick of the light. Well, that's what the anchorite glimpsed
and heard. Barak the monkey, scampering around the nave before
he escaped, slipping swift as a darting shadow through the Devil's
door during the removal of the stone. Little wonder, Sylvester,
that you did not mourn Barak or discuss his escape, as that might
provoke three embarrassing questions. Firstly, why was Barak in
the church that night? Secondly, if he was there, were you also
present, Sacristan Sylvester? And thirdly, if you were present,
what were you doing in your abbey church at the dead of night?'

'I agree,' Norbert declared. 'Your silence about your darling
pet is most mysterious. And what Brother Athelstan now tells
us is logical enough.'

'Brother Robert your sub-sacristan was, I suggest, also
suspicious,' Athelstan continued. 'The anchorite panicked

because when he left his cell, he found the Devil's door locked when it should have been left on the latch. Brother Robert took the blame for that, saying it was an oversight on his part. I don't really believe that and I think Brother Robert thought the same. He must have wondered what truly happened. How did that door come to be locked on that particular night? I wonder if he listened to the rantings of the anchorite? Did he reflect on the other mysterious events of that particular evening? Oh, the sub-sacristan could confess it was all his fault but, in his own mind, did he conclude that he had left the door unlocked? This in turn begs the question, and one which must have concerned Brother Robert. If he left the door unlocked, then who locked it? Who else had the key? And the only answer is you, Brother Sylvester.' Athelstan cleared his throat. 'True, the abbot and Prior Norbert hold keys, but what would they be doing in the nave of their church at the dead of night?'

'I, I, wouldn't do such a . . .'

'Stupid thing?' Athelstan broke in. 'Yes, it was a very stupid mistake. I suggest the escape of Barak clouded your thinking and you locked that door without a second thought. A truly hideous mistake, masked only by your sub-sacristan taking the blame.'

'So,' Cranston intervened, 'this mystery was secretly concocted in Scotland. Prior Sinclair is one branch of it. He discovers that Paltoc may know where the secret regalia of Scotland lies buried in a family grave in Southwark. They developed their plot. Paltoc would be in Southwark, lodging at the same tavern as the good prior. Paltoc's position is greatly enhanced by seizing the opportunity to assist me in my hunt for the Flayer.' Cranston laughed sharply. 'Both men are embedded deep in St Erconwald's like shrubs in a herb pot. Sinclair requires information for his chronicle whilst keeping you, Athelstan, under close observation, as well as helping Paltoc in his search for the treasure chest.'

'You have little proof, if any,' Sinclair protested, 'of an alliance between myself and the bounty hunter.'

'You did help him in his search for the family grave.'

'An act of kindness, Brother Athelstan.'

'And your knowledge of Paltoc's family? You knew the names of his father and mother, not to mention the precise dates of their deaths. You remember,' Athelstan raised his voice, 'when you and Paltoc visited my house, you provided such detailed information because you'd memorized it and could repeat it fluently. How could you do that? You and Paltoc must have conferred and conferred deeply.' Sinclair simply shook his head.

'And the second strand of this wickedness was being spun in the abbey,' Cranston continued. 'The removal of the stone, the escape of Barak, the door being mistakenly locked. The labourers who were really members of *The Bannockburn* crew. All of these are the ingredients of the murderous plot concocted at Westminster?'

'Oh, that's certainly true,' Athelstan agreed. 'And, Sir John, so easily done. Sacristan Sylvester is the one monk who can leave the abbey to buy supplies or indeed anything else. I believe, Brother,' Athelstan pointed at the sacristan, 'you did just that. Masked and cowled, you entered some apothecary shop where you bought poisons.'

'I did not!'

'Oh, but you did. And you brought your phials with you when you boarded *The Bannockburn*. You never had the opportunity to unlock and remove those phials. Your baggage was seized along with the stone. Only after all items had been fully inspected were they passed back to you. We found poison, Brother Sylvester, in your medicine coffer.'

'I resent and protest at such intrusions. A heinous violation of my rights.'

'Shut up, monk,' Cranston bellowed. 'You will have both the time and the opportunity to explain to anybody who cares to listen as to why a Blackrobe had phials of poison in his medicine coffer.'

'You are a poisoner,' Athelstan declared. 'And the reasons are obvious. First, Brother Robert had to be removed. He entertained his own suspicions and you knew that. Secondly,' Athelstan pointed at the red stone slabs, 'the Stone of Destiny was kept under the English throne at Westminster. Now, in accordance with ancient Scottish rites, the kings of Scotland would have the occasional formal crown-wearing ceremony during which, garbed in the royal regalia, they would sit or stand on the Stone of Destiny to be proclaimed. By tradition one of these ceremonies occurred on the fourth Sunday of Advent. On such a day the so-called Guardians of the Stone, Brothers Robert, Malachy, Fergal and Donal, would assemble in the sanctuary of Westminster Abbey, withdraw the stone from its place and conduct their own little liturgy, a rite of celebration. They were four Scots in exile, honouring a relic of Scottish kingship.' Athelstan rose and walked across to the table. He stood between the two sandstone slabs and placed a hand on each. 'The Bannockburn Slab is not the Stone of Destiny. All four Benedictine Guardians of the Stone would probably know every inscription and mark on this sacred relic. I suggest they would soon recognize a counterfeit stone.'

'And they would have done so,' Cranston agreed, 'on that last Sunday of Advent when the stone was taken out.'

'Are you sure of that, Brother Athelstan?' Prior Norbert demanded.

'Yes certainly,' Athelstan shrugged, 'maybe even before. Whatever, it was only a matter of time before the guardians realized something was dreadfully wrong: that the stone kept in Westminster Abbey was not the Stone of Destiny.'

'But surely,' Brother Norbert queried, 'if the Guardians of the Stone were Scottish, and we know they certainly were, surely they would have rejoiced at the Stone of Destiny being returned to its rightful owners.'

'No, no.' Athelstan shook his head. 'I don't believe that. They would see the stone as a sacred relic which should be formally and publicly returned. Concerned about what was truly happening, they would have raised the alarm. An investigation would take place and the matter ruthlessly pursued by the English Crown. Time was of the essence. We saw how swiftly *The Bannockburn* left, which is why we arranged for *The Firedrake* and *The Sanglier* to be prepared for sea. The stone had to be taken, but secretly and in plenty of time. It is a long and very arduous voyage from the Thames up through the Northern Seas, along the east coast of this kingdom to the port of Leith outside Edinburgh. The English Crown would have reacted vigorously to intercept *The Bannockburn* and recover the stone. Couriers would be despatched. Harbour masters alerted. English war cogs put to sea. No, no,' Athelstan shook his head, '*The Bannockburn* would have to be back in Scotland before the storm broke.'

Athelstan paused. He could not ask the one question which nagged at his mind. Did this enterprise, Brother Sylvester's plot, have the support of the Scottish King and his council? Athelstan returned to his seat. Cranston whispered at him to continue. Athelstan simply shook his head and sat down, still reflecting on the problem.

Prior Sinclair and his entourage had journeyed to England on *The Bannockburn*, a royal Scottish cog. Surely this must have been arranged by the Scottish King and his council? Athelstan shook his head: it was the usual ploy. If Sylvester's plot had succeeded. If the stone had been returned to Scotland, the English could protest but do no more. The Scottish Crown would simply point out that the stone was theirs, and indeed by the Treaty of Northampton, England had promised that the stone would be returned. Such a response would utterly crush any appeal the English Crown might make to the Papacy. On the other hand, if the English Crown accused the Scottish King and his council of being complicit in the murderous activities of Sylvester, they would simply wash their hands of it. They would reply that the enterprise had nothing to do with them, although they sympathized with the heartfelt attitude of Scotsmen who wished to return such sacred objects to their rightful owner. After all, this is what the English had agreed to at Northampton some fifty years ago. Athelstan, lost in his own thoughts, laughed sharply.

'Brother Athelstan!' The friar, startled, glanced at Sir John.

'Brother Athelstan,' Cranston whispered, 'we must proceed.'

'The murders,' Athelstan raised his voice dramatically. 'Ah yes, the murders! Sir John, I apologize to you for my silence, as well as for the fact that a number of you here have clearly demonstrated how the murders at Westminster Abbey actually took place.' Athelstan's words created a deep silence. Sacristan Sylvester, who had sat through most of the recent discussions with his face cupped in his hands, now glanced up, letting his hands fall away. He turned and whispered to Prior Sinclair, who just shook his head angrily.

'Brother Athelstan?'

'My Lord Coroner. Before these proceedings began, I asked for small trays of sweetmeats, hardened honey wafers, to be placed around this judgement chamber, including on the table before you.'

'Yes, yes, and they were quite delicious.'

'Precisely, and how many of you,' Athelstan raised his voice, 'have, often absentmindedly, picked up such a comfit and eaten it without a second thought?' Athelstan smiled. 'I hope you enjoyed such a simple pleasure, believe me those sweetmeats are wholesome and they are free. So how many of you did eat one?' Most of those in the chamber raised their hands. Flaxwith, leaning against the door, loudly confessed he'd crammed his mouth with them.

'I agree, I agree,' Athelstan replied. 'I have done likewise and I have recently seen the same in my house. I had a gift from Merrylegs' shop. I was quite surprised at how many people, when they see a tray of sweetmeats or comfits, simply pluck one up. Indeed, people take and eat before they even reflect.'

'It's common enough,' Cranston agreed.

'And that is precisely what happened at Westminster. Remember, Advent was approaching. The great fast was imposed. All the brothers would be hungry, very hungry, eager for any morsel. Our assassin realizes this and decides to exploit it. Sinister and sly, he leaves out a sweetmeat, some small delicacy on a wafer-thin base, honey or fruit, a delicious mouthful which can be consumed so quickly. Brother Robert may have found his in the sacristy, Brother Fergal in the scriptorium, Brother Malachy anywhere he happened to frequent, Brother Donal sheltering in the sanctuary and the anchorite alone in his cell.' Athelstan paused. 'Just think,' he declared. 'A small sweetmeat on its wafer-thin base. Brothers Robert and Malachy may have found theirs in their room. I noticed how the doors to the different cells are left open so anyone could enter. Think of Robert and Malachy, both ravenous. They pick up the sweetmeat and pop it into their mouths without a second thought. Brother Fergal goes to his desk in the scriptorium and finds the same. Brother Donal in the sanctuary would have been the easiest victim. Yes, Sylvester?' The Blackrobe did not look up. 'Donal was in sanctuary,' Athelstan continued. 'I understand the sacristan has sole responsibility for such individuals. Donal was so agitated he would be easy prey. The same is true of the anchorite, hungry, even famished. He even asked me for food. I suspect the anchorite found that venomous sweetmeat left on the ledge of the squint hole of his cell. He would take it, as the others did, as a gift from some charitable brother, who worked in the kitchen, buttery or refectory.'

'But we found no stains on their lips or mouths.'

'Of course not, Brother Norbert. Listen.' Athelstan rose and pointed at the platter of sweetmeats close to Sir John. 'Do you remember,' he asked, 'as a child helping yourself to something in the kitchen, a piece of pear or a slice of apple. a sliver of roast meat or a drop of sweet fruit?' Athelstan paused at the murmur of agreement. 'I certainly remember such occasions. I always tried to hide the evidence by cleaning my mouth and wiping my lips. Brother Norbert?' Athelstan waited for the prior to raise his head. 'I see you are embarrassed, don't be,' Athelstan declared. 'These victims cleaned their lips and mouths to ensure they removed all evidence from their sharp-eyed prior that they had infringed the great fast.' Athelstan picked up a goblet from the table in front of him. 'All the victims hid their petty breach of the great fast by cleaning their mouths with water and, perhaps, when hidden from view, using their finger as a cloth. We know that Brothers Robert and Fergal were seen to drink from a common source before they died. Donal was in sanctuary – you, Sylvester, would give him both the poisoned sweetmeat and the water. Indeed, Donal was like Malachy and the anchorite, sprawled dead by themselves for some time. You could easily have ensured that all was as you wished it. Armed with a wet rag, it would only take a few breaths to wipe their lips and clean their mouths. I do not know what poison you used, but it caused a thick froth and that too could hide any sign of what had been recently eaten.' Athelstan waved a hand. 'A most subtle and deadly poison, contained in the shell of sweetmeat, so easily taken and so easily disguised.'

'Sir John, Brother Athelstan.' Sylvester rose to his feet with as much dignity and grace as he could muster. 'Brother Athelstan,' the sacristan's powerful voice echoed across the chamber. 'How those people were murdered, poisoned may well be as you say, but you have no specific evidence that I was the one who poisoned them.'

'Listen then,' Athelstan retorted. 'First, on that fateful Wednesday night, if Brother Robert did not lock that door, then who did? We know you were there. That,' Athelstan pointed at the Stone of Destiny, 'was being stolen. The anchorite heard it being moved. Secondly, we know you were there in the nave of your abbey, and your monkey was with you. The animal escaped, but in circumstances which you would not wish to be known. Thirdly, you removed that stone to *The Bannockburn*, and you intended to flee back to Scotland on that cog to seek out your reward: an abbacy or some other similar wealthy, powerful benefice. Fourthly, poison was found in your medicine cabinet. Fifthly, on the Friday morning before the first Sunday of Advent, you asked Brother Michael, the abbey pastry cook, to immediately prepare a tray of delicate sweetmeats.'

'I did not . . .' Sylvester broke off, chewing his lip. 'Yes, maybe I did,' he stammered, 'I-I am becoming confused.'

'No, you are not confused, Sacristan Sylvester. You've quickly recalled that Brother Michael keeps a most detailed register of what he bakes. He showed Sir John that. I asked my Lord High Coroner to seek out Brother Michael and question him. You asked him for at least a dozen sweetmeats. Why? Why then? So close to the start of the great fast? Brother Michael himself was curious. He asked you why you needed such delicacies. You, of course, exerted your authority, declaring it was none of his business. You then added, in the form of an apology, that you needed the sweetmeats for visitors. Which visitors, Brother? When?' Sylvester just gazed blankly back. 'And sixthly,' Athelstan continued, 'you abducted me.'

'You fell asleep. We had to put to sea. We—'

'Nonsense, you kidnapped me. You realized I knew the truth. My researches at Westminster Abbey, my close scrutiny of the stone alarmed you. You concluded that I had discovered

the truth, so you had to silence me.' Athelstan drew a deep
breath. 'God knows what you intended. The murder of a
Dominican priest? The killing of a personal friend of the Lord
High Coroner of London?'

'Brother, Brother!' Prior Sinclair, hands flapping, threw a
hateful glance at the sacristan as he sprang to his feet. 'Brother
Athelstan, I assure you, you would have been kept safe.'

'Oh, I am sure I would have been. However, I would have
also been kept prisoner until *The Bannockburn* reached
Edinburgh and your journey was complete, the game over and
won!'

'I shall demand . . .' Sylvester rasped, breaking the silence.
'I shall demand proof positive that I actually administered poison
to my brothers, or indeed to anyone else. Norbert,' the sacristan
gestured at the prior, 'would you not agree?'

Norbert, sitting with his face in his hands, let these drop
away. He sighed noisily, crossed himself, leaning back in his
chair. 'Brother Athelstan, Sir John,' he declared, 'I will go on
oath, over the Eucharist, that I have no knowledge of the murders
carried out at Westminster, or that I was involved in Brother
Athelstan's kidnapping. Do you believe me, yes or no?'

'Yes,' Athelstan replied.

Norbert turned to the sacristan. 'Brother Sylvester, two
questions for you which, on your obedience, you must answer.
First, could your pet monkey Barak enter and leave your
chamber at will? Yes or no?'

'Yes. There is a narrow lancet window sealed by a little
wooden door. Barak could push this open and close it, a simple
trick I taught him.'

'Good, so when Barak escaped, why did he flee out of the
abbey precincts? I mean, he was a pet, not feral or wild? He'd
get hungry surely and return home? You must agree with that?'
Athelstan smiled to himself. Prior Norbert was sharp as a cutter
and was raising issues he had overlooked. 'You would agree?'
Norbert repeated.

'Yes, and your second question?'

'Barak wore a coloured cape, scarlet, blue and gold. I will
be honest, I did not like it, a monkey wearing the royal colours
of England.'

'No offence was intended. Your question?'

'There were pockets in that cape, why?'

'Oh, I trained Barak to put things there. Items he picked up. Prior Norbert, what is all this?'

'*Pax et bonum*,' the prior replied, turning to Cranston. 'Sir John, I journeyed here on a cart, hence my delay. I brought a casket, I must show you and Brother Athelstan what is inside. The cart stands in the courtyard below. Would you please arrange for the casket to be brought up here?'

A short while later, Flaxwith and two other bailiffs, their faces swathed with pieces of cloth, brought the casket into the chamber and laid it on the floor before the dais. Even from where he sat, Athelstan could smell the horrid stench of corruption, which deepened as Norbert shifted the lid. Pinching their nostrils, Cranston and Athelstan came round to inspect what was lying there – the decomposing corpse of a monkey, still garbed in its tawdry cape. The animal, eyes popping, lay sprawled on its back, rotting lips curled back to reveal yellowing teeth.

'Look.' Norbert picked up a small pointed cane from inside the chest. He pushed this against the corpse.

'Hard, rigid,' he murmured, then tapped the animal's mouth. 'Notice the stained froth. This monkey was certainly poisoned. Probably the same potion used in the murders.'

'Nonsense,' Sylvester muttered. However, the Blackrobe now looked truly frightened.

'Oh yes,' Norbert replied. 'I have examined the animal's corpse, the popping eyes, the rigid muscles and that dirty froth filling the mouth and staining the lips. It's the same.'

Athelstan also noticed the marked contusions around the right wrist, much clearer than similar marks on the corpse which had been brought to St Erconwald's.

'More importantly . . .' Norbert stretched down and, using the small cane, opened one of the pockets of the monkey's cape. He dug in the pointed cane and brought out a small blob of sticky substance. The prior held it up for all to see. 'I have examined this mess carefully. I believe it is a sweetmeat, a comfit, perhaps two moulded together by decay.'

'And the conclusion?' Athelstan remarked.

'Is that these same sweetmeats are poisoned. Hence Barak's

death and the symptoms he presents.' The prior glanced at Sylvester, who now sat a broken man in the face of the evidence pressing against him.

'I think it is best, Sir John,' Athelstan offered, 'if we adjourn for a while. I need to reflect.'

PART SEVEN

'Let us hasten quickly to our country.'

Cranston agreed, ordering Flaxwith to keep a strict watch on both Sylvester and Sinclair, as well as look after Prior Norbert. He also ordered the corpse to be removed and fresh herbs to be sprinkled on the fire and braziers, so as to sweeten the air. He and Athelstan then washed their hands and broke their fast.

Afterwards, Athelstan excused himself and went round to scrutinize the stone brought from *The Bannockburn*. He examined it very carefully, then looked at the one Cranston had brought from Westminster.

'What is it, Brother? Is there something wrong?'

'For the moment, Sir John, leave it. Let us keep to the issue in hand.' And Athelstan swiftly summarized what they had learnt from Norbert. The prior was brought up to answer a few more questions, Athelstan eventually declared himself satisfied and the coroner swiftly reconvened the Inquisicio.

'It would seem,' Athelstan began, once everyone had taken their seats, 'that the drama I depicted was not complete. The Stone of Destiny was removed on the Wednesday with all the eerie occurrences I have described. Barak the monkey did escape and cavorted around that nave, where his shadow darted and flitted in the poor light. Then Barak disappeared, probably through the Devil's door. No alarm was raised, was it, Prior Norbert? Could you just confirm that for me?'

The prior nodded in agreement.

'And why should the alarm be raised?' Athelstan continued. 'Barak could come and go as he wished as he did probably on that Wednesday evening, going in and out of that lancet window.' Athelstan lifted a hand. 'However, I suggest that sometime on Friday, before the first Sunday in Advent, Barak returned to his master's chamber. Scampering around, he came across the platter of sweetmeats already primed with the most deadly poison. He ate one of these and put others in his pocket, then fled his master's chamber to enjoy the spoils. Of course the poor creature falls ill and, weakened by the poison, cowers in some hiding place. Prior Norbert, during the adjournment, you informed us that the corpse was found three days ago.'

'Yes, yes it was.'

'So we can conclude that you, Sylvester, prepared those poisonous sweetmeats, your pet monkey ate some and only then did he disappear. Naturally it was not an issue you wished to be investigated. You must have realized that Barak had taken some of the poisoned sweetmeats and would die. Hence the story of Barak's escape became common knowledge over that Friday, Saturday and Sunday. Just one of those unhappy occurrences. As for the corpse of the monkey brought into St Erconwald's, that was mere coincidence. Pet monkeys are common enough in London, especially amongst the rich of Cheapside, whilst it was difficult to make out any distinguishing mark, especially on either wrist. People believed a monkey had escaped and a monkey was found dead. They put the two together and left it at that.'

'Where did you find Barak's corpse?' Cranston asked.

'In God's Acre, some of our lay brothers were collecting holly to decorate our halls and green our chambers. The poor creature must have crawled in there and died . . .' Norbert's words hung in the air, a deep silence broken by an occasional sob from Sacristan Sylvester.

'Brother Athelstan, Sir John, this Inquisicio is finished, yes?' Cranston glanced at Athelstan, who nodded.

'In which case,' the prior stood up, 'I need urgent words with you alone.'

Cranston agreed. The chamber was cleared. Sylvester and Sinclair were taken into custody by Flaxwith's bailiffs, while Sir John's henchman stood on guard outside. Once the judgement chamber had emptied and the door closed, Prior Norbert retook his seat before the dais. 'Sir John, Brother Athelstan . . .'

'Prior Norbert,' Athelstan interrupted. 'Sir John and I thank you for your intervention and support. It is deeply appreciated.'

'I had no choice. Barak's corpse was discovered some time ago. I grew deeply concerned when I listened to your indictment against our sacristan. I became convinced of his guilt, even though this is only an Inquisicio, not a trial.'

'That is correct,' Cranston barked, drumming his fingers on the manuscripts before him.

'Sinclair,' Norbert continued, 'is guilty of nothing more than . . . well,' the prior spread his hands, 'deception whilst trying to retrieve and recover a treasure which, in truth, belongs to Scotland. Sinclair's greatest mistake is that he failed. Let him go . . .'

'I would agree,' Cranston replied. 'Moreover, Sinclair enjoys status and privileges as the accredited envoy of King Robert. Consequently, any further intervention with him would be fruitless. Sylvester, however, is a killer, an assassin responsible for the deaths of five innocents. He deserves to be hanged, drawn and quartered.'

'He is a Blackrobe, a Benedictine,' Norbert retorted. 'Sylvester will plead benefit of clergy and, in public at least, he will be supported by our Lord Abbot, the entire Benedictine Order, not to mention the bishops and . . .' Norbert added wearily, 'Even the Holy Father. Now Sylvester has not confessed, but the evidence presses firmly against him. On the balance of all probability he is a murderer, most worthy of death, of being strangled on a gibbet. Yet, Brother Athelstan, as you well know, there are other sharper living deaths. Sylvester will be tried and judged by our Lord Abbot. I will be sitting at his right hand. Sylvester will undoubtedly be found guilty but he will not die, not yet. He will be taken to a small island off the Cornish coast, a rocky outcrop where the great storms roll. He will live on bread and water. He will be forced to reflect on his overweening arrogance and ambition. He, I am sure, devised the plot to return the Stone of Destiny to Scotland. Many would applaud him, Scots in particular. Sylvester, however, did not really care for the country of his birth, its prince or its people. Sylvester was motivated by bounding ambition. He wanted to bring home the Stone of Destiny and use that achievement to advance his career even further. Brother Robert and the others were just obstacles to be callously removed.' Norbert paused to catch his breath. 'Believe me, Sir John, Brother Athelstan, our former sacristan, will live a life of hard penance on that rock. The time will come, sooner or later, that he will pine for death.'

'We accept your assurances, Prior Norbert,' Cranston declared. 'Now this business has finished. We have a hanging to attend.'

'The mills of God, eh Brother Athelstan?'

'The mills of God, Prior Norbert,' Athelstan agreed. 'They grind slowly but they never stop.'

Cranston and Athelstan hurried up Cheapside. Already the crowds were swollen, all thronging up to the formidable House of Iron, Newgate, the nightmare prison. A place of stygian darkness, its narrow stone passageways glistening with filthy grease and reeking constantly of a foul stench. A world of the most profound darkness, where lunatics and madmen roamed the galleries, half naked, loaded with chains. Remart the killer, the self-confessed Flayer, was dragged from this place of perpetual midnight. He was fastened to a sled pulled by an ancient dray horse. Remart, garbed only in a loincloth, had been dragged through the City, along the thoroughfares of Cheapside as well as the filth-packed narrow runnels of Whitefriars. Here the dark-dwellers lurked, a surging mob crammed into rotting houses, thick as lice on a slice of rotten meat. These denizens of the night forgot their own misery to heap on insults and hurl whatever rubbish they could over the prisoner. By the time the execution party returned to the soaring gibbet outside Newgate, Remart was a living wound, covered in dirt from head to toe. When Cranston and Athelstan met him, with the Hangman of Rochester, on the platform beneath the lofty gibbet, Remart was groaning and protesting, though his eyes still glistened with malice.

The condemned man rested against the gibbet ladder placed alongside the one the hangman would use. Athelstan stared across the platform and repressed a shiver. The purveyors of death had arrived. Walter Brasenose, master butcher and leading member of the Fleshers Guild, was preparing for the gruesome ritual. The lords of the Guildhall had decreed that Remart, known as the Flayer, would hang, choke to death, after which his corpse, because of his own heinous crimes, would be flayed, peeled, and the skin nailed to the door of the gatehouse on the Southwark side of London Bridge. Brasenose and his two apprentices, their faces concealed behind grotesque masks, their bodies covered by thick red leather aprons, were laying out the knives, cutters, slicers and prongs of their grisly trade. They would show each item to the crowd who would roar their approval. Athelstan moved away, closed his eyes and quietly prayed. He hated such occasions, yet many Londoners viewed them as a holiday. Indeed, despite the iron-hard cold, the City had turned out in droves to watch the Flayer die. The usual tinkers, traders, cunning men, felons, naps and foists were also in attendance. Hot-pot girls and pastry boys pushed through the crowd, offering food and drink. The Choir of the Damned sang mournful songs whilst Friars of the Sack and other charitable groups intoned hymns of mourning. The crowd was a sea of moving colour and constant noise, surging up against the high platform on which the gibbet reared black against the sky.

The execution ground was guarded by two rings of Tower archers, under the personal command of Sir John. These stood behind a line of City pikemen, war bows notched and ready. The braziers close to the scaffold flared into life as the butcher boys, Brasenose's apprentices, poured on oil. The air turned rancid. Black smoke billowed backwards and forwards. Guildhall trumpeters came up the steps on to the scaffold.

'Sir John, Brother Athelstan.' The Hangman of Rochester sauntered across. He pointed back at the condemned. 'Remart wants words with all three of us.' Cranston looked at Athelstan, who nodded, and they went across. Remart, bruised and wounded, forced a smile, his battered lips curling back like those of a dog.

'I am to hang?'

'You certainly are,' Cranston retorted.

'Slowly?'

'As slow as I can make it,' the hangman replied.

'Brother Athelstan, Sir John. One boon.' Remart's lower lip trembled. The prisoner leaned against the ladder, as if listening to the clamour of the crowd roll across the scaffold.

'What?' Athelstan demanded. 'Remart, do not waste our time.'

'The treasure chest from the Savoy Palace,' Remart blurted out. 'I was there, but,' he shrugged bony shoulders, 'I did not see it taken. Ursula did. She claimed she glimpsed a cowled masked figure, on that hot summer afternoon, push a barrow into St Erconwald's cemetery and bury what it contained in Paltoc's family grave.' Remart paused, blinking and wetting dry lips.

'The candle burns,' Athelstan warned. 'In a word, What?'

'Ursula dug the chest up, she carted it away. She then came back to disguise what she'd done but by then the rebel army had swept through St Erconwald's.'

'And then what, briefly now?'

'Well, priest, Ursula forced the locks and clasps, pushed back the lid to find nothing, except old pewter cups, goblets, dishes and platters.'

'What!'

'That's what she found. She sold the contents to Joscelyn at The Piebald. You can ask him yourself and see what she sold.'

'Oh, I know that already,' Athelstan retorted. 'They were being used on that evening when those two rogues Halpen and Mildew were lavishly entertained. So I know that's the truth, whilst Benedicta found the coffer – the treasure chest – hidden away in Ursula's house.' Athelstan closed his eyes then opened them and glanced at Cranston. 'Sir John, you can see the chest for yourself, the work of a true craftsman, and the same goes for its many clasps and locks. Ursula broke those. She also chiselled away any insignia which might betray the true origins of that chest. Well I never.' Athelstan walked away and came back, aware of the crowd, the noise surging like the sea. Crows and ravens circled beneath the dull grey sky. Master Brasenose and his apprentices were sharpening their knives, the scraping sound echoing eerily across the execution platform. The trumpeters were now waiting. Cranston had taken the Proclamation of Death from his wallet. The hangman already had one foot on his ladder, his assistants eager to push Remart on to the other.

'Is that all you can tell us?'

'Yes, priest, and me?'

Athelstan nodded at the hangman. 'When the moment comes,' he murmured.

'I'll send him to hell,' the hangman retorted. 'And he can tell the Lord Satan I sent him there.'

'No,' Athelstan replied. 'Giles, when Sir John decides, send our prisoner as swiftly as you can to God. He's been expecting him.'

Athelstan and Cranston walked away to the far end of the scaffold.

'Remart told us the truth,' Athelstan murmured. 'But why was that chest full of cheap kitchenware?'

'Think, Brother, last June Gaunt left London for Scotland. The last thing he wanted was a war in the north. A Scottish invasion across the March into the northern shires. He knew as we all did that London was about to erupt. So he had to escape the City, as well as placate the Scots.'

'True, true,' Athelstan murmured. 'And I suspect Gaunt took the Scottish regalia, including the Crown and the Black Rood with him. I believe he offered these as a peace offering to King Robert.'

'In truth, Brother, yes. He probably intended to deal with the issue on his return. However, during his absence, he did not want some spy, some snoop to notice what was missing. Remember, Gaunt may have his minions, but they also have their price, and they are ready to sell their master for the right one. Indeed, Paltoc the mercenary is a fine example. He once served Gaunt but, when he was turned out, he became Gaunt's enemy. Now, be that as it may, to anyone who looked in the arca, the treasure chest was still there, heavily locked and firmly bolted. If anyone lifted it, it would be heavy. To all intents and purposes there was nothing wrong. If the revolt had not occurred, if the Savoy had not been pillaged, the truth about the regalia might have stayed hidden for decades. Little wonder that Gaunt was so furious that his palace was sacked. He must have been secretly worried that the false treasure might come to public notice.' Cranston shook his head. 'God knows, Brother, where the regalia really is.' The coroner laughed sharply. 'All such scheming, tangled and twisted, all brought to nothing by Ursula the poor pig woman.'

'Oh, Sir John, I think there is more.' He tugged at Cranston's sleeve, drawing him even closer, for the noise and clamour of the crowd thronging around the scaffold had grown, although it would hinder the sharpest eavesdropper.

'Brother, what is it?'

'This is all a nonsense, my Lord Coroner, we still don't have the full truth.'

'Brother?'

Athelstan pointed across the scaffold.

'Look, Sir John, let's hasten this malignant to judgement then use all your power and influence. We need to meet Prior Sinclair urgently, not at Westminster but in your private chamber at The Lamb of God.'

'Brother, what do you intend?'

'Sir John, trust me, and we will have the truth of all this.'

'My Lord Coroner?' The hangman called out. 'The sheriff's men are waiting.'

Cranston patted Athelstan on the shoulder and joined the other officials gathered at the foot of the gibbet. Trumpets brayed time and again and that deep silence which occurs just before a hanging descended. Again the trumpets. A drum began to beat. The hangman and his assistants pushed Remart up to the top of the ladder. The hangman followed nimbly on the one alongside. Remart, hands bound, was made to turn. The noose was put over his head and tightened. A trumpet shrilled. The hangman and his acolytes swiftly descended. All remained silent. The hangman gripped the ladder holding Remart and abruptly twisted it. The murderer's body fell like a stone, ending in a sharp crack as his neck was broken.

'God help you,' Athelstan whispered. 'But you have gone to judgement and I will be off to The Lamb of God.'

Athelstan and Cranston made themselves comfortable in the luxurious solar of The Lamb of God. Opposite them sat a rather nervous and subdued Prior Sinclair, who picked at the meat on his platter then turned to take a deep gulp from his wine goblet. The day had drawn on. Athelstan had left the execution ground. He had paused to say a prayer in a nearby church, then came to sit in the quiet of the tavern while Sir John brought the proceedings outside Newgate to an end. Remart had gone to God, though his naked corpse still dangled from the lofty gibbet outside the prison. Nevertheless, it was finished, and the crowd which had flocked to watch Remart die had dispersed to the many taverns along Cheapside. Once proceedings were over, Sir John had visited Westminster armed with all his warrants. The coroner had secured Prior Sinclair's release from his chamber prison, and brought him here to be wined and dined but closely questioned.

'Prior Sinclair.' Athelstan dabbed his mouth on a napkin and leaned across the table. 'I thank you for coming here.'

'I had little choice,' Sinclair retorted. 'And now I am here, why should I discuss matters with you? I am finished, I am done. I have to return to Scotland.'

'Hush now,' Athelstan murmured. 'Prior Sinclair, why make enemies of us? All we have done is what we were supposed to do. Sacristan Sylvester is responsible for those hideous deaths, not us. We have dealt with you justly and fairly. You owe it to your dead and to us to speak the truth, honestly and directly.'

'On a more practical basis,' Cranston interjected, 'if you cooperate, we will always regard you as a *persona grata* to London. We are not here to force the truth, Prior Sinclair, but to reach it. Naturally you can object. You can insist that the lay brothers who escorted you here take you back now, but if you prove difficult, so will I. You plan to return to Scotland. However, I could delay that by months with this obstacle and that. Sacristan Sylvester's murderous plot has been discovered. He will meet with judgement. We have no issue with you, Prior Sinclair, and what you tell us here is only a matter for us, no one else.'

'Listen,' Athelstan declared, 'I know, we know that you are an accredited envoy of King Robert and the Scottish council. You had a mission to secure, by whatever means possible, the return of the Stone of Destiny and the Scottish regalia from London. The first being held in Westminster Abbey, the second somewhere in John of Gaunt's palace of the Savoy. I am correct, am I not? Yes or No?'

'Yes.'

'I am of English stock, Prior Sinclair, but if I were Scottish, I would certainly sympathize with your desire to secure the return of very sacred relics, which are really yours by right and law. However, like you, Prior Sinclair, I do not compose the

music of the world, I simply dance to it. Where possible I will
try to do what is right, and that's another reason we are meeting
here. I will be blunt, honest and direct. I beg you to do the
same. First, let me assure you that the treasure chest you and
Paltoc were searching for was a will of the wisp. What lay
buried in that cemetery was a very expensive coffer crammed
not with relics but with cheap tawdry kitchenware. The chest
was found by Ursula the pig woman. You must have seen her
and her pet sow wandering St Erconwald's cemetery.'

Sinclair just gaped.

'My Lord Prior, I speak the truth.'

'You mean,' Sinclair gasped, 'that was the so-called treasure,
cheap kitchenware?'

'Yes, it certainly was. In brief, I believe Paltoc took the coffer,
sealed, bolted and locked from the arca in the Savoy Palace.
At the time he truly believed it contained treasure, but it didn't.
Paltoc removed the coffer during a season of great violence.
He simply didn't have the time to open, check the contents,
and hide the treasure away. Instead, he brought it across to
Southwark and buried it in his family grave. Ursula, who haunts
the cemetery, saw what happened, immediately dug it up, broke
into the coffer, kept that for herself but sold the contents to The
Piebald tavern.' Athelstan laughed sharply. 'You may have even
eaten from this kitchenware during your stay there.'

Sinclair sat gaping in astonishment.

'This is the truth?' he gasped.

'Prior Sinclair, I would swear on the Eucharist, the most
solemn vow a Christian can make. But there is more.' Athelstan
paused to take a deep breath. 'Before the Inquisicio earlier
today, I had the two stones brought to the Guildhall. One from
The Bannockburn, the other from Westminster. Now, I had
studied the one from Westminster, indeed you saw me do so.
However, during the Inquisicio, as I studied the one taken from
the cog, I suddenly realized that too is a replica, a very clever
one, but still not genuine.' Athelstan pointed at Sinclair. 'You
know I studied the manuscripts in the abbey library. According
to the texts, two crosses were cut into the side of the real Stone
of Destiny, I mean the genuine one.' Athelstan smiled. 'The
side being to the right or left depending on how you look at

the stone. The first cross was clearly etched in the right-hand corner. The other cross in the centre bottom. Now, the latter cross is there in both stones but the former, the one to the right-hand corner, is missing on both.'

'Never,' Brother Sinclair stuttered. 'The Guardians of the Stone, my good brothers, murdered in the abbey, would have noticed it.'

'No.' Athelstan shook his head. 'Remember the light in the abbey sanctuary is very poor. The cross is small and both sides of the stone are hidden because it is placed beneath the English throne. I only noticed what was missing in the full good light of that Guildhall chamber. In addition to the poor light, the Guardians of the Stone were fairly old men, their eyesight failing. Of the two stones, the one kept in the abbey was a finer copy. The one brought from *The Bannockburn*, however, was certainly not a perfect replica. I suggest it would have only been a matter of time before the exchange was discovered. But by then of course you would be back in Scotland.'

Sinclair picked up his goblet and sipped carefully. 'Of course,' Athelstan continued slowly, 'you would expect that the stone brought from *The Bannockburn* would be a perfect replica, but I suggest two things. First, when Edward I seized the genuine Stone of Destiny, he also took all the manuscripts from Scone Abbey where the stone was lodged. These manuscripts were brought south and entrusted to the library at Westminster Abbey. The Scottish Crown would find it difficult therefore to fashion a replica.'

'I know what you are going to say, Brother Athelstan, and let me assure you, you will speak the truth. We did have a detailed description of the stone sent to us by no less a person than Sacristan Sylvester.'

'Of course,' Cranston breathed. 'Sylvester was sacristan. He could pull that stone in and out whenever he wished. He could measure it, take careful note of its markings, and despatch such information in confidence to the Scottish Crown.'

'Yes, yes he did,' Sinclair replied wearily. 'But he made a mistake.'

'Very good, Prior Sinclair,' Athelstan declared. 'You have been honest. I will give you my explanation.'

'Before you begin . . .' Sinclair raised his hand as if taking an oath. 'I swear, Brother Athelstan, that I had no part whatsoever in the murder of my brothers at Westminster.'

'I believe you, Prior Sinclair.' Athelstan lifted his goblet in toast. 'To return to the matter in hand: last summer, London and the southern shires teetered on bloody revolt. A short time before this occurred, John of Gaunt travelled north to treat with the Scots. I believe he took the real Stone of Destiny and the regalia of Scotland with him. I believe such precious items are still in his possession. I assure you of that.' Athelstan pulled a face. 'More than that I cannot say. You, a member of the Scottish council, must know what happened next.' Sinclair cleared his throat and glanced nervously around.

'You're safe,' Cranston murmured. 'We are alone, no one can eavesdrop.'

'For your ears alone,' Sinclair retorted. 'Only for you.'

'We can suspect what happened,' Athelstan offered. 'It's a matter of logic. If my Lord of Gaunt had handed those treasures over, we would not be sitting here.'

'True, true, Brother. Well.' Sinclair's voice dropped to just above a whisper. 'In brief, Gaunt travelled north because he was frightened, terrified of the coming storm. He was caught between two pressing dangers. On the one hand the growing boldness of the peasant rebels to his rule in both London and the surrounding shires. On the other hand, Gaunt was also aware of the curdling hatred of the powerful English lords, nobles such as the Earl of Arundel and others. Gaunt was trapped. He came to ask for a Scottish army to move across the border and place itself under his command. He would then march on London and shatter his opponents. He would get the army, and in return he would hand over the Stone of Destiny and all the regalia of the Scottish Crown.' Sinclair shrugged. 'That was it. Nothing more, nothing less, nothing else.

'Satan's tits,' Cranston breathed. 'You must be romancing, exaggerating?'

'Sir John, nothing was put in writing, but I was there at that council meeting. Gaunt made that offer, the Stone of Destiny and regalia in return for knights, hobelars and men-at-arms with proper provision. King Robert and the council fiercely debated this, then the Great Revolt broke out in London. The news we received was of a violent uprising, yet it seemed confined to London, Essex and Kent. King Robert's advisers warned him that the northern shires remained fairly quiet, whilst the revolt in London was being bitterly opposed and short-lived. You know what happened. Your young King confronted the rebels and their cause collapsed. King Robert's council also argued that it would be disastrous if a Scottish army crossed the border and became trapped. In the end, King Robert broke off negotiations, saying he could not commit himself.'

'And Gaunt?'

'He was furious, and his anger deepened further when he received news about the destruction of the Savoy. You must remember, Gaunt's visit to Scotland was not a hurried one. He lodged at Melrose Abbey and the proceedings between us took time and careful scrutiny.'

'Heaven be my witness,' Cranston declared. 'If all of this became public knowledge, Gaunt would face charges of high treason. People would ask what really was that Scottish army for? To quell the revolt? To crush the nobles? Or, God forbid, remove his nephew from the throne and seize the Crown for himself?'

'Gaunt made himself very vulnerable,' Athelstan declared. 'And that is not like him.'

'Ah yes.' Sinclair smiled bleakly. 'Gaunt demanded nothing should be put in writing and he protected himself well. He warned us in no uncertain terms that if his offer was ever published or proclaimed in any way, he would personally destroy both the Stone of Destiny and the regalia which, for the future, would remain firmly in his grasp.'

Sinclair spread his hands. 'Gaunt, full of fury, left for London. We recognized his threat and the council decided to act. We would secure the return of what,' Sinclair fought to remain calm, 'what in God's name is rightfully ours. You know what happened, I can say no more, except to grieve over what tran-spired. We were stealing a replica and replacing it with another. What a disaster! What a cost! All those poor souls sent into the dark; God have mercy on them and bring Sylvester and Gaunt to judgement.' Sinclair drained his goblet. 'Sir John, Brother

Athelstan, I have told you the truth. There is nothing more and I must go. Lay brothers wait for me in the taproom to escort me back. One final word.' Sinclair got to his feet and leaned over the table. 'Be careful of Prior Norbert, they say he is Gaunt's spy.'

'Do they indeed?'

'Yes, my Lord Coroner. Now I must go.'

Athelstan lifted his goblet. 'God speed you then, Prior Sinclair.'

Once the Blackrobe had left, Athelstan just sat shaking his head.

'Brother.'

'Sir John, I am intrigued. What we have discovered here tonight is that our noble regent helped himself to the stone and took it away from the abbey. But how could he do that? How did he have the time and the means to recreate such a replica?'

'My good friend.' Cranston smacked his lips. 'We've touched on this before. Earlier this year, do you remember, the English throne in the sanctuary of Westminster Abbey was refurbished. People thought it was in preparation for a royal occasion, perhaps the young King wearing his crown. Now we know that the throne was refurbished, during which the stone must have been moved.'

'Of course, of course,' Athelstan breathed, 'and it was all supervised by Master Thibault. He would have had the original Stone of Destiny taken to the sacristy to be carefully scrutinized and examined by some master mason heavily bribed by his masters. Thibault would have ensured that Sylvester and the rest were firmly excluded from the process.'

'I believe the same,' Cranston agreed. 'The refurbishment was a pretence so Thibault could make careful note. You see, Brother Athelstan, Gaunt knew what was coming. He had sown the tempest and he would have to reap the whirlwind. He needed Scottish troops and so he prepared. As for removing the stone and making the exchange – well, I have already scrutinized the records of the abbey. Gaunt demanded that the abbey church be closed for a short while, so he could pray safely, securely and serenely for his journey to Scotland. He also brought presents in great caskets, pure beeswax candles and linen cloths for the different shrines and altars. He handed over those presents, but I am also certain that he took the replica stone into the abbey in one of those coffers. He and Thibault made the swift exchange and the real Stone of Scone was loaded into a chest and removed.'

'Very, very clever,' Athelstan declared. 'Yes, it all makes sense. And so we have it. The English throne is refurbished, the stone is scrutinized, careful note being made of all its markings. The replica is fashioned. Gaunt uses his desire to pray to disguise the removal of the original stone from the abbey and its replacement by a replica. Very subtle indeed.'

'God knows, Athelstan, the full truth of all this. It does make me wonder.'

'Sir John?'

'Gaunt has made his move on the chessboard and he was blocked. Think, Athelstan! Sinclair returns to Scotland with empty hands, but at least he knows the truth of the situation. Will Gaunt make the Scots a second offer? Only this time will they agree? More importantly for us, if Gaunt ever learns that we know what he has done, that would make us the most dangerous men in the kingdom.' Athelstan leaned over and squeezed Cranston's hand.

'Very good, Sir Jack, then let us walk very carefully, very prudently through the dark.'

AUTHOR'S NOTE

he Stone of Destiny is, of course, a work of fiction, but I have tried to faithfully depict a busy medieval parish in Southwark during the last decades of the fourteenth century. Athelstan lived at the time of the great poet Geoffrey Chaucer, and if you really want to find colourful medieval characters, study his Prologue. It certainly was an inspiration to me in writing this and other novels.

The Great Revolt of 1381 was soon crushed by the great lords, who made sure that the rebel leaders were either hanged or hunted out of the kingdom. Nevertheless, reading the legal records provides some interesting perspectives. Men and women who ranked prominently in the ranks of the peasant armies were often very successful in avoiding exile and execution. For example, we have individuals deeply involved in the destruction of the Savoy being given pardons and even rewards from Gaunt and other ministers. This in turn makes you reflect about who was fighting for whom. Gaunt's palace, however, was devastated and its ruination complete. The rebels indulged in a frenzied orgy of destruction. Plunder was either burnt or thrown into sewers or into the Thames. The Savoy embodied all that the peasant armies hated. The opulence, the luxury, the wealth, as well as a callous indifference by the lords to the welfare of anyone else.

John of Gaunt was not in the Savoy or in London during the uprising. He had, as the novel describes, decided to leave the City and journey north to negotiate with the Scots. Many commentators have argued that Gaunt, who was a born intriguer, could have simply decided to put himself out of harm's way. If the rebels had captured him, execution would have certainly followed. Ostensibly Gaunt and the Scots negotiated over the usual complaints from both sides: petty raiding across the border, the theft of livestock, hostile incursions and so on. However, there is also a very strong possibility that Gaunt may have been looking for military help to resolve the sea of troubles confronting him.

The Flayer is also a product of the times and a theme I often touch upon in my novels. England went to war with France. Pillaging French towns, and plundering their contents, almost became a way of life for many of the great English milords. They in turn needed troops. Men were reluctant to leave their fields and farms for a season of war in France. The great lords became more and more dependent on the sweepings from English jails as well as the free companies, cohorts of mercenaries who sold their swords to the highest bidder and, when the money ran out, so did they. The cruelty of these men was unbelievable. One historian argued that their savagery was even greater than that of the Nazis during the Second World War. Little wonder, as Catholic historians point out, that God had to raise a saint, Joan of Arc, to deliver France from this scourge. Joan did not pull her punches. English mercenaries perpetrated horrific atrocities, including flaying the skin from their victims. On one very famous occasion, Joan, who tried to act with all humility and gentleness, lost her temper with one English commander. She marched up to the castle gate and screamed, 'Glasdale, come out, so I can send your soul to hell.' The Flayer mentioned in this novel would have found comrades richly deserving of him.

The Stone of Destiny, or the Stone of Scone, is and was a source of sacred mystery and one of the most important Scottish national icons. We do not know its true origins. Rich legends about the stone abound. Some claimed it was the stone used by Jacob to rest on when he had his famous dream of heaven opening and angels ascending and descending. According to this legend, the stone ended up in ancient Egypt in the possession of Scota, daughter of the Pharaoh of Egypt, who pursued Moses and drowned with his army in the Red Sea. Scota's husband, however, survived this catastrophe. He, his wife and the stone then wandered Europe before they ended up in Scotland.

However, the most probable origin of the stone were quarries close to the abbey, where it was kept before it was seized by Edward I and taken south to Westminster. Under the terms of the Treaty of Northampton as well as the Treaty of Edinburgh of 1328, the English Parliament authorized the return of the stone to Scotland, but this did not happen due to the opposition of the London mob. It remained in England; Scotland, however, never forgot its great treasure.

At the beginning of the twentieth century there was a move by prominent people in Scotland to secure the return of the stone. My novel mentions it being stolen; that could have been a strong possibility. In the mid-twentieth century such a theft did occur when four Scottish students succeeded in removing the stone from Westminster Abbey on Christmas Day 1950. They entered the abbey as visitors, cleverly concealing themselves until the abbey closed. They then dragged the stone from the Coronation Chair on a coat through the abbey to a waiting car. Once the theft was discovered, the police and the authorities launched a major hunt but with little success. Three months later, on 11 April, the stone was found in Arbroath Abbey. The theft provoked further debate about where the stone really should be. Eventually, in 1996, on the 700th anniversary of the stone's removal from Scotland by Edward I, that sacred relic was formally and with great ceremony returned to Edinburgh Castle.

The return of the stone on St Andrew's Day 1996 certainly marked the end of a long exile. Whatever the stone's origin, it was regarded as highly sacred and played a major role in the coronation of Scotland's kings. The chronicler Fordun described one such coronation which emphasizes the truly sacred nature of the stone itself. Fordun's description is as follows: 'There they set him on the royal throne, which was decked with silken cloths inwoven with gold; and the bishop of Saint Andrews, assisted by the rest, consecrated him king, as was meet. So the king sat down upon the royal throne – that is, the stone – while the earls and other nobles, on bended knee, strewed their garments under his feet, before the stone. Now, this stone is reverently kept in that same monastery for the consecration of kings of Scotland; and no king was ever wont to reign in Scotland, unless he had first, on receiving the name of king, sat upon this stone at Scone, which, by the kings of old, had been appointed the capital of Scotland.'

The Stone of Scone has now assumed its rightful place. However, bearing in mind all the drama of its 700-year exile from Scotland, I do wonder if the right stone was returned.